Sophia is a new fictional author, mother of two, wife, scholar, and university instructor who aspires to tell the stories of the poor and marginalized via fictional accounts. Her roots in the Caribbean provide her with a plethora of opportunities to witness many untold stories. Sophia believes these stories must be shared so others can learn the true meaning of resilience.

This book is dedicated to the people who live in ghettos across the globe. The world has much to learn from your strength, grace, and resilience.

Sophia Sophie

YELLOW BRICK ROAD

AUSTIN MACAULEY PUBLISHERS™
LONDON • CAMBRIDGE • NEW YORK • SHARJAH

Ordering Information:
Quantity sales: special discounts are available on quantity purchases by corporations, associations, and others. For details, contact the publisher at the address below.

Publisher's Cataloging-in-Publication data
Sophie, Sophia
Yellow Brick Road

ISBN 9781645362449 (Paperback)
ISBN 9781645362456 (Hardback)
ISBN 9781645368601 (ePub e-book)

Library of Congress Control Number: 2020908899

www.austinmacauley.com/us

First Published (2020)
Austin Macauley Publishers LLC
40 Wall Street, 28th Floor
New York, NY 10005
USA
mail-usa@austinmacauley.com
+1 (646) 5125767

Thank you to my two most precious gifts: Tori and Jon. Audrey Lynn, you are forever with me.

Chapter One

"Nika, you sleepin'? Nika, it's me. Wake up. I come to shoot marbles with you."

I roll over and look up at the naked bedroom window. I see Makalo's narrow, black face pressed against the web-covered window screen. He smiles when he sees my eyes open.

"Nika, I come to shoot marbles with you. How come you still sleepin'?"

"Makalo, why you come so early? What time it is now?" My hoarse morning voice is rough.

"Time to get up, that's what. Come on, Nika. It's already seven o'clock."

I sit up then rub my eyes to get rid of the sleepiness.

"Nika, you look funny when you wake up. You gat two plaits stickin' up on top of your head." Makalo laughs and then presses his small face against the dusty window screen.

"You look like a monkey, Makalo. Wait for me. I comin'."

I run out to the side yard to meet Makalo whose presence makes this a typical morning in July. Makalo comes to play with me just about every day. His long, lanky frame and charcoal skin is what shows on the outside but inside he is a meek lamb. A lamb with a shark's smile. I never understand why he smiles so much but I like it. Makalo is always happy. His bright smile is a sign of his permanent cheerful mood. Makalo's teeth are even happy. They line up perfectly inside his big mouth. Even though he neglects to brush thoroughly and regularly, they are so white, and his gums are so pink.

"Makalo, you know I don't have any marbles. You win all from me the day before yesterday. You ga gimme some marbles?"

"Here. Take these." Makalo hands me ten small marbles.

"But I want a big, fat rollie pollie. I can't win without a rollie pollie." I put my small, brown hand out to Makalo.

"I can't give you a rollie pollie. I only gat one left. Don't worry, Nika. I won't use the rollie pollie this time." Makalo kneels in the dirt and uses his long, boney, pointer finger to draw a circle about the size of a large bowl. We put our marbles in the circle.

"You go first, Nika." Makalo gathers some dirt in one hand and sprinkles it in his other hand. He rubs both his hands together and wipes them on his thin bare chest that holds his boney ribs. I kneel. Take my first shot but I miss all the marbles in the circle.

"Dang it! I missed." I look at Makalo.

He smiles and prepares to take his first shot.

Makalo has the best aim. I watch as he kneels in the dirt on one scrubby knee. He squeezes a big, fat marble between his thumb and pointer finger. He shoots. Immediately, he hits three of my marbles out of the circle. Makalo wears the same dirty, navy blue shorts from yesterday. Yet, his face screams of contentment.

"Hey, you said you wouldn't use a rollie pollie. You cheat, Makalo."

"Oh, yeah. I forgot about that. I won't take those three marbles. Go ahead, Nika. Put them back in the circle." Makalo points at the marbles outside the circle. I quickly grab the three small marbles and put them back in with the others. Makalo shoots again, this time, with a small marble.

"Yes!" Makalo hits one marble out of the circle.

"Miss, miss... Please let him miss." I press my hands together in a prayerful position. I look over at the tall coconut tree that bows his head when he sees me. The crooked, rigid tree trunk winks at me. I wink back because the shade he gives provides much relief from the sun on the hottest days.

"Yes! I got another one." Makalo smiles. He picks up the marble and puts it in his pocket. He walks over to the coconut tree and kisses the rigid brown trunk for more good luck. I think I hear the tamarind tree sigh because she wants a kiss, too.

The yellow Caribbean sun grows brighter and the blueness of the sky makes the scene so beautiful. Makalo and I play for thirty minutes. His pocket bulges as he puts his winnings inside it. Black, dirty, boney bare feet are evidence of his determination to win. He wipes the sweat from his forehead with his dirty, skinny hands after the game ends. He returns home with his pocket full of marbles he wins from me.

The next morning, Makalo returns. Bare feet and bareback, wearing the same dirty shorts. He repeats his kind gesture and gives me some marbles.

"You can have these," he says.

Makalo is kind to me. So, I am kind to him. At school, if he asks me to help him with math or reading, I gladly assist. Numbers and words are a challenge for Makalo. The teachers say he is a slow learner. I wish the teachers could see him shoot marbles. They would see how smart he really is.

Makalo and I have a lot in common. Apart from being playmates, we are both eight years old. We are in the same classes at school. Marbles in the dirt and hide-and-seek are games Makalo and I like to play. Bat-and-ball is our favorite.

Today, the game ends when Makalo runs into the bushes to retrieve the tennis ball. He encounters the jewels of the violent ghetto. Sparkling pieces of colored glass bottles hidden in the bushes. Makalo returns with a wound in his right foot that gapes and spews black blood like a water fountain. His big, beautiful smile goes away. A look of worry comes that causes lines to form in his forehead.

Makalo does not cry but he says, "I'm going home now."

He hops along and leaves, a blood trail I see the next morning. It reminds me that ghetto children play barefoot games at their own risk. We hold on to the old, rotting piece of lumber, with rusted nails along each side. We eagerly await the tennis ball. We swing with a smile and hope the ball sails high enough. The smile quickly exits when we realize the ball crosses over into the forbidden yard of the grouchiest neighbor. The game ends because no one dares retrieve the ball.

A week later, Makalo's foot is better. He finds a tennis ball in the bushes and brings it when he comes to play with me. After a game of marbles in the dirt, we play bat-and-ball. Makalo throws the tennis ball. I hit it with the old, rotting piece of wood that is my bat. I run to touch the three rock bases with my thin, dust-covered bare feet. I head for the empty soda can that marks home.

"Ouch!" I scream because I feel the sting of the tennis ball at the center of my back.

"Makalo, that hurt!"

"You're out, Nika. I got you." Makalo holds his growling belly while he laughs.

"Makalo, why you laughin'? You hit me hard with that ball. Don't worry. You ga feel it when I pork you with the ball." I try to reach my hands to rub the painful spot on my back.

Makalo continues to laugh. I smile. Then I giggle.

"Nika, you should have seen your face. Look like someone put you in a tub full of snakes. Why you make a squirmy face like that? You always makin' me laugh, Nika."

"Keep laughin'. Don't worry, Makalo. I'll have the last laugh. Get the bat. It's your time now."

I pitch the tennis ball. Makalo swings. He hits the ball so hard. It sails through the air and crosses over the fence into Mr. Roker's yard. Makalo doesn't run because he knows the game ends now.

"Oh, no! No, no, no. Game over, Nika." Makalo tosses the rotting bat into the tall, littered bushes.

"Go, get the ball, Makalo. Please. I still wanna play."

"You crazy. You think I would cross that fence and go into that crazy man's yard. You go get it." Makalo points at Mr. Roker's fence.

"Me. Not me. I wouldn't go over that fence if you paid me a million dollars."

"A million dollars! I would do it for a million. What! I would jump that fence in a flash." Makalo smiles and pretends to jump the fence.

"Nika, you remember what Mr. Roker said last time I jumped his fence. He said, 'Makalo, get your stinkin' black ass out of my yard.' I jumped over the fence and out of his yard so fast because Mr. Roker is a crazy black man."

"Yeah! He is. I am so glad he gat a good fence to keep his mean dogs in. I think those dogs would eat us if they ever got out."

"Yeah. Those dogs would bite anyone who stupid enough to cross that fence. So what game you want to play now, Nika?"

"Let's play hide-and-seek but this time, Makalo, I want to count. You go hide."

Makalo and I are realistic. We don't dare attempt to retrieve the ball because in the world of a Caribbean ghetto, good fences make mean neighbors. They sit on their porches and watch with their pot cake dogs on guard duty. They protect every inch of their land and patrol their hog plum trees. Children are enemies of their fort.

"Get your stinkin' ass off my fence," are the words of these mean neighbors. Sister says they believe their grumpiness saves them from the vileness of their surroundings. The sounds of gunfire and police sirens cannot penetrate their negativity. Threats to "beat your ass" are made to even the youngest who dares to cross the fence to retrieve the tennis ball. Only the angel of death can soften the hearts of these mean neighbors. Who upon their death beds beg forgiveness to the woman who nurtures the children they curse.

******

My name is Nika. I'm eight. Anika is my real name, but everyone calls me Nika for short. You can call me Nika, too. I like it when people call me Nika. It makes me happy. But today, I'm not happy. I'm sad because my favorite cousin, Makalo didn't come to shoot marbles with me. Mother says Makalo has worms in his belly and he feels sick. That's why he can't play today. I hope Makalo feels better soon, and I hope his wiggly worms don't wiggle too much in his scrawny, black belly. Sometimes I get wiggly worms, too. I hate wiggly worms in my belly, but I mostly hate when they wiggle out of my bum when I poop.

After Mother tells me Makalo is sick, she says I should play with my sisters today. Mother says God blesses me with many playmates with dark, brown skin and nappy heads, just like me. Mother doesn't understand. Seven sisters are not a real blessing because I don't like playing with my sisters. Stacey and Belinda only like to play in the dirt because they're younger than me. Edith is too grumpy. Chrissy doesn't like playing marbles. Regina says she's too grown to play marbles. Mia says she would play with me, but she is too busy cleaning the house and washing our clothes. Matilda wouldn't play with me because she lives with her boyfriend and we hardly see her. My little brother Matt only plays dollhouse with me because he doesn't know how to shoot marbles yet.

Makalo is the only one who plays marbles with me. He's my best friend. Edith says I can't call him my best friend because he's my cousin. I never listen to my sister Edith. She's such a grump. I know she doesn't like me because she tells me to my face whenever we have a fight. I don't care if Edith doesn't like me. I don't like her, either. Edith's ten and I'm not scared of her.

Today is so boring without Makalo. The only things I can do are play dollhouse with Matt and hide-and-seek with Belinda and Stacey. I can't wait until tomorrow because Makalo comes then. We have so much fun playing marbles.

This day is so long and I'm glad when night time comes, and Mother tells us to go to sleep. I have good dreams. I dream about Makalo. We shoot marbles in the dirt and he smiles all the time. Whenever I have good dreams the night passes quickly. I can't believe how fast the morning comes.

******

"Nika, come here." Makalo motions with his hands for me to follow him.

I run behind him to the yard of some neighbors who live just three houses up the alley. A woman and her husband argue. Makalo and I join the ten other nosey neighbors who come to witness the dispute.

"I'm tired of your cheatin' and your foolishness," the woman says. She pokes the man's hairy, bare chest with her sweaty pointer finger.

"Woman, take your hand off me." The man grabs her finger. Pushes her away.

The woman is persistent and resumes her poking immediately after she recovers from the push.

"I'll fuckin' touch you when I want. What you gonna do, asshole?" The man feels the spit fly from the irate woman's mouth when she speaks. He pushes the short, heavyset, yellow-skinned woman again.

The woman recovers. Uses her hand to brush back her disheveled, short, curly hair. She jumps on the man's sweaty, charcoal, muscular back and begins to choke him. "I told you never to put your hands on me. Why you so fuckin' stupid?" She yells in the man's ear.

The man shakes the big, heavy woman off his broad back. Slams her down on the black dirt. Her white t-shirt has red blood and black dirt as the new design. The wild woman gets up. She picks up a melon-sized rock. Throws it at the man but misses.

The man chases the woman up the road, "Mother fucker, you better run." His beer belly jiggles and sweat pours down his face, neck, and back.

I run home. Makalo follows me. I hear marbles jiggle inside his pocket. We run to the side yard where we play marbles and sit under the tamarind tree.

"What you think he will do to her when he catches her?" I ask Makalo.

"Beat her up." Makalo's eyes widen. The lines in his forehead appear.

"I hope she can run fast so he never catches her." I lower my head.

"Me too." Makalo pulls some marbles out of his pocket. "People so fuckin' crazy round here," he continues.

"Yeah. They're fuckin' crazy." I say this only because I want to sound like Makalo.

Cursing is the first language of the ghetto. We pretend not to speak this language in the presence of elders.

"To give a fuck" or "not give a fuck" are powerful words in the mouth of a ghetto girl. People around her know she embraces the dark side of her soul. I never speak this ghetto language much. The language is dirty in my mouth. I only use it when I'm most angry, or when I try to be like Makalo. As a ghetto child, I prefer the language of the Queen. Makalo laughs and mocks me because I try to be something I'm not. So, I use the second language of the ghetto instead – the English dialect white visitors find amusing. It takes less time to say more in dialect. Even though I know the words are mere modifications of English words, I speak them with reverent authenticity.

I say, "gimme" when I mean to say, "give me." "Gurn" translates to "going," and "dat ein yours" means "that's not yours." Sometimes Makalo and I mix our dialect with proper English words but most times we use only our dialect because it's our mother-tongue. To speak it comes so naturally.

I don't understand why the preachers in the ghetto churches don't speak the dialect in their sermons. They preach like their audience is educated and civil. They use fancy, proper words to persuade the ghetto people to take up the cross. It's amazing how many do. Even at the tender age of eight, I give my heart to the Lord and hope for immortality. To walk on streets of gold and to feast with angels is a wonderful desire ghetto children cannot resist. Deep down inside we want to be pure and holy, but our graffiti-covered surroundings remind us that here on earth we are unclean and unworthy of God's love.

I go to church every Sunday and listen to Brother Leo speak about Jesus at Sunday school. Brother Leo is ninety years old and wears a smile of pink gums alone. The lines in his forehead are few for a man of his age. I think Makalo will look like Brother Leo when he grows old. I could picture his tall slender frame as it hunches over, slow steps, and black, wrinkled hands that always tremble. The only difference is Brother Leo wears a clean, dark coat suit and his white shirt smells of chlorine. Makalo's clothes are often dirty and stinky.

Every Sunday morning, Brother Leo gets up early, dresses, and walks to the small, white church just down the road. His passion for teaching ghetto children the "good news" gives him something to live for. He is a "Brother" in the ghetto church and is respected by all. This holy ghetto man does not use fancy, proper words because he is like Mother. He only attends school up to grade five, but we understand his every word in dialect. Brother Leo teaches us that we love ourselves more than we love our neighbors and we should strive to love them as we love ourselves. Do ghetto children love themselves? Yes. Indeed, we do. Even amidst all the chaos, filth, violence, and sadness, we are the happiest children alive.

Chapter Two

I sit under the tamarind tree in the side yard and make drawings in the black, dusty dirt with my calloused finger. First, I draw a flower. Then I use my hand to erase. Next, I draw a happy face because I think of Makalo. I'm not alone under the tamarind tree. Right next to me are my four-year-old sister, Belinda and my two-year-old sister, Stacey. They dig holes in the dirt with sticks and bare hands. Next to Stacey is my six-year-old brother, Matt. He cries because he wants my sixteen-year-old sister, Mia to bathe him. Matt hates being dirty. Edith, my ten-year-old sister, chases my thirteen-year-old sister, Chrissy around the tamarind tree.

"Tag, Chrissy. You're it." Edith shouts with her prissy, loud voice.

"Nika, look at me," Belinda calls. Her light brown skin is covered in black dirt. She wipes her dirty hands on her two, short, messy braids.

"Careful, Belinda. Don't get dirt in your eyes," I reply. Then I return to my drawing. My happy face looks a lot like Makalo. I smile because I think of how much fun Makalo and I have when we play.

Stacey throws dirt on the rotting white clapboards that are the siding of our small house. She uses her hands to paint the boards with dirt, and giggles because Belinda tickles her.

"Chrissy, get the other children and come inside. It's getting late," Mother calls from the squeaky, termite-filled front porch.

When I hear Mother's voice, I get up right away. I run in quickly because I can tell Mother's in a bad mood. Belinda, Stacey, Matt, and I wash our dirty hands and feet in the small tin tub Sister fills with rainwater. Sister's real name is Mia. I always call her Sister because Mother would often say, "Get your sister to help you."

Mother sends us to bed and I obey without hesitation. I lay my eight-year-old body across the bed I share with Sister. This night, I become intimate with thirst. My dry mouth and arid throat caress me. I feel weak. My thirst is intense. It has a deep desire to fill me. I gather frothy spit in my mouth and hold it for a while so that it moistens my throat as I swallow. The dryness of intense thirst is like holding my breath underwater. Except, it's water, not air, I crave.

Thirst seduces me this night because the government water pump is shut off for repairs. Mother cannot afford to buy bottled water. We have no water pipes under our clapboard house and the well water smells like a soft, brown, bodily waste. I finally fall asleep after my erotic desire for water passes. My dreams are happy. I dream about Makalo. We play marbles, hide-and-seek, bat-and-ball, and his big smile never fades.

The next day, I awake and drink the rainwater Mother boils in an iron pot over the gas stove. Thirst is satisfied but hunger begins his teasing. Luckily, food in our home is a scarcity but never absent. I'm thankful for all we have. Hunger does not have the opportunity to fully consume me. Mother gives me a small plate of grits. Before I eat, I perform the ghetto food ritual.

Lustfully, I gaze at the white, lumpy grits. I dig my spoon in. Scoop up the first bite. I enjoy the corn fragrance it gives before my mouth engulfs the spoon. Sluggishly, I pull the spoon out removing every speck of grits from it. It shines like silver because it's entirely unoccupied. I churn the grits inside my mouth. Half swallow. Regurgitate. Swallow again. This skill we ghetto children learn without lessons. Makalo is even better at it than I am.

All other food encounters today will awaken my five senses. The smell of the food as it cooks will alert my eyes to seek it out. My lips, tongue, and the inside of my mouth will experience the texture and taste of the cuisine. My ears will bear witness to the crunching and clashing of my teeth.

For now, my senses are fully engaged with the grits on my plate. As I chew, Makalo races inside. As usual, he smiles.

"Nika, you comin' to play marbles with me?" A big grin follows his words.

"Makalo, wait until Nika finish her food. She'll be out in a little while," Mother says.

I shove the last spoonful of grits in my mouth. Then I say, "See. I'm done. Can I go play now?"

"I don't know why you always have to play with Makalo. You have so many sisters and brothers to play with. Why don't you play with one of them today?" Mother asks.

"Because me and Makalo are having a marbles contest." I put the empty plate on top of the dirty pile.

"Okay. Go play." Mother raises her right hand in the air. She flicks her wrist as her get-out-of-here signal.

Makalo and I run out to the side yard. I kneel to draw the circle in the dirt.

"Makalo, why you didn't come earlier today?" I put some marbles in the circle.

"Because I was tired. I sleep too long. Last night, I stay up late shooting marbles with some boys who live on my street. I am lazy today." Makalo continues to smile.

"You feel lazy. That's a surprise. I thought I was the lazy one."

"You still the lazy one. Don't worry, Nika. I'll be here bright and early tomorrow." Makalo kneels and rubs his hands in the dirt. All day long, Makalo and I play marbles, hide-and-seek, and bat-and-ball. Then he goes home to eat dinner.

The evening comes and I'm thankful for white rice in the iron pot and corned beef in the pan. Mother always makes enough to feed all fifteen of her children. We each get an undersized serving. Grateful is what we must be because the growls of our bellies are less. Besides, Mother teaches us to be thankful. We give thanks for the government water pump, the avocado and dilly trees down the road in the empty lot, the buckets that catch water from the leaky roof, and for the many wonders of nature.

******

I rise with the sun the next morning and run up the alley to meet Makalo. We, two ghetto children, hurry our sleep so we can meet at our special place – the waterhole. Smiles consume our faces as we watch the tadpoles swim in the water-filled hole that one day holds a septic tank. Tadpoles are beautiful creatures to ghetto children. The mystery of their transformation fascinates and boggles the mind. We catch them in old, cut-off, plastic, water jugs and hope to witness the miracle. The temptation to touch them is irresistible. We put our fingers inside the cut-off jug of water and press softly against their slimy bodies. They do not like our touches and so they try to escape them.

"Look, Nika," Makalo says. He puts his finger inside the jug, and the tadpoles swim around in a flurry.

I put my finger in, too. The tadpoles are even more agitated.

"They look scared, Makalo," I whisper.

We remove our small, dark fingers from the jug and give them the space they require to transform. These teeny creatures are smaller than a pea, but they grow bigger each day right before our eyes. Legs appear. Tails drop off. Skin changes color. Eyes bulge. Yet, we do not witness the actual moments of change. God does not reveal his mysteries to us. We marvel at them. Eventually, the tadpoles become green frogs. We are sad the miracle passes. We set the frogs loose because they have nothing to offer. When they are tadpoles, they give us something to look forward to. But frogs, they only want to escape.

We ghetto children want to escape, too. Car rides with my wealthy aunt Martha who drives us to her church to sing in the choir are a short escape. Auntie Martha arrives around six o'clock to pick up four of my sisters and me. We are happy to go because the treats at the chicken restaurant after choir practice give us something to dream about. I wish Makalo could come with us. Auntie Martha says there's no room in the car for him. I wave goodbye. Makalo whispers, "Bye, Nika. See you tomorrow."

More dreams are made a week later when a local politician offers me a job selling raffle tickets. The man says Makalo can't help because he's a boy. So, another eight-year-old ghetto girl and I are the luckiest. We sit for nine hours outside a food market selling raffle tickets for a criminal in disguise. I wish I was home playing with Makalo, but Mother says I must work today.

******

"Miss, you wanna buy a raffle ticket?" I ask the tall, skinny, well-dressed woman who approaches the food market's entrance.

"What's the grand prize?" She walks over to the small, wooden table.

"A car," Pamela, the other little girl speaks up.

"Really… Let me have a look." The woman takes the raffle book. Her eyes read the list of prizes.

"So, Miss, you wanna buy one?" I ask.

"I'll take two." She pulls out two dollars from her pink, suede, medium-sized purse and gives it to Pamela. I give her a pen. After the woman writes her name and phone number in the raffle book, I rip off the tickets and pass them to her.

"Here you go, Miss. Thank you." My smile is brief. I'm not happy. I don't want to sell raffle tickets. I want to play with Makalo.

"You two cute, little girls should have no trouble selling tickets. I only came over here because the two of you are so cute." The woman smiles at us.

"Thanks, Miss." Pamela makes a big, fake smile. I can tell she doesn't want to be here, either.

The nine hours go by at a snail's pace. Finally, the man comes to pick us up. Turns out he lies about the raffle and never pays us a dime. He goes off to his big-time, office job and pockets the money we collect from the raffle ticket sales. His big wide nose, charcoal skin, and grey coat suit are the perfect masquerade. He pretends to be honest and passes for an honorable man. Ghetto children are his peons who work nine-hour shifts in the smoldering heat just for a ride in his fancy car.

Mother says, "Nika, I knew that man was a crook. I can't believe he would cheat you, small children. What is this world comin' to?"

The next day, Makalo asks, "How did it feel riding in that nice car?"

I say, "It felt smooth and the car smelled so clean."

Cars are the gem of the ghetto. BMW's, Corvettes, and Mercedes sit in the front yard of houses that lean to one side. Dilapidated houses of the ghetto are not a priority. If the drug-selling sons park their shiny cars in the front yards, life is great in the ghetto. Respect comes when ghetto boys drive around with shiny rims. Respect comes when ghetto boys wear the most expensive running shoes and have a mouth full of gold. Ghetto folks are not immune to vanity. I do not understand our values. It's so easy for ghetto boys to involve themselves in the drug trade. The trade that promises big money is an irresistible lure. Dirty, evil money blinds us like sun rays in a mirror. Some say it's the root of all evil. Indeed, it is the evil that roots our ghetto.

Chapter Three

"Nika, wake up."

I open my eyes and see Makalo's squished face up against the window screen. I smile. Then tell him to wait.

"Hurry, Nika." Makalo uses his hands to clean off the mosquito-filled spider webs that grow on the window screen.

Sister rolls over, "Makalo get away from that window. Why you have to come here so early, Boy?"

"Go back to sleep, Sister. He didn't mean to wake you."

I put my finger on my chapped lips as a signal to Makalo to keep quiet. I tiptoe out of the room, but the old floorboards still squeak. I run outside to meet Makalo.

"What do you want to do today?" I ask.

"Hey, why don't we play marbles for a while then we can play hide-and-seek?" Makalo replies.

We play for an hour and Sister calls for me to come in.

"Nika, it's time to get ready for church."

I say goodbye to Makalo. He runs home.

"Sister, I comin'." I run inside.

I think the path of my life changes its direction when Sister takes me under her wings. Sister and I are inseparable. She is the maternal figure that provides me with the selfish attention I require. Sister is a bright scholar and speaks the Queen's English like a London native. Her long, skinny legs are shapely, and her pretty, oval face makes her a vision that is easy on the eyes. She is eight years my senior and takes a particularly special interest in my upbringing because she feels sorry for me. My need for attention is obvious to her. She knows she can provide what Mother has no time to give.

My first sister, Matilda moves in with her boyfriend. Her bedroom passes down to the next sister in line, Mia. My baby sister, Stacey still sleeps in a crib in my parent's room. My four other sisters have to share a room. My seven brothers all share a room. I'm lucky because Mia shares her bedroom with me. When Sister extends the invitation for me to stay in her room, I realize how much Sister likes me. I'm overcome with joy when I hear Sister's words that day.

"Nika, you can stay in my room."

"Sister, are you serious?" My smile is almost as big as Makalo's.

"Yes. I want you to stay with me," Sister pronounces her words like a news reporter.

"Mia, can I stay with you, too?" My fifth sister, Edith asks.

"Sorry. I only want Nika with me."

Sister smiles at me.

"Mia, you sure you want Nika in there? You can't change your mind later. You better be sure. Once Nika is in there with you that's it," Mother says.

"I'm sure," Sister nods.

"She only wants Nika because she always calls her Sister. Nika knows how to suck up to people," Edith pipes up.

"Don't mind her, Nika. She's just jealous."

Sister pokes Edith's forehead.

I gladly accept Sister's invitation and move into her room. The four walls of this petite bedroom witness our conversations about the birds and the bees. Conversations develop into loud laughter and quiet giggles. These giggles follow us into the weirdest circumstances. Sister teaches me how to tongue kiss a pillow. She shares a cigarette (she steals from Father) so her favorite little sister can taste the bitterness of nicotine. Sister knows I desperately need her affection. She also knows I'm very helpful and can wash laundry on the hard ridges of the wooden, scrubbing board in the tin tub outside in the back yard.

Clothes hang upon the line and people say, "It looks like an adult hung those clothes." I'm a perfectionist even at the age of eight. I hang the clothes neatly in a line and make sure each item is a bit longer than the one that hangs before it. This is a sign of the great care I put out as I complete a task I truly enjoy. I'm a natural caregiver. I change bedding. Fold laundry. Dust dresser drawers. These gifts I exchange for Sister's love. I do everything for this special sister whose laziness becomes more important than having a room just for her. The only thing I leave for her to do is wash the bloody rags she uses for her period.

******

Today, Sister comes home from her summer job and is delighted to see all the chores are done.

"Nika, you did such a great job cleaning the room. The clothes on the line are perfect." Sister looks happy.

I'm on my knees organizing Sister's second hand, high heeled shoes in the closet. Sister is lucky her feet are the same size as rich Auntie Martha's.

"You think I did good, Sister?" I look up at her.

"Yes, you did really well, Nika."

I smile.

"Tonight, I'm going out," Sister says.

"Why, Sister? Why do you have to leave me home? Why can't I go with you?"

"Because you're too young. I'm going to a party. They don't allow children."

"Fine. I'll stay home then. I don't like it when you go out."

Sister dresses. She wears high heeled shoes, tight jeans, and a shiny, gold tank top. She leaves. I sit on the bed feeling sad.

"Why you look so sad, Nika?"

I look up and see Makalo's face pressed up against the window screen.

"Makalo, what you doin' here? I thought you weren't allowed to play today. Why you come by so late? It's already seven o'clock."

"Mom says I can spend the night here." Makalo wears his usual gigantic smile. He presses his face against the window screen. Makalo sticks out his long, pink tongue. He asks, "What do I look like, Nika?"

"You look like a fool, Makalo. Come inside. Let's play hide-and-seek."

Makalo comes in. I hear Mother's voice, "What you doin' here, Makalo?"

"Mom says I can spend the night." He runs to find me. I remain seated on the bed.

"Nika, what's wrong? Why you look so sad?" Makalo sits next to me.

"Because Sister went to a party. I wanted to go with her."

"Don't worry, Nika. When you grow up you can go to the party with me. Come on. Let's play. You go hide and I'll count." Makalo covers his eyes with his hands and counts. "One, two, three, four, five, six, seven, eight, nine, ten. Ready or not, here I come."

"I'm not ready yet, Makalo. Count to twenty." I crawl under the bed.

"Ten, eleven…thirteen…" Makalo pauses because he can't count past eleven. "Thirteen, eleven, thirteen." He pauses again.

"Ten, eleven, thirteen, twenty. Ready or not, here I come."

"Not yet, Makalo. I crawl out from under the bed and hide inside the tiny closet."

"One, two, three, four, five, six, seven, eight, nine, ten, eleven, thirteen, twenty. Ready or not, here I come."

Makalo and I play hide-and-seek for twenty minutes. The only places to hide are inside the door-less closet or under the saggy double bed. Both Makalo and I choose to hide inside the closet. We cover our eyes and pretend to be invisible. Our invisibility doesn't last very long because we both find each other in a matter of seconds. One time, I pretend not to see Makalo, so he thinks he really is invisible. Eventually, the game begins to bore us. I realize we mess up the shoes in the closet, so I make Makalo help re-organize them. Afterward, we lie on the bed together looking up at the leaky roof. Makalo tells me scary, ghost stories. In time, the vertical lines of the paneling mesmerize us, and we fall asleep on the bed. When Sister comes home, she lifts Makalo off the bed and puts him on a shaggy blanket on the hard floor.

Chapter Four

My fourteen siblings and I come home from the summer talent show and we all laugh. Sister knows she is the one who provides us with reasons to cackle. She performs her solo, "Memories." She fails to hit all the right notes. Sister is so humble and admits she's no singer. Memories of her song make her chuckle. Sister doesn't mind when I imitate her in our petite living room whose capacity is five but holds fifteen. I pretend I'm Sister and sing "Memories" in front of a pretend crowd of one hundred people whose shouts are only a farce.

Sister knows her talents are English and literature. It's better if she recites poetry or reads from Romeo and Juliet. Singing is not one of her fortes. She is a fantastic long-distance runner and this hobby keeps her thin. Her hip bones protrude through the spandex, running pants she wears but her best assets sit firmly on her chest. A ghetto girl who wears "D" cups attracts both nosey and wicked watchers. Sister is the luckiest of all. She has a sharp, pointy nose like white folks. She is not beautiful like my fourth sister, Chrissy but she is pretty. Her oval face and wide smile make her look like a model on the front cover of Ebony magazine.

Sister is extraordinary. For a while, she is even more special than Mother. Mother is always at work. She always smells like dirty dishwater. She never smiles. She is too tired to smile. Yet, she does not wear a frown either. She wears the expression of the ghetto mother who has too many children and a husband who hides in the shadows.

Mother cannot hide and has no desire to do so. She must remain visible – even if only to her children. She is invisible to the people who make her work graveyard shifts. Every day, she prepares food for the foreign hotel guests only to return home to more hungry mouths. She fills her pockets with leftovers and hopes security does not get a whiff of them as she leaves. Mother comes home from work and inspects the bare, rotting, wooden floors. She whips Sister, Regina, and Chrissy, if they still hold yesterday's tracks.

"Ain't no shame in being poor but there is shame in filth," she utters with firm conviction.

A woman who works hard all day long has no time for cosmetic moments. Mother's cheeks or lips are never red. She does not wear make-up, but she wears old-fashioned clothes. I wish she dresses a bit younger. Her big, round glasses make her look even older, but people say she looks good for a woman who has fifteen children. They expect a woman like her to be fat and heavy, but she remains average size even though she does not exercise.

"I'm on my feet all day and I walk where I need to go," she tells people when they question how she keeps the weight off. Mother is a woman on a mission to earn her keep and to ensure her fifteen hungry children eat.

Mother can't attend the summer talent show because she has to work. She comes home and finds me and my seven sisters in the living room.

"How was the talent show? Mia, how did you do?" Mother asks.

I jump up and squeal, "Memories, memories."

"Misty, water-colored memories," Sister jumps in.

We all burst into laughter.

"I guess, it was bad." Mother gives her puzzled look.

"Memories, misty water-colored," I continue.

"All right, Nika. That's enough. Time for bed now." Mother's mood changes because she's too tired for jokes.

******

The next morning comes quickly, and my usual visitor is prompt.

"Nika, come see." Makalo presses his face against the window screen.

I roll over and I'm glad Sister is already gone to work.

"See what?" I manage to speak despite the frog in my throat.

"Tadpoles. There's so many. Come see. I have a jug. Let's go catch some." Makalo presses the cut-off, plastic water jug against the window screen.

"Okay. I comin'." I sit up on the bed. Rub my crusty, brown eyes. Run out to meet Makalo. We race up the alley to the waterhole. After we collect some tadpoles in the water jug, I hear Mother calling, "Anika, Anika."

I know Mother is losing her patience because she calls me by my full name.

"Anika, Anika," Mother calls even louder.

"I have to go now, Makalo. Come by a little later. Okay."

I race home, and Mother tells me to eat some grits. She begins one of her long speeches, "Why do you and Makalo have to go to that waterhole so early? You should know better. Suppose one of you was to fall in and drown? No one is around to save you. You better listen, Nika. Don't go down to that waterhole so early. You hear me?"

"Yes, Ma'am," is my reply. Mother continues her elongated speech and then tells the story of the little girl who dies because she accidentally locks herself in a refrigerator and no one is around to open the door to let her out.

I often obey Mother's wishes because she knows a lot. We learn so much from Mother. I learn that cleanliness is next to godliness. Mother demands that her children not eat from certain people who are "dirty." But everyone eats at our house. Mother is famous for good cooking and offers the little she has to anyone in need. She offers prayers, too. The woman has a heart of gold. The teaching of Jesus influences her narrow perspective. Her five years of formal education provide her with basic literacy. She reads her Bible. She writes without punctuation. Has no difficulty counting money and understands the rules of addition, subtraction, multiplication, and division. As long as she is healthy enough to work, her children can eat.

We are the most important people to Mother. Her hungry children inspire her to dream. She dreams about a better life for us. Then she dreams about the days we walk the yellow brick road. She has no dreams for herself. I know Sister's wise words are true, "We are Mother's dreams."

Mother has fifteen different dreams and only one reality. She is a ghetto daughter, a ghetto wife, a ghetto mother, and a ghetto grandmother (my first brother Vincent already has a bastard son). Mother is fortunate to have such a long life – a life that reveals to her that some dreams do come true. She has much to rejoice over. Most times she rejoices. Sometimes, poverty steals her joy.

Makalo thinks Mother is wise. He often reminds me to obey, "Nika, you better listen to your mother."

Whenever I plan to disobey, he says, "Nika, you might get in trouble. Didn't Auntie tell you not to do that? You better listen to Auntie."

******

Later in the afternoon, Makalo returns and we resume our play as if he never left.

"Race with me, Nika." Makalo tugs my right arm.

"Come, Nika. Let's race." He pulls me to the end of the alley. "On your mark, get set." Makalo takes off.

I run behind him yelling, "You didn't say go. You cheat. You cheat, Makalo."

Makalo slows down and then stops. He turns around and says, "Sorry. Let's start over."

We walk back to the end of the alley. I say, "On your mark, get set." I take off. Makalo runs behind me. Suddenly, he passes me. I say, "You win, Makalo. You win."

We race some more and every time Makalo wins he says, "That's okay, Nika. Next time you'll win."

Makalo and I are tired after the races. We sit under the dilly tree in the empty lot up the alley. We rest for a few minutes. Makalo says, "You want a dilly?"

"Yeah. Let's climb up and get some." I stand up and put my hand out to Makalo. He takes it. I pull him up, too.

"Nika, you go first. I'll help to push you up."

Makalo helps me get up the tree and then he climbs up like a monkey.

"Who teach you to climb dilly trees, Makalo?"

"No one. I just know how."

"I wish I could climb like you, Makalo."

"I wish I was smart like you, Nika." Makalo smiles and then picks a dilly and passes it to me. "Here, Nika. This is for you."

I take it and bite into the sweet, fleshy fruit.

"What do you think happened to that woman who had a fight with her husband? Do you think he beat her?" I ask.

"I think so. He was so mad at her. I bet he smashed her head with a beer bottle." Makalo claps his hands to demonstrate smashing.

"I hope she got away. I hope he didn't kill her." I look at Makalo who still smiles.

"Don't worry, Nika. Don't worry about that."

Sister says so many lives are lost in the ghetto and are forgotten too soon. The woman who walks the streets in rags trades sex favors for money. She is a mother of three. The boy who sleeps in a tree, who sells roasted peanuts at the red light is an only son. The man who has one leg who gets high on cocaine is a father to a beautiful daughter. I see the emptiness in their eyes when I pass them on the streets. I think they know something eats them from the inside out. Mother says the day will come when they are dead and gone – merely faint ghetto memories. Sister says ghetto memories are invaluable nightmares. They remind us that the world is full of evil. They remind us of the delicate balance between goodness and wickedness. Our existence weaves itself with threads of both.

I ask Sister, "How do you know all of this?"

She tells me, "From library books." Mother does not read library books and the only books in our home are the school books Sister brings home. I ask

Sister, "Can I read some of these library books?" She says, "Yes. In a couple of years, I'm sure you will be able to read them."

Chapter Five

Mother is African by ancestry and my father is of mulatto roots – his mother, a vision of light skin and dark blue eyes. I do not know my maternal grandparents. They are in heaven and my birth comes many years later. My paternal grandfather is in the other world as well. I have visions of his corpse from the memories of myself at age seven. My paternal grandmother is gone, too. Not much matters about that because fond memories are the last things I have of her. I remember words like "our skin is too dark for her liking" or "our mother's past relationships and bastard children who bear dark chocolate skin turn her off." In her feeble years she manages to utter "she loves us."

Mother says her great grandfather was a slave and we are fortunate to have our freedom. Sometimes she sings a song around the house, "*I'm free. Praise the Lord. I'm free.*" Makalo says freedom is a ghetto treasure. I know he only repeats words his mother says because when I ask him what he means by treasure he tells me, "Nika, I mean we have to dig up our freedom because the white people bury it somewhere."

I think we are free to say and do whatever we please. I know that such freedom comes with great consequences. So, I choose not to be free in the ghetto. Freedom takes what it wants when it wants it. Freedom says and does what it wants when it wants to. Sister says the boy who fires a gun into a crowd is free. The man who spreads diseases to his sixty-five lovers is free. The preacher who cheats on his wife and sleeps with teenage girls is free. I dislike freedom and I prefer to abide in the confinements of the law. Ghetto people dislike the law and all who wear its uniform.

Corrupt police officers are the enemies. They arrest Sister and my fifth brother, Ron because they pick grapefruit off a tree. The evil policemen drive Sister and Ron home in the police car. They are fully aware that a night in reform school is no punishment for hungry ghetto children. Instead, they bring them home to Mother to receive lickings from the rod. Sister and Ron are innocent. They commit no crime so do not accuse them of theft. They are only ghetto teens who long for the sweet taste of pink, fleshy grapefruit.

Ghetto people believe petty crime is our entitlement. Our circumstances leave us with no other choice. Who can chastise the man who steals a loaf of bread to feed his starving child? Mother fills her pockets with leftovers from work. This does not mean she is a criminal. Real ghetto crimes are violent crimes of passion. Ghetto people kill each other. They are like black crabs fighting each other without reason. Thankfully, the daylight often subdues the violence. At night, though, no one is safe. The darkness extracts the evil that wanes in the daylight. Even former ghetto people stay away from the ghetto at night. Taxi drivers refuse to drive you home. They make you pay and get out at the street corner under the bright, street lamp because they don't trust turning onto dead-end streets. They send a young, unarmed woman off into the darkness while they drive off quickly to save their own asses. The young woman races down the dark alley and prays she does not encounter any familiar faces.

******

I don't mind seeing familiar faces when daylight comes. I especially love seeing Makalo's face in the morning. Today, I awake and see him before he presses his face against the window screen. Sister is still asleep, so I quickly get up and press my finger on my lips to motion to him to be quiet. I tiptoe out of the room and then race out to the side yard.

"Good mornin', Nika." Makalo's smile is even bigger.

"Mornin', Makalo," My reply is unenthusiastic.

"Wake up, Nika." Makalo grabs me by the arms and shakes me. "Nika, wake up."

"I'm up. I'm up," I try to sound lively.

"Nika, do you want to go to the waterhole today?"

"Yes. But not now. Mother says I shouldn't go there until later." I manage to emphasize the word "later."

"Okay. What do you want to do now? Shoot marbles?" Makalo is excited.

"No. I don't feel like it. Can we just sit for a while?" I grab Makalo's hand and pull him to sit down with me in the dirt. My eyes close after I get a glimpse of Makalo's big smile. He put his arms around my shoulder and says, "Rest, Nika. We can play later."

My sticky, dark brown eyes are shut for ten minutes. When I open them, Makalo still sits next to me.

"Okay, Makalo. Draw the circle. But you know you have to give me some marbles because I don't have any," I mumble. Makalo understands me.

"You wake, Nika?"

31

"Yes, Makalo. Just draw out the circle." I don't look at Makalo. I hear his smile.

I have a regular day with Makalo and then he goes home.

******

The orange sun sets this evening and ten of us sit on the porch with Mother who tells us a humorous, olden-day story. Her story begins with a hilarious introduction. Mother jumps from a tamarind tree and tries to induce the labor of her first child. She tries to get the baby out as she forces vomit from her mouth. She does not understand why the baby refuses to come up with the vomit. Her grandmother explains to her that babies come from the place she receives them. Mother is shy and only receives this child because her father tells her to share herself with a man he chooses.

This man who promises to marry her gives her two more sons after the first but beware – a promise is never kept in the ghetto. The man goes off to work on "the contract" – picking oranges in Florida and returns to accuse her of cheating.

He tells her, "Light-skinned children cannot come from a man like me." Mother curses his words and clings to her distrust. The skin of Mother's first three sons darkens as they grow but the man leaves her before he sees his sons wear the skin that is dark like his.

Mother meets a second man who makes more promises. He is a cheat who stays a very short while. The second and third men deceive Mother and give her three more babies. Her distrust hardens her soul. She curses the lies she hears from married men and cheating womanizers who spread their seeds on any fertile ground. She makes a promise to raise her six children on her own. A promise she cannot keep. In a year's time, she opens her heart to another man. This one makes no promises. She trusts him. She receives nine more babies and then receives his name.

Mother's story ends, and I see my favorite aunt in the distance. She carries garbage bags across her broad shoulders. I smile. Run to greet her. I know the bags contain old clothes she brings for us from the Salvation Army. I'm so happy to receive the clothes. I try on item after item and beam with excitement because they fit my body perfectly. No other eight-year-old feels such joy until she understands how trash becomes treasure. My aunt feels she does a good deed. Her wide nostrils flare. Her large breasts jiggle. Sweat pours from her dark skin. Her big belly shakes as she laughs. She is happy to know this thoughtful act brightens the eyes of her ghetto niece. Auntie Zelda's heart feels whole.

"Nika, spin round for me. Let me see how pretty you look." Auntie Zelda uses her hand to demonstrate how I should spin.

I twirl and smile, "Like this, Auntie?"

"That's it, Nika."

I continue to spin, "Look, Auntie."

Auntie Zelda laughs because I fall. "Child, you're too excited."

I get up and continue to spin. "Weeeee…"

"That's enough, Nika. Stop that spinnin' before you hurt yourself," Mother breaks her silence.

"Yes, Ma'am."

******

I have a happy sleep this night because I wear the cotton pajamas I get from Auntie Zelda. The next morning arrives and so does Makalo.

"Nika, wake up."

I open my eyes and see Makalo at the window. Sister is already gone. Makalo looks different today. He looks sad.

"Hi, Makalo." I sit up on the bed.

"You comin' to play with me?" His tone is so somber.

"Yeah. I comin'."

I go out to the side yard to meet Makalo.

"Hey, what's wrong, Makalo?"

"Nothin'." The look on his face tells me otherwise.

"Makalo, I know you. Something gat to be wrong. How come you are not smilin'?"

"Nothin' wrong. I just feel sick today. Worms come out with my poo this mornin'. I still feel them wigglin' inside me. That's all."

"Did you tell Auntie?" My voice is soft.

"No," The response is quick.

"Why you didn't tell? She could give you medicine to get them out." I reach out to hold Makalo's hand.

"I don't like worm medicine." I feel Makalo's hand relax in mine.

"Why?" I pull him down to sit with me in the dirt.

"Because the worms come out even more. Last time I take medicine for worms and they all come out when I poo." Makalo makes a squirmy face.

"But they have to come out, Makalo."

"I know. I just don't want them to come out today."

"Makalo, you scared? Don't be scared." I squeeze his hand as a sign of my support.

"All right, Nika. I won't be scared." Makalo's smile returns. "I'm goin' home to take some worm medicine. I'll see you later. Bye, Nika."

"Bye, Makalo."

Makalo leaves and does not mention anything about my new pajamas. Worms consume his mind today. The last time Auntie Zelda brings clothes from the Salvation Army, Makalo notices right away.

"Hey, Nika. That's a new shirt you wearin'. Auntie Zelda give you that?"

"Yeah, Makalo. You should see all the other stuff she brings. Come inside, I'll show you."

But today, Makalo takes no notice of my new pajamas. His mind is preoccupied. I hope he feels better. He goes home to get medicine for his worms. This is the last time I see him this summer. Makalo does not come to play for a week and then summer ends. I'm sad summer is over because I miss spending time with Makalo. I'm glad Makalo goes to my school. He doesn't come to see me in the mornings. I see him at school. We play together at recess and at lunch.

Mother says, school is important, and she makes sure we go every day. I like school because the teachers tell me, I'm smart. They put me in a special reading group for gifted students. Makalo is in the group with the other children who can't read well. Sometimes I help Makalo with words, but he always forgets them by the next day. I tell him he has to remember them, so he could move up to my reading group.

He says, "But Nika, the words are too hard for me to remember."

The months go by so quickly. September, October, and November race pass. December comes and thoughts about the jolly season guzzle me. Makalo and I get into the Christmas spirit. At recess, we sit and talk about what we want for Christmas.

"I want a bicycle for Christmas," Makalo says.

"Makalo, you know Auntie can't afford to buy you a bicycle." I give a discouraging look.

"You don't know, Nika. Maybe she could." The big grin makes its appearance.

"I don't think so. Don't get your hopes up, Makalo."

"Well, if I don't get a bicycle, I want a water gun."

"I want dress-up jewels," I jump in.

The bell rings for us to go in. Makalo and I run to line up with the rest of our classmates.

******

Three weeks speed by and today we go to the Christmas party at the fancy hotel that employs Mother. Employees' children and grandchildren under the age of ten are welcome. My nephew Jacob, my youngest brother Matt, my two youngest sisters Belinda and Stacey, and I are still young enough to attend. Makalo can't come because his mother doesn't work for the hotel. Mother says he's not allowed to go. She tells me because I'm the oldest one who attends, I must look after the youngest – my one-year-old nephew, Jacob who cannot sit still. I perform my baby-sitting duties with great pride and do the job like someone teaches me the ways of childrearing. But this, too, is something we learn without lessons in the ghetto. Even Makalo knows how to do it.

Mother puts us on a bus and we ride to the fancy hotel. When we arrive, I take charge and make sure everyone is safe.

"Matt, Belinda, and Stacey you three hold hands." I pick Jacob up and walk with him on my hip.

"Nika, look. Look, Nika." Matt points at the overgrown Christmas tree that is overly decorated with lights and tinsel.

"Pretty, Nika," Jacob says.

"I wanna see it." Belinda runs off toward the enormous tree that sits in the hotel lobby.

"Belinda, come back here," I call after her, but Matt and Stacey run to the tree, too.

"Pretty, Nika." Jacob points and wiggles out of my arms. He runs to join the others.

After I gather the four of them together, we go to the dining hall where hundreds of other children gather. A hotel employee takes us to a table that has a sign with Mother's name on it. There are five chairs around it. We sit and wait for about ten minutes and then our mouths salivate when the workers bring out food for the buffet. It's like a magic trick because thirty servers come out of nowhere with trays of ham, turkey, potatoes, carrots, rice, fruit, and salads. I don't regurgitate my food today because I know I could have seconds and thirds.

After dinner, Santa Claus arrives in a motorboat and we go out (all two hundred of us) on the dock to greet him. We laugh and point as we anxiously await the gifts he bears. He "ho, ho, ho's" and wishes us a Merry Christmas. We do not question his authenticity. Even though his skin is the color of charcoal, we still believe in his magic. His red suit and long, white beard persuade us that he is real. The crowd of eager children rushes back to the dining hall to listen for the roll call. When at last they call Mother's name. Belinda, Matt, Stacey, Jacob, and I race to the overgrown Christmas tree to collect our gifts. We are happy and quickly rip the gifts open.

Dress-up jewels are what I really want, but instead, I get a game of Jacks with a bouncy ball and six neon-colored pieces. I am happy and sad. The Jacks are something I can use to occupy my time after school when Makalo can't visit. But I really want dress-up jewels. They are on my mind all the time.

******

The next day, I go to the corner store with Makalo to buy bubble gum with the dime I find along the roadside. I see the dress-up jewels on display in a far corner. Makalo says, "Look, Nika. Dress-up jewels. You said you wanted them for Christmas. Maybe you'll get them. Look, Nika. Look how pretty they are."

I stare at the dress-up jewels for a long time and then plan to take them without asking or paying. The freedom of the ghetto tempts me.

"What if I take them, Makalo? Would you tell?"

"No, I wouldn't tell. But, Nika, you might get in trouble. Auntie might beat you." Makalo makes a squirmy face.

"I know. Let's go, Makalo."

The fear of Mother's scolding subdues my itch to be free. I leave the store without the jewels but take with me the images that dance around my dreams. This night, I smile in my dreams because I wear my dress-up jewels. I dream that Makalo compliments me and says, "Nika, you look divine. The pink, dangly earrings make you a princess who has servants at her beck and call."

I wake in the morning and eagerly anticipate the next night that brings more sweet dreams of my dress-up jewels. Dreams of my dress-up jewels are even better than dreams about fried chicken. I don't have to share my jewels with siblings or worry that I'm selfish.

Chapter Six

Christmas morning arrives and I'm still hopeful. I have a strong feeling my dress-up jewels hide under the tall, yellow, electric lamp we dress up as our tree. I wait and wait. Finally, Sister tells me to open the gift from her to me. Inside are the jewels I pray for. I care not how Sister earns them. Perhaps she takes them without paying when I tell her how much I want them.

I scream then shout and squeeze as I hug her.

"Thank you, Sister. I love you so, so much!"

A happier child than me does not exist. My life is complete and my joy overflows as I clip on my pink, dangly earrings. I slip on the fake bracelet. I pull on the fake pearls. I parade around the house. Christmas is magical and a time of gladness that I deserve. I'm a princess not a ghetto child and my servants fetch all I need. They fold laundry, wash dishes, dust furniture, and care for younger kin. I sit on a chair, sip pink lemonade, and do nothing else but breathe.

Breathing is something we forget to do at Christmas during mealtime. We inhale the food without pause. We do not talk as we eat. We eat then we talk. We drink merrily together. We forget all our woes and have hope for the future.

Sister says without Christmas we die without the true experience of life. Gift-giving is a virtuous thing. Although gifts in the ghetto are not expected but welcome, and our thankfulness is indeed grand. We smile and receive all with deep appreciation. Mother is happy for the Rubik's Cube we give her. We hope she has fun as she solves it. She does not complain and receives nothing from her husband. Complaints are a rarity at Christmas and are quickly shut down if they threaten the joyous celebrations.

This Christmas is just like the last five I remember because the carnival comes to town. I know someone is patient and kind enough to take me. Each time this kind soul is different. Perhaps an aunt, an uncle, a cousin, or even just a family friend fills this role. I'm fortunate nonetheless.

This time, Sister takes Chrissy, Edith, and me with her on a bus trip to the carnival. She lets Makalo come with us, too. Makalo and I ride the merry-go-round once or twice. We enjoy the bright lights and do not dare complain.

Instead, we are happy to be away from the ghetto even if only for some, few hours. We ghetto natives blend in with regular folks who cannot tell who we really are. The feeling of disguise makes us walk with our heads high. Even though it's night time, we are happy to see familiar faces. Elation is what we feel when we brag to each other about the thrills of the joy rides and show off whatever new clothing we wear.

A week later, the carnival leaves and Christmas is over. It's time to get back to real life. Money worries, job losses, and violence return to the ghetto with supreme force. Happy times in the ghetto cannot last here. They visit and then they move on. The world seems off balance when the ghetto is happy for seven days in a row. It seems strange when ghetto people feel joy that lasts a whole week. Sister says it's odd that the people feel anything but disgust for a country that fails them – a country that claims to honor God.

Even Makalo is fed up with our ghetto life. He tells me, "No one cares about us, Nika, especially the politicians. My mother says politicians only look out for their children." I know Makalo repeats what his mother says because he couldn't come up with these words on his own.

I copy his words, "Yeah, politicians only look out for them, not us."

The politicians are not ghetto people, though some have roots and ties that they hide. They frequent the ghetto only when they are up for election. A songwriter declares, "They come out of the woodwork like worms."

They are spineless creatures who prey on the poor. But Mother thinks one is worthy. She swears, preaches, and brags about Brown's good works, and gives him her vote each and every time. Mother is happy when her party wins. She even smiles when she hears the results. I'm happy when Mother is happy. She deserves so much more than she has. Yet, she is content with her situation and swears never to leave. The ghetto is all she knows. It's home.

Although cliché it's true. "A home is not a house and a house is not a home." Our clapboard house with rotting boards is not the home Mother swears to keep. She is ready at any moment to bulldoze the thing if she could. To her, home is familiarity. She knows what to expect and understands the ghetto. Mother knows the woes of the people. She consoles neighbors and prays for all. Her role as a strong believer gives her a duty she thrives upon. The people of the ghetto need her, and she needs them equally. They are her sisters and brothers who share her story and who truly understand. Life in the ghetto is her calling and theirs, too. It's not a choice to choose or not. To leave the ghetto after so many years would be most difficult for a woman who roots herself deeply. It would be a catastrophic event to lose her ghetto status. What else could Mother be? A ghetto woman is all she knows and ever wants to be.

******

The recess bell sounds and we run outside to play. I see Makalo.

"Makalo, are you coming to play after school today?" I expect the usual response but do not hear it.

"No. I can't come today."

"Why not, Makalo?"

"Because Tito and Jeremy want me to play marbles with them." Makalo smiles even though his words disappoint me.

"But you played with Tito and Jeremy yesterday. Can't you play with me today?" I expect him to say yes.

"Nika, I play with you all the time. Tito and Jeremy say girls and boys shouldn't play together so much." Makalo continues to smile. I don't understand why he smiles when he knows I feel sad.

"Don't listen to them. They don't know anything," I sulk.

"Nika, I'll come to play tomorrow after school. Okay."

Makalo smiles even bigger, and then hits me on the shoulder and yells, "Tag. You're it."

Chapter Seven

I don't see Makalo often nowadays. He has taken to playing with boys and only visits me on Saturdays. I really miss Makalo, but I have a new friend now, Paulina, the young woman who lives around the corner. She takes the time to talk to me and listens to my every word. Paulina is twenty and the oldest in her family. She lives in a one-bedroom house with her parents and her three siblings. Her language is different because she is one of those illegal immigrants. After school, on this hot day of January, I go to visit Paulina, and she waits for me on the front porch.

"Hello, Paulina," I say.

"Hello, Nika." Her French accent is noticeable.

We embrace like mother and child.

"I wait for you, Nika," Paulina tells me.

"Thank you," I reply.

Paulina offers me some benne cake. "Here, Nika. This is for you. How was school today?"

"It was good. I played tag with Makalo at recess and guess what, Paulina? One of his wiggly teeth fell out."

"Really. Tell me more about it, Nika."

A big round face and terrible acne cannot conceal Paulina's inner beauty. Her dark chocolate pores are wide like fish gills and her heart is big like a whale. She has oversized breasts, a big, round bottom, and walks with a slight waddle. The floral-patterned, cotton cloth around her head covers her short afro. She is a vision of ghetto beauty in my eyes. Her voice is soft and nurturing. At times, I feel like her child. I'm special to her. I'm her favorite.

Paulina, the lonely stranger, is a different kind of ghetto woman. The kind the rest of us despise. The Haitian immigrant who crosses the ocean in search of what we have. She wants a better life, just like we do. Heroic is a name she befits. She puts her life on the line to become a ghetto woman in a land that's not her own. Hundreds of others like her drown in their pursuit. They pack themselves like sardines on tiny sailboats and pray for land before they sink. A titanic goes down in the Atlantic every month and aboard are no rich or upper class. Without life vests, sleeping quarters, or a qualified captain, Haitians gather to their escape vessel and they do not leave any who come behind. I wonder, do they welcome death like cancerous patients or do they fight to stay alive.

Paulina befriends a little girl like me. I'm a tadpole in her eyes. She watches and waits for my miracle to unfold before her. I'm delighted to be in her company because it occupies my time. The less time I'm at home, the better. I prefer to socialize with a lonely woman because Makalo hardly visits and Sister works full time. She is like Mother, never home much. My new friend is my favorite and she gives me all the things I need. Her home is peaceful, quiet, and clean.

Paulina and her family do not learn the violent ways of the ghetto and they are more civil than we give them credit. People mock the smells that come from their kitchen and poke fun at the funny way they talk. Even Makalo laughs when I tell him about Paulina. He says, "Nika, that woman has put voodoo on you."

"Stop it, Makalo. Paulina is a nice woman," I reply.

I like Paulina. I teach her English words and learn some of her Creole language, too. I learn, *Kijan ou ye. Mwen byen.*

I tell Makalo Paulina's dad works hard. He laughs and says with a French accent, "Cut grass. I cut grass for you. Two dollars."

"Stop it, Makalo," I nudge him.

We use these strangers as peons. They receive two dollars to mow our lawns and pull weeds. They walk around with lawnmowers and machetes, tools for work alone. Ghetto folks think they are better than these strangers who work harder. They slave in the heat all day long pulling weeds, so they can eat. What do they get from us in return for their labor? People curse and bully them.

"They'll take all our jobs," even the drug dealers agree. Yet, these strangers do the jobs ghetto boys and men refuse.

******

Early Friday morning, I go to Paulina to invite her to my school's assembly. I have a speaking role and I desperately want someone special to me in the audience. Both Mother and Sister have to work. Paulina tells me she is busy today because she has errands to run. I beg her and beg her to come.

"Paulina, please come watch me perform today."

"Today is not good for me, Nika. Sorry, Dear. I can't make it." Paulina's French accent is thicker than usual.

"But you must be there, Paulina. It's so important to me."

"I really would like to be there, but I can't. I'm really sorry." Paulina gives me a hug and then kisses me on the forehead.

She understands my childish plea, but her errands are very important, and her father depends on her to get them done. I beg some more and plead with her to come, see me perform. She is sorry and cannot commit herself. My stubborn childish ways do not waiver and I plead some more. I even make a big smile and blink my eyes fast to try to convince her to come. She is consistent in her demeanor and continues to refuse.

"Nika, I really wish I could make it, but I can't. I will try to come to the next one."

My mood changes instantly. The big smile goes away. I feel the soreness of my core. Rejection. A bullet that speeds through my thin brown skin and it lodges itself between the muscles of my little heart.

I sit in a chair. I feel stupid.

"But, Paulina."

She looks at me and says, "Sorry, Nika."

My smile is not enough to persuade Paulina to abandon her duties.

"Okay. Bye, Paulina."

I leave the house and pretend to be fine but inside I ache like the flu. Pride masks my disappointment. The attention of Mother, Sister, Makalo, and Paulina are things I seek because I carry conceit, self-importance, and arrogance in my heart. Empty promises I do not make. I swear to myself, "I'll never let anyone in."

I go to school and I'm sad. Makalo says, "Nika, what's wrong?"

"Leave me alone, Makalo." I run off to be alone.

I cry warm, slow-moving tears.

I hear Makalo calling me, "Nika, Nika."

I see him. He runs toward me. I quickly dry my eyes. Pretend to be fine.

"Are you okay, Nika?"

"Yep." Before I say anything else, the morning bell sounds for us to go in.

Makalo gives me a hug, "Don't worry, Nika." He holds me but does not squeeze. My arms remain at my sides. I don't squeeze, either.

Chapter Eight

An eight-year-old child cannot understand rejection. I pity the kids of divorce. My mind only understands: You're not coming; You're not here; and You're gone. Ghetto children feel pain when we are lonely. I think Sister is wise because she knows children who are surrounded by others can be terribly lonely. She sees my loneliness. I can tell. To be lonely and alone makes so much sense. The loneliness of a twelfth child perplexes the soul. The ghetto is full of lonely souls. We seek something to fill us, indeed.

Some turn to drugs and alcohol in their loneliness and others to promiscuity. But food is most useful in the ghetto and its company a welcome addiction. We save every dime we find to purchase greasy chicken and French fries. The fries, we smother in ketchup, then we pour on the hot sauce to make them spicy. A cold bottle of Vita Malt washes everything down to our content bellies. At the end of the meal, the loneliness is gone.

"Belly full and ass glad" is a wonderful thing in the ghetto. We gather on the street corner to commune with our friends – children, teenagers, and adults. We talk about good jobs, nice clothes, hairstyles, and relationships. With our bellies full we have no worries. We smile and laugh and enjoy the company of everyone who joins us. We exclude no one. Even the Haitian man who sells "numbers" joins in the typical evening event and he brings with him the answer to this ghetto question, "What fall today?" His reply is a number between one and one hundred.

******

After school today, I go straight home. I'm still sad and hurt. I do not wish to visit Paulina because she might suspect something's wrong. I see Mother enter the doorway and she looks different. Today, she smiles! "I catch it," are her words as she enters.

Even a holy woman is a gambler in the ghetto. Gambling is not a sin because to win you merely catch the number that falls from the sky. Sometimes, Makalo and I look up at the sky for a really long time and hope for a number to fall. But none ever does. Mother says number catching is a way to earn fast, clean money. There is no shame at all to share this news with others. Yet, it's better to keep this news "hush, hush" so people don't expect you to share. Mother does not mind sharing. She tells everyone her news. She puts aside some money for church collection and then she shares it out to friends and family in need.

Ghetto people like to share. They are most kind but those who are not bear mean labels, "niggerly, greedy, and stingy." People ostracize those with these labels because there is nothing worse than a Negro who doesn't share. The ghetto's survival depends on kindness, so you dare not threaten the lifeline for all. Without kindness, ghetto dreams can't come true.

******

My eyes light up when I see Makalo walk in.

"Nika, I come to play."

I run to Makalo and we embrace. Makalo holds me but does not squeeze. I squeeze him, though.

We go outside and play a game of marbles. But this game is not like our usual game because I beat Makalo.

"Makalo, how come you lose today? You never lose."

"It's okay, Nika. I'm happy you win because now you're smilin'."

"You let me win, didn't you? I squint and my lips pout."

"Well, kinda." The big grin follows.

"Makalo, you so crazy." I give him back the marbles.

"Nika, why you were crying today at school?"

"Crying. I wasn't crying."

"I saw you, Nika."

"Makalo, you lie."

"No." Makalo looks me in the eye. He smiles but his eyes tell me he is not happy.

"Don't worry, Makalo. It was nothin'."

"I don't believe you, Nika."

"Fine. I was crying because Paulina said she couldn't come to see me perform."

"That's why?" The big smile follows.

"Yeah. See. I told you it was nothin'."

Makalo doesn't say anything else. He just smiles.

"Why you smilin', Makalo?"

"I told you that woman put voodoo on you."
"Quit it, Makalo."

45

Chapter Nine

They say the eyes are the window to the soul. In the ghetto, eyes lead to evil. People watch your comings and goings. Nosey watchers are like harmless mosquitoes, but the wicked watchers are the ones I fear. The packing boy is a wicked watcher. He presses himself on me from behind as I push the grocery cart home. I do not like the way his touching feels.

Mother sends my fourth sister, Chrissy to buy groceries. She takes me along for the company. Chrissy walks alongside the trolley while I push from behind. The packing boy from the grocery store helps me push and walks behind me. He bumps my small behind with his frontal. His frontal hardens each time he bumps me. I don't say anything. He continues his casual conversation with Chrissy as if he does nothing. Finally, I say, "I don't want to push anymore." I run to take Chrissy's hand.

I don't tell anyone at home about the packing boy's frontal touching me. Shame swears me to secrecy. I can't tell Makalo because he's a boy and it's embarrassing. I want to tell Mother but I'm too afraid she might say it's my fault. So, I tell Violet, the ten-year-old girl who lives next door. Rumour goes around that Violet spit in the packing boy's face because he put his hands on her private.

"That packing boy is wicked," Violet whispers to me.

"Yes. I know," I reply.

"Do you know what we call him?" Violet continues. She sounds so grown up for a ten-year-old. "My friends and I call him the 'fresh boy.' He likes to touch little girls. Be careful. If you ever see him, Nika, just run away."

The packing boy is fifteen. He's tall for his age. His short afro, dark skin, thick lips, white teeth, broad nose, and wide eyes make him a typical, ghetto boy.

Only two days after the packing boy touches me with his frontal, I see him on my way home from school. He comes to me almost in tears. He says, "Please help me find my way through the bushes. I got lost on the trail behind the ghetto school."

I remember Violet's words. "If you see him, run away."

"Nika, come with me in the bushes so you can show me the way. Please, Nika. I really need your help." The packing boy looks at me. He pouts.

I know it's a trick. The sound mind of an eight-year-old, ghetto girl is sharper than a knife.

"Sorry, Fresh Boy. I don't know the way." I run home as fast as I can.

I escape but the "fresh boy" goes home and rapes two of his cousins in his back yard.

Life changes in a decision in the ghetto and the decision to run is often the best one. The ghetto gives much running practice and I'm grateful God blesses ghetto children with speed. We race home before nightfall. We race home when we get our first black and white TV. We race home to escape Mother's scolding.

******

The next day, I play in the front yard of Makalo's house. A familiar face approaches and I know. I'm in trouble with Mother. Mother dislikes when I go to Makalo's house without asking her permission. Her logic I can't understand. To ask an invisible woman's permission is something I never learn.

She sends Chrissy, my fourth sister (who is five years my senior), to get me. She is the sister whose hand I grasp after the packing boy touches me with his frontal. Everyone adores Chrissy – not for her ways but for her good looks. Her smooth yellow skin, long, soft hair, perfect white teeth, shapely body, and pretty face – features every ghetto girl wants. Chrissy walks by my side as we head home to Mother. She understands why I'm scared. She says, "Rub your arms together. It's a ghetto ritual that protects children from switches."

I walk slowly, side by side with Chrissy who tells me, "I feel sorry for you." She knows Mother is angry and waits at the door for me to arrive. I rub my arms together until they burn, and I hope this is the only burn I feel today. Mother's tamarind switches not only burn but they sting and leave ridges on the skin.

Each step we take brings us closer to home. Chrissy worries. She whispers to me, "When Mother sends you to choose a switch from the tamarind tree, choose one that is medium-sized. If you bring a small one to her, she will go to the tree and choose a bigger one for you."

These words of advice come from a sister who has lots of experience with Mother and switches. Chrissy is in trouble with Mother at least four days a week for late arrivals at home after school. Ghetto rumor reveals my sister has a boyfriend she meets and spends time with after school ends. I know the rumors are true because they are words people speak in secret behind Chrissy's

47

back. I don't care about the rumors. They mean nothing to me. Chrissy is older. I cannot judge her. All I know is she loves me enough to share kind words of advice that lessen the pain that awaits me.

We continue our walk and our steps are slower when we reach the alley that takes us to Mother. Chrissy shakes her head and says, "I wish I could help you but there's nothing I can do for you now. Pray the beating ends quickly and keep rubbing your arms together."

With the support of a loving sister, I take the final steps that bring me to the front door. I see Mother's face as I enter. I know she is pissed-off and full of rage. She tells me to undress and so I know the serious nature of my wrongdoing. It has nothing to do with going to Makalo's house without permission. I undress quickly and hope my willingness to obey will please Mother. I keep my eyes low because Mother clenches a tamarind switch of her choosing in hand. She is ready to discipline. The first lick comes down hard and it leaves a red line across my back that is twelve inches long.

"Mother, please stop. Please don't beat me," are the first things I say.

The second lick is firm. This time the red line swells up almost immediately. I cover my head and a flood of tears rush out. The third lick comes quick and is relentless. This time the red mark is horizontal. It's better if I stay in place so the marks match each other. The horizontal one intersects the vertical ones that ache and sting.

Mother says, "A liar is a thief. A thief is a murderer. Is that what you want to be, Anika?"

The fourth lick comes with a vengeance and is grueling. Thick tears come from my eyes and my nose. Jesus, I understand the pain and suffering when they whip you that day and mock your Holy name.

The fifth lick is loud and troublesome. It stings like a deep, open wound as it receives pure alcohol. "No, Mother. No. I didn't steal it. I found twenty dollars on the floor. You dropped it after you did the counting. I should have given it to you. I'm sorry. I'm no thief. I promise I won't steal anymore."

I make the wrong choice when I use the word "promise." Mother knows a promise is a lie. The sixth lick comes down with its pitiless wind. A razor-sharp pain follows. I feel electricity pass through my back. My tiny nerves expend flame.

I bear five more violent, noisy, rigid, corrosive, solid licks that split my raw skin open. Scabs form at the site – the bare back of a ghetto child who learns what is right from a mother who is so wrong.

The English translation of my cries to Mother does them no justice. My real words you may not understand. "Mommy, I ein steal dat. I fine dat twenty dollars on da floor. You did drop it when you finish countin'. I shouldda give it ta you. Sorry. I ein no tief but I promise I ein ga tief no more."

My eyes lead me to punishment. The money I see isn't mine, but I take it and run off to the market with my fifth sister Edith who is two years my senior and wiser than me. I tell her my secret, "I found this dollar bill on the floor." She tells me the bill isn't one dollar but five and it buys us an arm full of candy. Turns out, the bill is all of twenty. Mother's "asue payout" she is to give to the weekly drawer.

Shame on me. I deserve this licking. I know better. To take something I know isn't mine. One dollar or twenty, it's Mother's bill. Not a keeper's joy to find.

******

I hide for days in the bedroom. My pride never waivers. A thief in the ghetto is a leper. Except our wounds go away without medicine or treatment. No one nurses my back or my pain.

This experience is one of discontent but it's one that teaches me much. I learn my actions have consequences and I suffer them alone. I understand the hefty displeasure of a ghetto girl who is wrong. I hate being wrong. I go to enormous lengths to be right but what a challenge it is to live with this burden.

Burdens dissipate if we surrender. At least this is what the church goers say. But without burdens, we cannot claim to be fully human. We understand right from wrong and this is in itself a burden. We carry the burden to be righteous or we live with malevolence in our hearts. My heart cannot carry the weight of wickedness because pride consumes it like prey. I drown in a sea of conceit and the ghetto shakes its head in disapproval. I cannot even pray for humility because this requires true confessions from the heart of a ghetto girl whose arrogance is sinful.

Mother prays for me. I pray for her. She raises her children with the rod and cannot see the flaws that are intertwined in her switches. She is merciless as she raises her hand to discipline her own flesh and blood. Yet, her God shows his favor and mercy each day. But perhaps, ghetto children do not deserve mercy. We learn callous lessons the hard way. Respect is a really important lesson and so we learn to respect our elders with a back-hand slap. You better learn fast or things get really ugly. A broomstick breaks across the back. This is the least of our worries in the ghetto. We don't dare push the buttons that conjure up unpleasant feelings in the minds of ghetto mothers who use the rod. "Yes, Ma'am" and "No, Ma'am" are words to expect from decent, mannerly ghetto children who must practice what they never learn from the actions of their mothers.

Chapter Ten

Seven of Mother's eight daughters are my father's. They say we seven look so much the same. Yet, there are so many little differences we see from a close view. Sister is polite and proper. Regina is overly religious. Chrissy is flirtatious. Edith is a smart ass. I'm a loudmouth. Belinda is a tattletale and Stacey is a girlie girl. Shades of brown, yellow, and red make up the hue of our skin. Some are more yellow, and some are more refined, but all are good looking. We have small, healthy frames and pretty faces. A house full of ghetto beauties attracts nosey watchers and wicked watchers stalk us like prey.

My first sister, Matilda is different. She is like Mother. Her milk chocolate skin and thick lips we do not have. We do not share the same father, but she is our sister. We love Matilda and she loves us back.

Love between ghetto sisters is nebulous. It's strong but subsides in catty fights over chores and closet pickings. At the end of the day, though, we protect each other against any outside attacks from nosey or wicked watchers. Together we always stand strong. The times when our fights separate us, we manage to forgive and move on. There is something so precious between sisters. We are fortunate to have a wealth of this rich ore. Life is never dull because something interesting happens to at least one of us.

Today, Chrissy, Edith, Belinda, and I sit in the living room and take turns playing Atari games. The box is a gift from a well-known drug dealer who woos my fourth sister Chrissy. Mother lets us accept the gift. She says, "If he wants to be generous, I won't stand in his way."

I like to sit and watch my fifth sister, Edith, play Atari because she is so good. She beats Pac Man and Donkey Kong again and again. I watch in awe of how she moves the controls. She is so pretty. I admire her but in secret. I cannot let Edith see the soft side of me. I'm the tough one. I never back down in a fight. My loud voice scares off the tallest of them who dares cross the line or make a rude remark about Mother.

"Edith, it's my turn." I reach my hand out expecting her to hand me the control.

"Here. Take it. I know your turn won't last long because you suck." Edith's sarcasm is intentional.

"You two, no fighting today or I'll have to pray for both of you. God wants us to get along," Regina yells at us from the bedroom.

My third sister, Regina is the tall one (she is six years my senior). I do not envy Regina's lanky frame. Her large mouth and high cheekbones make her very unique. She has a terrible overbite because she sucks her thumb for many years. Regina is most like me – not her looks but her ways. She cleans everything with a fine-tooth comb and hates when my big brothers fight till they bleed. Education is important to Regina. She is hardworking and smart but not as smart as Sister. Sister is so smart she earns respect from all of us.

Mother tells us, "We earn everything in the ghetto. The good and the bad come from toils."

Mother's right because her long days on her feet, earn her varicose veins. She is rich if the veins carry cash. Though, richness is not her desire.

She says, "My desire is to live and that's all." Mother wants enough to feed her children. Any extra money she has a plan for. She pays for Sister to attend a private school because her grades meet the mark the teachers demand. Mother manages to pay school fees because my first brother Vincent works as a carpenter. He gives her his entire weekly paycheck. Mother's gambling luck provides money as well.

Mother tells us she plans to send all four of her bright scholars to private school. The four bright scholars comprise of three girls and one boy. Sister is the first bright scholar. Her reading and writing abilities are supreme. I'm the second bright scholar. Matthew (Matt) is the third, and we think Stacey is the fourth.

Matt is my seventh brother. He is a chubby, round-faced child with rosy cheeks no one can refuse to squeeze. His skin is more yellow than mine and his eyes a bit brighter. I think he is a vision of ghetto royalty. People marvel at his cuteness and wit. This boy-child is lovable and cuddly. His smile is absolutely radiant. Not one ounce of evil enters his heart. He is honest and curious with a desperate desire to please. He loves to be clean and complains when Sister refuses to bathe him. He is happy to learn and is smart as a whip. Matt asks lots of questions and has many answers for the ones even Mother doesn't know.

I remember the day so vividly. I'm five and Matt is three. We play in the shopping cart, up and down the alley. We hope the collector forgets to pick it up. It's our car that takes us on joy rides, just my chubby little brother and me. We smile in the sun and have so much fun as we race the cart up and down. Matt says, "Nika, jump on. I'll push and give you a ride." I hold on and pretend we speed down a highway in a brand-new convertible with the top down on a summer's day. He is so innocent and so pure, the best brother anyone could have. I'm the luckiest ghetto child who spends her days with a beautiful creature. The brother I truly love.

I take Matt with me to the corner store to buy bubble gum. I hold his hand when we cross the road. On our way home, he lets go of my hand and everything around me spins. When I see the fast car strikes him, I hold my breath and pray it's only a nightmare. But it's real. It's painful. I run to him. I grab hold of his little hand. I do not know what comes when I feel his hand go limp. His eyes close and I hear every breath I take. People gather, and the ambulance arrives. Everything is a blur around me. I think Matt is dead. I'm the cause.

Time passes. I do not notice. Slow-motion slows things even more. They take him away and I cry like a baby because Mother tells me to go home. She rides with him to the hospital. I go home to suffer alone. Fat, heavy tears roll down the sides of my face and I shudder when I think Matt is gone. A loss like this is no surprise to a ghetto child who at the tender age of five knows that real-life gives steady, hard punches. Even an angelic, precious, rosy-cheeked child cannot withstand the impact of hard, cold metal that moves quickly.

I think it's inevitable to lose Matt because good people do not belong where we are. My heart is heavy, and my soul is empty because my brother who brings joy is no more. Matt is better off in heaven because he is an angel on earth whose good works earn him his wings. God sends me an angel, even if only for a little while, to be my brother, companion, and friend. Now the angel has wings and can fly up to heaven. Fly away, Matt, and tell Jesus I love Him. He has to believe it if he hears it from you. A wretch like me waits for the day Jesus takes me away. I'm patient in my yearning. I cannot be complete until Matt and I meet on the heavenly shore behind the Eastern Gates, *"in the sweet, by and by."*

Great joy gives me strength to take normal breaths when Mother returns to tell us Matt's fine. They keep him one night in the hospital and I know he is so, so glad. He's out of the ghetto for an evening and receives care and oodles of attention. Perhaps he gets a second serving of food he enjoys with a smile those fat, rosy cheeks produce. This child is a ghetto prince who does not know of his wealth. His richness is a natural talent for learning new ideas and concepts, a talent that singles him out. Of my seven brothers, Matt is the one I really like. Perhaps it's because he and I are so close in age (I'm two years his senior).

******

53

Makalo and I like to play marbles, but Matt and I play dollhouse. Makalo refuses to play dollhouse with me because he says dollhouse is for girls. Matt plays with me, though. I roll up a sweater to make the doll and we play inside the big cardboard box outside (our neighbor George gets a new stove and tells us we can keep the box).

"Matt, you're the dad and I'm the mom." I climb inside the box. "Pass the baby to me."

Matt picks up the sweater doll with one hand and it unravels. "Oops. Sorry, Nika."

"That's okay. Give it to me. I'll roll it up again." I reach my hand out and Matt passes me the sweater.

"Nika, whose sweater is this?" Matt asks.

"Mine. I got it from Auntie Zelda."

"Where did Auntie Zelda get the sweater?" Matt continues.

"The Salvation Army." I hold the sweater baby doll in my arms like it's a real baby.

"What's the Salvation Army?" Matt's curiosity grows.

"It's the place where rich people give clothes they don't use, and poor people go to get the clothes they need." I sit down inside the cardboard box.

"Is Auntie Zelda poor, Nika?"

"Yes, Matt. Now come in the box so we can play."

"Are we poor, Nika?" Matt climbs in.

"Yes." I rock the sweater baby in my arms. "Here, Matt. You take the baby now."

"Why are we poor, Nika?"

"I don't know. You have to ask Mother."

Matt grabs the sweater baby from me, climbs out of the box, and runs toward the front door. I hear him yell, "Mother, Nika said we're poor. Why are we poor? Nika said you know why."

Chapter Eleven

The ghetto tempts me when I walk home from the corner store. I see Tamika, the girl who constantly teases. She says I'm ugly and I wear hand-me-downs. The bully knows she is in the ghetto on a temporary billet and her family builds a new home far away. Tamika calls me ghetto trash. She says my clothes are stinky and tattered. We are eight years old, but she calls herself mature and responsible. I'm the immature ghetto girl who still plays outside. Her rude comments are offensive, and they hurt me so deeply.

She says, "Your mother is a whore."

Her finger points at me as she laughs with her friends and calls me a beggar's daughter. She says Mother is popular for her ghetto, whorish ways and the rich, white people write a nursery rhyme about her, *"There once was an old lady who lived in a shoe. She had so many children she did not know what to do."*

My tormenter at school and my harasser at play, I cannot escape Tamika's oppression. She is a descendant of a malicious, obnoxious, nasty pot of clay. No one deserves the title of ghetto bully more than she does. She even bullies me in my sleep. My dreams are full of her vile mockery that fuels ghetto rumors. Her filthy tongue speaks horrible words my ears do not enjoy. The day arrives, not soon enough, when I teach this bully a lesson.

I surrender to temptation. I run after Tamika. I punch her at the back of her head. The ghetto ways engulf me. I do not resist and forget Mother's teachings. We fist fight each other and I grab and scratch her black face. I choke her scrawny neck until she pushes me away. I pull one of her thick, black, long plaits like I want to remove it from her head.

Other children gather to cheer and encourage, "Fight, fight. Beat her. She deserves it." The same effort I use to hang clothes in a line is the effort I use to pound her. I hate her so much. She treats me like garbage and parades around like she's better. I thrash her like garbage and I feel hot inside. The ghetto's rage is resilient. It consumes even a bright scholar who is content in a violent moment.

Tamika eventually escapes, runs home, and cries, "I'll tell on you. You in trouble now, Nika."

I race home, and hope fear gives her silence. In less than fifteen minutes, Mother calls me to come outside. She talks to Tamika's mother who is upset with the news she shares.

"Did you do it?" asks Mother.

"I'm sorry," is my reply.

Mother sends me to the tamarind tree to choose the rod she cannot spare because she raises a ghetto child. She beats me and teaches a lesson of irony – to inflict pain on another is wrong. I learn the ironic lesson but question its merit because ghetto bullies need to learn important lessons. Zero tolerance is the law to obey. If you don't you face painful consequences and even death if ghetto demons join their forces. But demons are not the only forces in the ghetto. There are godly forces that unite and encourage. Cookout sales for the sick and fashion shows for the scholars who head off to college are forces that dull the evil. The arts are good forces, too, and ghetto children are natural artists. We dance and sing without lessons or teachers. We love pageants and are ready to perform our talents on stage.

Only two weeks after I pummel the bully, I step on stage for the first time in my first ghetto beauty pageant. It does not surprise me that Mother lets me go even though she is still mad at me for beating up Tamika. She knows prizes are awarded to the winners, so she lets me go. But she warns me that if I get into another fight, she'll whip me again.

My right foot steps up on the stage and I like the feeling. I feel special and important and I know I shine like a diamond under the bright lights because the audience cheers and they tell me, "Nika, you look great up there." The announcer gives me the most difficult question and I'm ready to answer because Sister's help, for months, makes me ready. I do what people expect, memorize the answers my big sister prepares. The announcer asks, "At what time should children go to bed and why?" An eight-year-old gives her older sister's reply.

"Children should be in bed by eight because their rested bodies are important to their everyday activities. Honorable judges, distinguished guests, ladies, and gentlemen, my name is Nika and I hope you all have a fabulous evening."

The audience cheers. People say I'm a genius. Then everyone waits for the judges to make the announcement. The announcer calls me the first-runner-up. Makalo's sister Trish shouts out, "You cheaters, Nika is the queen and you all know it!" Her ghetto rage breaks my trophy in two halves. Makalo runs on stage and gives me a hug.

He says, "Nika, don't worry. They cheat but everyone knows you're the best."

They crown the winner, a ten-year-old niece of a popular politician. The sad part is she does not know the name of the minister of tourism who serves with her uncle in parliament. She freezes on stage and someone yells the answer. She speaks it in the microphone and pretends not to hear. She is the winner. I'm the second-best. She lives on the outskirts of the ghetto in a stone house. She is a more suitable queen. Real ghetto girls like me are poor choices, not beauty queens, even if we win fair and square.

******

Makalo comes to visit the next day. We sit in the dirt and talk under the tamarind tree.

"Makalo, why you think they cheat me?"

"I don't know."

"You think I did good?"

"Nika, you did so good. Everyone thought you should be the queen."

"So, if they thought that, why did they cheat?"

"My mother said they cheat because you are a nobody. The girl who win is a Thompson."

"Yeah. Her uncle is a big-time politician."

"Don't worry, Nika. Next time you'll win."

"Makalo, how come you hardly visit?"

"Because I'm busy."

"Busy doin' what?"

"Stuff."

"What stuff? I bet the stuff is Tito and Jeremy. Why you always have to play with them, Makalo?"

"Because."

"Because what?"

"Because I'm a boy. Tito and Jeremy say boys should play with boys."

"Don't listen to them. Makalo, you know we have a lot of fun when we play."

"I know. But I have to play with boys too, Nika." Makalo stands up.

"Makalo, you leavin'?"

"Yeah. Bye, Nika. And don't worry. You did the best in the beauty pageant. Even Tito and Jeremy think so. Don't be mad, Nika."

"Makalo, stop smilin' when you say stuff like that."

"Sorry, Nika."

Makalo leaves and the tears stream down my face. I cry quietly and then I hear Sister's voice.

"Nika, where are you?"

I dry my eyes then yell, "Under the tamarind tree."

Sister comes out and sits with me. My face reveals I'm not in the mood for talk, so Sister takes my hand and we sit in silence for a long time. Then Sister tells me about her conversation with the organizer of the ghetto beauty pageant.

"Did they cheat Nika out of the crown, or was she really first-runner-up?"

The woman says, "I'm sorry to have to tell you but Nika should be the queen, not her. One of the judges befriends the politician and tells him not to worry. His niece is queen and that's that."

I feel better after Sister talks to me. She says, "Fame's not important, so don't mind them." Sister's right so I let this one go. We don't get our earnings in the ghetto because the ones who don't need always receive. But I'm happy to know I'm talented enough to be a ghetto, beauty queen.

Chapter Twelve

I'm really happy tonight and the full moon shines bright to make this a glorious evening. Thousands gather at the Fort that overlooks the calm, blue ocean to take in the performances and fireworks of the July celebrations. Ghetto folks, middle class, rich ones, blacks and whites all come together to share in a national event. The flag waves high and the police band plays calypso music. People dance like there is no tomorrow. Police squads perform on motorcycles and their uniforms are so crisp. Crowds stand behind the barricades and toddlers sit up high on the shoulders of their moms and dads. The dignitaries arrive in their five hundred-dollar suits in black limousines that are shiny and clean.

I don't have to stand with the crowds who come only to observe. This ghetto girl is one of the performers, one of the lucky citizens. I get to go up on stage because I'm one of the dancers in the Independence Day celebrations. The Queen and Prince Charles are attendees and all the members of parliament are present as well.

This is the second time Her Majesty, the Queen of Britain sees me perform. It's no big deal. She comes to the Commonwealth to wave at the people and to remind us we are not fully free. Our ties to colonialism never leave us and our country bows down to her throne. She is welcome, and we honor her presence but an eight-year-old, ghetto girl cannot fully appreciate her. Important people don't mean much to ghetto children unless they take time to really spend time. A wave from afar is not enough to get me excited. I want these important people to come to my house, share a meal then join in with our game of rope skipping.

The first time I meet Her Majesty she comes close. She shakes my hand at the musical's curtain call. I'm one of the little girls in Sammy Swain the big-time musical production that people pay big money to see. Father says, "They better pay you or you'll never return." Mother tells him the money comes soon and gives me permission to go. We wait for two months and receive one hundred dollars.

The money is "oh-so-important."

The Queen watches from afar and I think she smiles at me. We dance in our pink leotards and tights to the music of the blind man who beats the goat-skinned drums. The costumes are free from the government. They tell us they're ours to keep. The dance of the conch is what we perform, and it requires us to move our backs like we are spineless. I'm so good at this conch-dance and the teachers are really impressed. They bring a woman to watch me who looks very familiar. She is the director of the National School of Dance. They tell her I'm a ghetto child whose talents in dance are supreme and they ask her to give me a scholarship, so I can dance at the National School with trained teachers. Her eyes open wide when she catches a good look at me. I'm the ghetto girl whose crown she steals to give to the relative of a politician. She cannot bear her own shame and is restless at night as she acknowledges her wrongs before God. She gives me a full scholarship to dance until I'm eighteen.

Dance is one of my passions. But it's really my way to escape the hard truths about my life and my ghetto. I forget every pain, every tear, and every misfortune when I dance. I love ballet and jazz but contemporary is my favorite. They all make me feel pretty. But the mean rich girls at the dance school poke fun at me and say, "You're not wanted."

"Who invited you to our dance school?" The ring leader, Beatrice says to me.

I just look at Beatrice. I can't find the right words to say.

"We know you live in the ghetto. You smell like the ghetto. We don't like ghetto smell." Beatrice turns up her nose at me.

I continue to look at her, but the words still don't come. This is one of the rare occasions when I'm speechless.

"You're not wanted. Go back to your ghetto, Miss Raggedy." Beatrice calls her dance friends together and they whisper, laugh, and point at me.

They don't understand why I stay in a place I don't belong. Even outside the ghetto, people know who I am. My ghetto halo glows and they see me, daytime or night. I never expect acceptance in this cruel world of ours. I hold on to my courage and swallow my nine-year-old pride. I dare not let my ghetto rage take over. I retreat into myself and ignore the mean jokes they make about me and my family. They are not worthy of ghetto rage, they are jealous of my talent.

I continue my dance lessons despite the bullying. Summer ends and I look forward to school because my school uniform makes me feel like I belong to a community of people who accept me and my "ghettoness."

******

"Who's up? Who's that?" Mother calls from her bedroom.

"It's me, Mother. Nika," I reply.

"Nika, what are you doin'?" Mother's curiosity makes her voice screech.

"Ironing my school uniform," I reply.

"But Nika, it's only five o'clock in the morning. Girl, go back to bed." Mother is impatient.

"Yes, Ma'am."

I get up early today because I have a deep desire to hide my "ghettoness" under my school uniform because my Salvation Army clothes cause people to pick on me. Beatrice says she can tell I'm from the ghetto because of my clothes. When I tell Makalo this he says, "That Beatrice sounds mean. You should beat her up like Tamika."

I say, "Trust me, Makalo. If it wasn't for Mother, I would."

I wonder what Beatrice will say when she sees me in my school uniform. I bet her jealousy will swell even bigger because people say I look so good when I'm dressed for school. My school uniform makes me blend in with the crowd and sometimes people even mistake me for the middle class. I'm eager to put it on. A grey, knee-length skirt with one-inch pleats and a white blouse with a folding collar are the items I wear five days a week. I love my netball uniform, too, because it means I'm a part of a team. Some days, I miss dance lessons to play netball matches and my dance teachers are not happy at all. "What a waste of talent," are the words they all say, and these words are so hard to hear because a ghetto child can never waste anything.

I struggle to choose between dance and netball and for a while my games take priority. But eventually, I return to the dance studio where the mean girls await me with glares that cut metal sheets. "Why did you come back? We said you're not wanted." Words a ghetto girl expects are my greeting. I listen and fight back the tears. Like my crown, they steal my joy of dance and leave me to wallow in pity.

I'm sad for two weeks and refuse to explain to anyone what eats away my joy. But Sister can get me to confess.

"Nika, what's wrong? You haven't been yourself lately." Sister sits on the bed and gently pulls me to come, join her.

"Mmm. It's nothin'," I speak with my head down.

"Come on, Nika. I know something's bothering you?"

"Nothin' is bothering me, Sister." I keep my head down.

"Nika, look at me."

I can't raise my steelhead. Sister reaches over and gently turns my face to hers.

"Tell me what happened, Nika."

The first teardrop falls, and Sister wipes it away.

"It's the rich girls at the dance school. They tease me and tell me I'm not wanted. They make fun of me."

Slow tears coast down my face. I see Sister's eyes get glassy. She embraces me, and I feel absolute comfort.

"Be strong, Nika. Don't let them get to you. Jealousy won't get them very far."

"What should I say to them when they tease me?"

"Don't say anything. Just ignore them."

"But when I ignore them, they don't stop."

"So, tell them to stop. Have you ever told them to stop?"

"No."

"So that's what you need to do, Nika. When they say stuff that hurts you, tell them to stop."

"Okay, Sister."

Sister cheers me up and tells me to expect a very special gift from her. She orders me a brand new, pink leotard from the "Bookman" who is really a traveling salesman.

I pick myself up and return to the dance school to reclaim my joy and be strong. When the mean words attack me, I take a few minutes to build courage and then I do something great. I contain my ghetto ways, smile, and say, "You all have serious problems."

I dance like no one watches and enjoy every step that I make. I whisper to the ring leader Beatrice, "Listen closely. Dance is my own and you little bitches can't have it!"

Ghetto children like to say, "is my own" when we really mean to say, "is mine." Dance is mine and I refuse to let Beatrice and her friends take it away from me. Sister says I need to be stronger than their words and remember she is always there for me. She says Beatrice and her friends must think I'm a threat because I'm so talented. From now on, I will not let Beatrice get to me. I will not let my ghetto rage push me to become violent. Besides, if I do get in a fight with Beatrice, Mother would whip me and I'm so tired of that.

Chapter Thirteen

Makalo doesn't visit much this summer. I take up a new summer friendship with Amy. Amy is nine (like me) and she lives on the corner of the alley across from ours. I think I like Amy so much because she looks just like Makalo. She even smiles like him.

This beautiful summer's day I play with Amy and we have so much fun but it's hot and we need to cool off. Amy says, "Nika, let's go down to the beach." I follow her like a fool. Mother does not permit us to go to the beach alone, but I go anyway. Amy and I arrive at the beach and it's truly a beautiful sight. I forget about Mother when I see the horizon. The line that separates blue skies and crystal-clear waters are most beautiful under the radiant sunshine. Amy and I strip down to our panties and run around with bare chests. Bras are not items we need yet.

The beach receives us gladly because it's lonely. No one visits today, only us two ghetto girls who are free to come and go as we please. We forget freedom comes at a cost as we bask in the sunshine and breathe in the pure, clean, fresh air. Amy and I sit on the shoreline of the most picturesque view. Only Sister's words can describe this scene. I see beautiful, serene, crystal clear, aquamarine waters, and white sand glistens in the warmth of golden sunshine. My dark brown eyes cannot fully capture the enormous clear blue sky because it gives off a rich prairie hue that is absolutely majestic. I gaze at the tall coconut trees that look down between the greenery of their long, narrow leaves. The leaves wave—like queens in the soft wind—and salute the pink and red hibiscus flowers that smile at the view. The scattered green leaves of the palm trees venerate this tranquil ambiance. Today is beautiful.

The water is cool. The waves are delightful. The sand feels so good between my toes. The seagulls fly overhead, and they sing their ocean-chorus that soothes two nine-year-old, ghetto girls. The water splashes between our thighs and we like the pleasure it gives us. Amy and I giggle, laugh, and touch each other's private parts. We dig holes in the white sand, collect pink seashells, make sandcastles, and relax in the shade of a coconut tree.

"Nika, help me build a wall around my sandcastle," Amy says.

"Okay," I reply.

Amy and I gather sand between our hands and form it into a wall.

"Nika, what do you want to be when you grow up?"

"A teacher."

"I want to be a teacher, too."

"You just want to be a teacher because that's what I want to be."

"No."

"Yes, Amy. I know that's why you said that."

"No."

"Amy, I don't care if you want to be a teacher, too."

"You don't?"

"No. I don't."

"Nika, I like playing with you."

"I like you too, Amy."

"Are you gonna be my friend forever, Nika?"

"Yeah, we should be friends forever." I nod my head in agreement then the mid-section of the sand wall collapses.

"Look, Nika. The wall," Amy shouts.

Then I see Marcus' evil grin of contentment as he straddles the seat of his old, rusty bicycle. Marcus speaks words that make me fearful, but he does so with pleasure, "Mother sent me to get you. Your dance teacher called the neighbors and left a message for you to come to rehearsal."

Not one word makes an escape from my lips. I put on my clothes in a flash and begin my trek home as I rub my arms together.

"Bye, Nika," Amy says.

My words fail to come out, but I say them in my mind, "Bye, Amy."

Marcus is the cursed one. His wide smile causes his eyes to squint and hides the wickedness behind them. He is a thief, a cocaine addict, and he has a passion for evil. His story is more sinister than mine. I do not even want to know it as I'm sure it reveals horrific tales that my mind blocks. His story includes a scene of a teenager who holds a man at gunpoint and forces him into the trunk of his own car. The man does not know the gun isn't real and the teenager doesn't acknowledge the evil he performs.

My evil brother, Marcus rides beside me and says, "You better go faster. Mother's angry and waiting at the door."

He giggles and shows no empathy for his sister who faces the threat of the rod.

"Run faster and you might become a sprinter who wins Olympic gold medals. Hurry because it's your turn to burn, Nika."

His words are mean, and I know he gets pleasure when he speaks them. I outrun his pedaling and my heart pounds as I get closer to home. He yells at me from the distance and makes the sounds of Mother's switches, "Whash, galash, whash, galash."

He's the devil. I know in my heart.

Each step brings me closer to home and I wish for any sister to be at my side. I know a sister understands me and shares my pain. Mother sends a cruel messenger, so this must be a sign. She is angry and gnashes her teeth.

I arrive on the porch. My heart throbs. I hold every second breath. Then I turn to look at Marcus. He winks, smiles, then shouts, "Mother, Nika's here!"

Mother gives me five whips with a hard leather belt then she gives me bus fare to ride to the dance school where all the kids hate me.

Hate is such a strong word and I don't like to use it. But sometimes it's the only word that makes my point clear. In the ghetto, we have to be sure our words are not open to misinterpretation. This is problematic for the speaker who has no time to retract. It's better to say what you mean and mean what you say in the ghetto or people think you're a fool or a cheat. Like that day last August, Chrissy's friend takes her gold necklace, but Chrissy is not clear enough. She lends it, but the friend receives it as a gift. A week later Chrissy asks her friend to return it and she "freaks." She claims it's hers.

"Chrissy, you gave this to me."

The girl flares her wide nostrils, puts her hands in the air, and warns Chrissy, "Don't fuck with me."

Her ghetto rage bubbles inside her and she picks up a rock at her feet. She hits Chrissy on the side of her head. I hear the rock as it pounds Chrissy's scalp. I see red, thin blood slide down Chrissy's left ear when she bends down to grab a handful of rocks. Chrissy chases the girl but to no avail. The girl runs inside her house and locks the door.

"This is not over," Chrissy threatens.

These words are the worst ones to hear. I worry Chrissy plans to attack the girl later and I worry about the outcome. Ghetto fights turn bloody and often there is one soul that never leaves the scene. They carry the body to the morgue.

Chrissy attends her bloody head and takes a nap. I hope this sleep calms her and gives her sweet dreams. I do not want Chrissy to fight her. I just want her to stay home with me. It's safer in the violent-filled house we call home than outside in the ghetto streets.

A few hours pass, Chrissy awakes with a peaceful demeanor. I'm happy she decides to stay home. She says, "She's not worth it. She can keep the stupid gold chain."

I'm happy because Chrissy contains the rage of the ghetto inside her that pushes people into their graves.

Chapter Fourteen

My earliest memory is one of a four-year-old who is afraid to go home to witness yet another violent episode between my brothers. The scariest recollection is of my evil brother, Marcus, high on marijuana. He throws a stone at Mother and it hits her with great force. Hot red blood rushes down the side of Mother's face. My father chases Marcus with a sharp machete in hand and threatens to kill him. In my mind, the threat is very real. Marcus uses the cheetah's speed to escape on foot. He runs into the street. Father chases after him with eyes like whips that are pulled back because they prepare to strike with lethal forces. After twenty minutes, Father returns home. He is hot, sweaty, and angry, "I'm gonna kill that boy. He better not let me catch him." Mother bleeds and Marcus escapes.

Amy tells me stories about her big brothers, too. They fight to the blood and her mother has to call the police to come, separate them. Amy says she has a brother just like Marcus. He steals money from her mother and uses it to buy a "hit" from the drug dealer up the road. Today, Amy and I play Jacks on her front porch. Mother allows me to go to Amy's house to play if I ask permission and come home before dark. Amy lives in a two-bedroom apartment above the corner store with her mother, older sister, and three older brothers. We play on the dirty, stinky concrete steps that lead to the broken, tattered door of their apartment.

"Here, Nika. Take the ball, it's your turn." Amy hands me the small, rubber, neon-colored, bouncy ball.

"Thanks, Amy." I pick up the six neon-colored jacks, shake them in my small right hand, and then toss them down on the concrete step.

"Awe, Man." I'm disappointed because my jacks fall too close together. "How am I supposed to pick up ones if they're that close together?"

"You can take another turn, Nika." Amy is so generous.

"Are you serious? I didn't let you take another turn when your jacks fell too close."

"That's okay, Nika."

"No, Amy. I won't take another turn because it's not fair to you." I throw up the ball, grab a jack, and miss the ball. "I'm out."

Amy runs down the flight of twelve stairs and retrieves the ball from below. "Yuck. It fell right in a mud puddle." Amy cleans the ball on her dirty, red shorts.

"Hey, Amy, wanna play tag?" I run down the stairs to meet her.

"All right."

"Tag, you're it." I tap Amy on the shoulder then run away.

Amy chases me. "Nika, slow down."

I run all the way home and sit under the tamarind tree. I try to catch my breath.

Amy arrives out of breath. "Tag, you're it." She barely gets these words out, taps me on the head, then sits next to me.

"That was fun," I speak when I catch my breath.

"Yeah, Nika. That was fun. But guess what? I dropped my ball while I was running."

"For real?"

"Yeah. Can you help me look for it?"

"Yeah, Amy. Let's go look for your ball."

"Nika, where are you going?" Mother sees me walking out of the yard with Amy.

"Amy lost her ball. I'm going to help her look."

"You come right back home after you find it. You hear me, Nika?"

"Yes, Ma'am."

Amy and I walk back to their apartment and do not find the neon-colored ball.

"Sorry, Amy."

"It's okay, Nika."

"You can have my ball. I have one at home. I'll give it to you."

"You'll give it to me? Really, Nika?" Amy smiles and reminds me of Makalo.

"Yeah." I smile then chuckle, "You remind me so much of Makalo."

"What! Why you say that?"

"Because you smile like him."

"Nika, you sayin' I look like a boy!"

I laugh. "No, Amy."

"What are you sayin'?"

"Nothin'." I laugh some more.

Amy laughs, too. "My best friend thinks I look like a boy. I just can't believe you, Nika."

I close my eyes, press my teeth together, and try to smile like Makalo. Amy laughs hysterically.

Chapter Fifteen

My arms are tired because I carry water jugs home from the government pump this late evening. It's better when the shopping cart collector is late. I push the gallons down the lane. But my muscles are strong because I carry these water jugs home. The orange sun sets and the air cools. I'm smart to do this chore late in the evening when the sun goes away.

I greet people and walk home – barefoot and dirty. The dirt is a sign of good fun. A game of marbles with Makalo, tag with Amy, and rope skipping with Edith and Chrissy, keep me physically fit. The games keep me busy and I stay out of trouble. Mother doesn't mind when I play outside in the side yard. But there is a woman who lives just behind us, her children cannot play outside. She protects them by keeping them prisoners. They stay inside their house all day long. I ask one of them to come, play. She says, "My mother says we can't come outside."

The five of them inside a small, two-bedroom house can only be up to no good. There is nothing to do – they have no toys, no TV, and no video games. I do not understand how they spend all their time inside their house. Inside a ghetto house, all day long breeds incest. The best bet is to go outside to play. Outside, there are no room doors to close, mattresses to sink, or bedsheets to hide below. Ghetto children are safer outside than inside and everyone knows it even if the words remain silent. Quiet shame, even ghetto stories refuse to tell. The silent words of the ghetto are the loudest and clearest. No one claims to misunderstand. Wicked watchers live inside, too. They are neighbors to others but family to you.

The other neighbor (Simon) comes to the wall to meet me. He comes outside but stays at the wall. Simon talks to me but that is all. He wants to play, and he seems so happy when he watches me mark out the circle in the dirt.

"Come shoot marbles with us," I call to him.

Then his father yells his name, "Simon, don't you cross that wall. Stay in our yard like I told you."

Simon obeys and watches me and Makalo play marbles from his view at the wall. He stands on a tall bucket, so he can see over it. Then, he leans on the wall. Rests his arms on top. Puts his chin on his arms, so his neck does not have to hold up his heavy head for hours as he watches us play.

Simon's skin is yellow like Chrissy's, but his features are very different from ours. He has an over-sized head, a pointy nose, and a mouth full of big, white, fang-like teeth. Normally, he wears a white undershirt when he visits us from the wall. His mother sells snacks from her fridge but sometimes Simon gives them to me and my sisters for free. Makalo and I go to the wall to place our usual order. "One cup and ten cents worth of salty sausage," is what we yell. "A cup" is frozen Kool-Aid that cools us off and makes our lips red.

My big brothers never go to the wall, but they send Matt and me to place their "cup" orders. Matt and I are the gofers. We go to the wall to place "cup" orders and to the corner store to buy cigarettes for Father. The cashier always remarks that Matt and I look a lot alike. Mother says we have so many features that are like Father's. But I don't look like my five older brothers because we don't have the same father. My five other brothers are much older than me. When I'm born, most of them are in their early teenage years. Although we all share the same house because none of them marry young, I do not establish a close connection with them like the one I share with Matt.

Only two of Mother's sons are Father's – Matt and Marcus. Their appearances fail to depict they are different, and they look very much the same. Handsome, ghetto boys, they are, indeed, with yellow skin, eyes that squint, thin upper lips, rounded-button noses, white teeth, and soft, curly hair. Marcus becomes more distinct when Mother throws a can of insect spray that hits him. His top lip splits open and heals with a scar. Later he cracks a front tooth playing rough games. Marcus is seven years my senior and he is the devil.

Matt and I have a lot in common. We both like to play marbles, catch tadpoles, and read books at school. My older brothers don't read books. They read wordless magazines. Matt and I sometimes find them in the garbage piles and in the bushes. The white women in them are so free. They pose in the nude with their legs spread apart and sometimes they pose with their own fingers inside their vaginas. These white models must be ghetto girls, too, because they forget freedom comes at a cost.

"Nika, what's that?" Matt points at the white woman's opened vagina.

"Matt, don't look at that." I grab the magazine and throw it back in the garbage pile.

I wonder if the mothers of these naked models are angry. Mother either kills me or dies from the shame if I pose in a book that requires no words. I do not understand the looks I see in the eyes of these magazine models. They look hungry for something, but I know fried chicken is not what they crave. I can tell they don't eat much because they are so thin. Perhaps they are sad deep inside and choose to pose naked, so their children can eat. A mother does what she has to and cares for her young. These white women are no different. Their lives mean something in the grander story that tells the troubles of humankind.

People who bully these white models must be happy because they have proof of the nasty things they say. My bullies have no photographs as evidence of the malicious things they say about me. To photograph poverty and a life of struggle is an impossible task. Besides, when cameras are ready, the biggest smiles appear on the faces of ghetto children and we say "cheese" with enthusiasm that echoes. Pictures reveal we are happy but conceal our sorrow. Our sadness hides far behind our eyes and to see it you must stare at them until the windows of our souls force themselves open.

They say the eyes are the windows to the soul, but ghetto folks keep their souls shut in. However, real windows are open during daylight in the ghetto and doors are open, too. But this is a risk we take. The story of the sleepy woman who unlocks her front door is another sad ghetto account. A wicked watcher comes in. Rapes her. Locks the door as he leaves. She is one of the many who suffer "under" ghetto men who believe they are free to take pleasure at their leisure. A ghetto woman suffers three times more than the average ghetto man. She suffers because she bares children and she bares shame but mostly because she is female.

Mother suffers, too, but she is strong. To bear fifteen children and maintain a sound mind is the accomplishment of a courageous female. Mother represents the vigor and power of ghetto women and she is the reason we are ghetto children with a clapboard house we call home.

******

"Nika. Is Matt outside with you?" Mother calls from the kitchen door.

"Yes, Ma'am," I yell back at her from the front yard.

"You two, come inside. It's getting late." Mother's words expect us to comply.

"Yes, Ma'am… Matt, let's go. Mother wants us to come in." I take Matt's hand and we walk toward the front door.

"Nika, when the sun starts to go down, I want you home. You hear me?" Mother waits for us at the door.

"Yes, Ma'am."

Mother wants us home because she knows it's unsafe to be out in the ghetto streets at night. Home is a safety-net in the ghetto, especially when it's dark. And schools are safety-nets, too. Mother's favorite politician does some good. He builds a school in the ghetto that looks like a castle. It's three-stories high and made of blocks and cement. Air condition and free lunch, the school is the best in the country. Too bad it only enrolls students up to grade six. The teachers are wonderful people. I don't understand why ghetto children come on the first day and they cry for their mothers to stay. This bright scholar does not cry on her first day of school. Education is something I need. The three-story, yellow schoolhouse is an omen. It hides Dorothy's secret maps inside. I'm eager to search for a hidden map that tells me where to find my yellow brick road that leads to my destiny.

Ghetto high schools have no maps on their walls and people know it because the students are lost. The high school students bear arms: handguns, kitchen knives, and baseball bats. I'm glad I do not have to witness all the violence because I'm one of Mother's four bright scholars. I go to the big yellow school with Makalo for some years but when I pass the entrance exam Mother sends me to the private school in the South. Unfortunately, Makalo doesn't pass the entrance exam even though I help him study.

Chapter Sixteen

I think I'm safe in my private school in the South, but ghetto ways travel everywhere. I walk outside my classroom after the dismal bell rings and a large stone misses my head by a fraction of an inch. "We're under attack," yells the tall, black, male, religion teacher. Then I see three ghetto boys throw rocks at students who wear the gray and white school uniform. I run back into my classroom.

"Shit. Fuck. Mother fuckers," are the words I hear as I hide behind the door. I hear rocks hit the outside walls of my classroom. I hear people scream. I don't dare leave my cover. I worry about Matt who is in the classroom at the front of the school where the intruders begin the attack. My little brother, I hope he is safe behind a door or under a table. I hope he does not try to be brave.

I say a prayer and hope Mother's God hears me. He is my God, as well. He better listen. *Please save Matt from harm and bring these attackers to their trial. They deserve to feel pain and do not deserve your mercy. Save us, Lord. Though I walk through the valley and the shadow of death, I fear no evil for you are with me.* I come out when I hear silence at last. I run to the front of the school to find Matt. He is safe and does not have any wounds. But there are others who bleed from their faces and whose spit is the color of red.

Our school principal is a great man and a religious leader. But he becomes a ghetto man when he realizes many lives depend on him. He grabs an attacker by the skin of his black teenage neck and drags him to his office where he beats him to the floor with his bamboo cane. I cannot say I'm sorry. The attacker gets what he deserves. My principal shares the same beliefs as Mother. Spare the rod and the child spoils like raw fish on a counter that sits for weeks in the heat of the Caribbean ghetto.

This religious, black man has a story that intrigues even ghetto folks. His shiny bald head, small waistline, impeccable shirt and ties, and sparkling leather shoes cannot contain his anxiety. He shakes like a man with Parkinson's disease. The trembles are the reminder of his loss that we learn about at a school's assembly. When government workers come from the Department of

Transportation to teach about road safety, our principal excuses himself from the presentation. In the end, he returns to tell us his story. He shakes because he receives a call one day from the police. They tell him there is a traffic fatality and the fatal victim is his only son.

I know this man is not from the ghetto because he has a heart that breaks. He weeps for his son and his life changes. The death of his son is a burden he carries and even though he walks upright and proper, speaks the Queen's English, and is intelligent, he hurts just like me. Ghetto pain is like the loss of a son every morning. The pain is wretched, abject, and miserable. In the ghetto, we soothe our pain with food on Sundays and we look forward to this weekly feast.

******

This October issues in its first Sunday and the feast begins around three o'clock. Mother dishes up seventeen plates of food but we don't eat all together. Some are in the living room, kitchen, outside in the front yard and Father takes his plate to Mother's bedroom where he hides.

Peas and rice, macaroni, coleslaw, potato salad, fried chicken, plantain, corn, and beets fill up our plates. We eat until our bellies swell. Sunday is the most sinful day of the week because ghetto people practice all seven sins: lust, gluttony, greed, sloth, wrath, envy, and pride. Sunday dinner makes it easy to sin. We lust after the food. Overeat. Take more than we need. Sit on our asses. Get angry if they forget to put ours aside. Complain because someone else's plate is bigger. And do not admit we are full.

"Can I have some more rice?" I ask Mother.

"Bring your plate, Nika. I'll give you some more." Mother takes the lid off the tall, iron pot and dishes up some rice.

"Thank you." I go sit at the kitchen table.

"Nika, you sure can eat." Chrissy pipes up.

"Yeah. Nika's a hog." Edith could not wait to jump in.

"You're a hog, Edith. Shut up," My words are quick and sharp.

"Enough. That's enough. If I hear another word from any of you, you know just what will happen," Mother quickly ends the dispute.

"Yes, Ma'am." Edith and I speak at exactly the same time.

"Just enjoy the food and thank God for it," Mother concludes her speech.

Edith gives me her evil look, but I pretend not to notice.

"Mmm… This rice tastes so good." I say this only to please Mother.

Caribbean food is delicious. Okra soup and peas soup and dumplings are the tastiest dishes we ghetto children enjoy. We are so fortunate that Mother is a good cook of local and foreign dishes. People come to her and ask her to make huge pots of food for cookouts, parties, and family gatherings. Mother is not good at anything else and she does not have any hobbies to speak of. But we ghetto children have so many. We especially love to play bat-and-ball to past time, and so we gather on the field of the big yellow school to play bat-and-ball almost every evening.

Twenty or thirty ghetto children show up around five o'clock this Wednesday in mid-October. Sister, Edith, Chrissy, Amy, Makalo, and I come to play, too. We divide ourselves into two teams. Old, rotting pieces of wood are the bats, large rocks the size of footballs are the bases, and a tennis ball is the target. Bat-and-ball is like baseball except you must hit the runner with the ball for an "out." Sometimes an "out" stings my skin. I learn to dodge the tennis ball when it races toward me. Adrenaline makes me happy when I play this game and even though I know I could take a ball to the face or back of the head, I'm always eager to join in.

The organizer of the games is a ghetto woman (Joanne) who lives with her two children. Joanne is spunky and fun. Sister admires her a lot because she is independent. Joanne raises her two sons without a man and she does a damn-good-job. Her children are clean, and they go to the big yellow school every day. Sister thinks Joanne is pretty. She has dark-chocolate skin and is tall and thin. Her long weave hides the real length of her hair and she prefers to speak like the Queen. Joanne uses the dialect on occasion when she wants to explain something well. She knows ghetto children understand the dialect better than the Queen's English that books force them to learn.

"Okay, kids. Let's do this right. I'll assign captains and then the captains will flip a coin," Joanne speaks to us like she is a school teacher. "Mia and Chrissy are the captains."

"Awesome! Sister, please pick me." I'm excited that Sister is team captain.

"Nika, you're always on Mia's team. I think you should be on Chrissy's team this time." Joanne sounds even more like a school teacher.

"Yeah. I agree. Nika you should play on my team today," Chrissy smirks and nods her head.

"But I like playing on Sister's team," I pout.

"Nika, it's okay. The teams need to be fair. You should play for Chrissy today." Sister agrees with Joanne.

"Fine," My response is subdued.

Chrissy and Sister pick their teams and we play. When it's my turn to bat, I hit the ball and make it to first base. Edith is the first baseman.

"You better watch out, Nika. If I get the chance I will pork you with the ball. You better not try to run." Edith is very serious.

I think Edith would make a good witch in a storybook. She reminds me of the wicked old woman in Hansel and Gretel. If I could perform a magic trick, I would put Edith in one of my storybooks at school. Perhaps she could be the evil stepmother in Cinderella. But then again, I wouldn't want Edith to ruin books for me. I think books provide hilarious tales. Stories of white people who live in countries where ice falls from the sky are so funny. Everyone knows the sun shines every day. Trains and mountains are made-up just like dragons and unicorns. The writers have incredible imaginations. These stories do not mean anything, but teachers are happy when I read the words out loud. I don't love the stories, but I love the words because teachers say I'm smart when I decode them. I wish Makalo could decode long words, so he could come with me to the private school. "I'm not smart like you, Nika," he says.

Long, complicated words are no challenge for a ghetto girl who aims to please. I decode the most complex and smile when I hear teachers say, "You're going to be somebody someday." The teacher takes my notebook and holds it up high for all the other children to see.

"Look at this book. It's neat, tidy, and it has no dog-ears. This is what I expect from the rest." Teacher is speechless when she hears me recite the sixty-six books of the bible in order.

******

"Ouch," I shriek because Edith hits the back of my left thigh with the tennis ball.

"Nika, you're out. I told you not to run." Edith is proud of her accomplishment.

"That's three out. Teams need to switch," Joanne calls out. She reminds me so much of my school teacher, Miss Curry. She even looks a bit like her.

I like Miss Curry, but there is another teacher (Mrs. Bain) at school who is like Mother. Mrs. Bain likes to discipline with the rod and gives long speeches about all the things we need to learn. This tall, heavy-set woman scares us. I do not understand why she teaches because clearly, she does not realize the importance of schools. Like an ogre or a troll, she is a beast if she discourages children or makes them want to quit.

Just a day ago, Mrs. Bain calls nine of us school children and says, "Line up and put your palms up." I go to the back of the line and watch as she licks the eight students ahead of me with her beating stick. Two licks in the right palm and two on the left. Students leave the line either crying loudly or silently. My turn comes, and I put up my right palm. She licks me with all her might. I feel her stout anger enter my palm, and it does not leave. It continues to sting for hours and then it slowly wanes. Mrs. Bain beats us because we play a game of "ring-circle" with boys and we shake up ourselves like adults do at parties.

Nine of us sing "ring-play" songs and when we are in the center, we swivel, grind, and shake our hips. With a partner, we bump and grind together. This childish game is not a bad thing. We are innocent, little children. The mean teacher punishes us because our game reminds her of the evil in fornication. It's clear that Mrs. Bain does not love children. She beats us every chance she gets. There is no joy or love in her heart.

"Nika, Nika. You day-dreamin'?" Makalo asks. "You better stop day-dreamin' so we could get Edith out."

"I wasn't day-dreaming, Makalo. And don't worry. I'm so ready to get Edith out. She is gonna get it."

Edith hits the tennis ball right at me. I catch it and then run toward her. I throw the ball at her. It hits her smack in the middle of her stomach. She drops to the ground and lets out a loud cry.

"Edith, you're out." I show her no mercy.

"Nika, you have no idea what you started." Edith manages to sound evil in spite of the pain.

I walk back to first base and Makalo says, "Nika, you hit her so hard. You didn't have to hit her that hard."

"She hit me hard first and whose side are you on anyway?"

"Yours."

"You don't know Edith. She's a bully. And for cryin' out loud, Makalo, stop that smilin'."

Chapter Seventeen

Love is something I do not take for granted. I know Mother loves us. Sister loves me. Sometimes I need a reminder that ghetto men love, too. Makalo and Matt love me, but my brother Marcus does not even love himself. Sister says no one teaches Marcus the important lesson. To love is to exist. We commit suicide when we refuse to love. Those who refuse to love are heartless. These people are the lowest in the ghetto. The heartless who curse everything is more dangerous than wicked watchers. When the heartless says, "Don't fuck with me," the evil in their eyes blinds you. They mean what they say and say what they mean. They do not make empty threats so don't test them.

If they say, "I'll kill you," take off as fast as you can. Many heartless end up in prison and I wonder if the prison cells give them time to think about their choices.

Love is a choice. We choose to love, or we die. In the ghetto, this choice is very clear. One day, Amy tells me she is unable to sleep because she enters the room where he slumbers in a blood pool. A ghetto man shoots himself in the head and splatters blood across his bedroom walls. The loud gunshot gathers men, women, and children who go inside whole but come out in pieces. They see the insides of a man's head as he lies on the floor. Bleeding arteries and veins. Pieces of human brain. Raw flesh. Exposed tendons. Muscles and bone. They leave to tell of this sight. A ghetto battle ends, and the only soldier is dead. The soldier refuses to love, even himself, and dies alone in a blood pool that desperately wants to give life. A sight like this, even nosey ghetto eyes cannot bear.

The ghetto is full of nosey watchers. It's no surprise the dead man gathers a big crowd of them. Mother says the nosey, old woman next door likes gossip more than pineapples, mangoes, and sweet coconut milk. She goes for nosey walks every day and pretends to look at her feet, but we all know she has eyes at the back of her head. Her nostrils are the widest and her hair is so grey it looks blue. She covers her head with a head-cloth but leaves room for her nosey eyes at the back. Short, nappy, tight curls sit at the top of her neck. Her long skirt covers her black, scrubby knees, and bedroom slippers do their job well.

A ghetto woman wears bedroom slippers so she is quiet when she walks past bedroom windows or stands behind you when you converse with a friend.

******

"Makalo, did you come to play today?" I ask.

"No, I came to bring the asue money. Mommy sent me, and she said to come right back home."

"How much money your mother sent, Boy?" The nosey woman interjects.

"Don't tell her nothin', Makalo. She's too nosey," I reply.

"You have a big mouth, Nika, for such a small face. Next time you talk like that to me, I'll tell your mother bout that time I catch you and Amy touchin' each other's privates. You Makalo, I'll tell your mother bout the time I catch you stealin' hog plums from Mr. Roker's yard."

Makalo and I run inside and leave the nosey woman to snoop around our front yard.

This nosey woman wants to know everything and gets in everyone's affairs. Her nostrils turn up when she judges the actions of all but her own. As she ages, her steps are slow but still quiet. She continues to see things people want to keep quiet.

"What you do in the dark comes out with the light," These are her words when we accuse her of nosey ways that make us all uneasy. I think she's the one who carries the blame for all the rumors that spread about Mother and my sisters. There is nothing we can do to make her stop. We live with an additional duty – to dodge a nosey watcher and conceal as much as we can.

God blesses the nosey woman with long life, hearing, sight, and a tongue that does not age with her years. Mother gives her much to take in when renovations begin on the old, clapboard house we call home. Before the renovations, the house sits on a foundation of blocks my grandfather leaves for his oldest. Mother gladly accepts her inheritance but with it comes six younger siblings she raises with her first three. The undersized house has four closet-sized bedrooms, a small open room for a living room and kitchen combination. There is no inside-plumbing but there is an outhouse and a well. The well gives water that stinks like shit. We are grateful for the government pump down the lane and happy for August and September when God gives us rain.

The house renovations are really wonderful, a job my father does all by himself because he is too impatient with my brothers. They tell Mother, "We're not helpin' that short-a-patience man."

Mother buys the materials with her gambling winnings, and Father does the best he can do. He uses his natural talents and bit by bit he transforms our house into something nosey watchers dislike. A house with five small bedrooms, two small bathrooms, and running water, gives the nosey old woman so much to infer. "The money is drug-money and one day the police will find cocaine stashes. Mark my words," is the rumor she spreads faster than HIV.

Chapter Eighteen

Young, black women of a Caribbean ghetto are endangered species because fornication is a typical, ghetto sin. The preacher in the small, white church says sex before marriage is the common cold in the ghetto. We all know there is no cure. Churches, prayers, and the bible cannot rid this from our community. This sin will remain in the ghetto until the ghetto dead rise from the dust of the earth. Sister says AIDS is rampant and takes young women down like war missiles. The common cold of the ghetto is mostly to blame. Unmarried sex without condoms is the "snowbird" that flies high with great speed and kills everything below.

This November evening, I walk past a house on my way home from the water pump and see my first AIDS patient. She sits under a lime tree in her front yard. I walk past and say, "Hello," and I look at my feet and pretend not to notice. I notice everything. She looks frail, tired, and lonely. Yet there is a peace she carries deep down inside. This nappy-head woman is no longer in need of a comb to "clear-out" her knots. HIV gives her soft, thin, curly hair like black babies. Her skin is smooth like a newborn's backside.

Mother says foreigners are responsible for these foreign diseases that kill ghetto girls and young women. The ghetto girls who are free to go to the cruise ships that dock in the harbor are culprits, too. They sell sex to horny white men who pay them twenty dollars to feel the sweet pleasure they hear a black woman gives a man when she lies on her back, raises and spreads her legs in the air. Ghetto men go to the ships, too. They give their pleasure for free to horny white women and then return to the ghetto with their pants full of germs. Foreign lands and foreign people have so much to offer but they only share their misery with ignorant Negroes who never suspect they come with diseases that kill.

I never suspect anything when a cousin comes to stay with us for a while in December. He's from Florida – the son of Mother's first brother who changes his name, joins the army, and spreads his seed across America. This cousin Devon who visits, I like him. We get along well. Devon confides in me,

"I'm gay and I wear makeup at night." I don't judge him but tell him his secret's safe with me.

Makalo comes to visit on Saturday and we play a game of marbles in the side yard. After the game, we sit under the tamarind tree and talk.

"How long is Devon staying at your house, Nika?" Makalo asks.

"I don't know. I think he is leaving in a week or so. Why you ask, Makalo?"

"Because my mother says she thinks he should go back to Florida because he's nothin' but trouble."

"What she mean, trouble"

"I don't know what she means."

"Devon ain't been no trouble since he came," I speak like I know for sure.

"Well, I don't know if he might be trouble. That's what my mother says."

"Makalo, stop repeating what your mother says because you don't know."

"I'm only saying, Nika."

"Sayin' what, Makalo?"

"I don't know."

"That's right, Makalo. You don't know so keep quiet. If you don't have something good to say, then don't say nothin'."

I defend Devon, but he wears out his welcome, overstays his time, and leaves huge, stinky messes in the bathroom for me to clean up. Months later, he goes back to Florida and we find out the whole truth he hides. Devon carries the deadly virus and is a male prostitute who sells his ass for cheap to any man who drives a car. I'm fearful that maybe I'm sick, too. I'm kind to Devon, and I share my can of soda, my straw, and my spoon with him. I never suspect he's ill.

Months later, we hear the news. Devon dies. The HIV gives him a terrible death. Before he passes, open sores cover his body, every nook and cranny, and the pain is so wretched that death is the only relief. I'm sad for Devon but happy for me. Mother says, "Thank heavens, HIV does not jump like lice from one person to the next."

It's so weird Mother makes this remark because Belinda (my sixth sister) comes home from school and she scratches her head. Mother checks her. She has a head full of lice. Mother kills them with the power of two thumbs she squeezes together – ghetto remedies are inexpensive but effective. She kills all the lice and they don't have an opportunity to spread through a house with seventeen heads.

Mother tells Belinda, "You're not allowed to play with the dirty girl over on the next street. I think she is the one who carries lice."

But this little girl is our friend. We cannot ostracize her. She's our playmate and she has cherry trees in her back yard. We love to visit her because we pick cherries, play hide-and-seek, and build cardboard forts with her and her little brothers. Touching games with her brothers are innocent fun. But none of us understand the feelings we have. We only know it feels good when we touch each other.

The feelings are different from the ones I get when an older boy touches. Older boys are wicked watchers and I don't trust them at all. On the first day of school in January, I encounter a wicked watcher on the jitney on my way home from my school in the South. The bus driver plays loud, reggae music that empowers wicked watchers to be free. "I'm dangerous," are the lyrics of the song he plays as he speeds down the road to be the first bus in line at the straw market downtown where hundreds of white visitors like to browse.

I call out, "Bus stop, coming up," and the speeding bus driver pulls over to let me out. I get up from my seat at the back and walk down the aisle in the center when the wicked watcher reaches out and squeezes my ass.

Immediately, I say, "Get your stinkin' hand off me!"

I look into his twenty-year-old eyes and he looks into mine. My ten-year-old eyes reveal the moment makes me heartless. He knows I'm ready to *kill*. He laughs it off and retreats. If looks kill, he dies quickly, and the murderer is a bright scholar who never finds her red shoes or walks the yellow brick road that leads people out of the ghetto.

I walk home and reflect on my moment of rage and my "heartless" conviction to kill the wicked watcher or die at his hands. I hate him and his touches. It becomes clear that we are all heartless at some point in time. An evil encounter pushes love out and replaces it with darkness and despair. But by the time I arrive home, the love returns, and I feel light on my feet because all I want is to live without torture. My ghetto is hell and I perish like the heartless, but my endurance is strong. I wait for the day when *my yellow brick road* reveals itself to me.

I do not share this evil experience with anyone, not even Sister, and I know she understands. Instead, I bury it in the graveyard inside my mind along with the shame of a nappy-head, ghetto girl who has many more evil encounters ahead.

Chapter Nineteen

Mother's brother comes to visit, and he lifts me up and tosses me high in the air. Matt says, "Uncle, do me, too." Uncle puts me down and then tosses Matt even higher than me.

I say, "Swing me, Uncle. Swing me like you did the last time you came to see us."

He firmly grasps my hands and spins me around. I fly in a circle five feet off the ground, and I love every minute. I'm dizzy when he puts me down.

Matt wants a turn, too, "Now me, Uncle."

My uncle swings Matt and he flies high.

When Uncle lowers Matt to the ground, I sit on his right foot and wrap my arms around his calf.

"Walk with me, Uncle, like you did last time."

Uncle walks around with me on his foot. He says to Matt, "Come sit on the next foot."

Then he walks around in circles with the two of us on his feet. Matt and I laugh and enjoy the foot-ride.

Mother says, "Now, let your uncle alone. Let him come in to have something to eat."

We love it when this uncle visits because he gives us joy rides. He is always happy to see us. But he does not come to the ghetto often. He lives with his wife and kids in a nice neighborhood. He is a good-looking man. So, lots of girls chase after him.

His smooth dark chocolate skin, muscular arms and chest, and handsome features make him popular. Rumour goes around that he cheats on his wife and has children with two or three other women. Mother says the cheating ways of a ghetto man never leave him.

I don't care about the rumors. I love Uncle. He lifts us up and plays games with us. Father does not do this. We enjoy the attention we get from Uncle. He makes us happy when he plays with us.

A cousin (Larry) comes to visit one day and he tries to spin Matt like Uncle does. Larry drops Matt on his face and causes him to be hurt. I say, "Don't try to be like Uncle. He knows how to spin us, and he never drops us."

Larry feels bad and apologizes for his mistake that leads to Matt's pain.

I don't know what to make of Larry. He comes to visit and denies the rumor that he is gay. I don't like it when gay people hide the truth. I like it when they are honest. The preachers say gay people are not heaven-bound. I don't agree. Some really nice people are gay. The ones who lie might go to hell. They need to be honest and not hide who they are.

I don't hide who I am. I'm proud to be a ghetto child. I tell everyone about our house renovations. I tell everyone I'm happy I don't have to use the outhouse anymore. The outhouse stinks. Inside, there is a wooden bench with two holes cut out in it. The bench sits over a hole in the ground that is more than ten feet deep. I look down one of the holes in the bench and I cannot see anything. It's really dark in the hole. But the smell, it's so awful. I can only imagine how much shit is down that hole.

******

Tonight, I have a tummy ache and I need to use the bathroom, but the water is shut off. Mother tells me to go outside to the outhouse. It's dark and I say, "But Mother, I'm scared." She tells me to light a candle and go.

I say, "Please, can someone come with me?"

Sister comes out with me. She waits outside the door of the outhouse while I take a poop.

"There's no toilet paper," I tell Sister.

She says, "I'll get you some."

Sister goes inside the house to find toilet paper. She comes back and says, "There isn't any toilet paper. I'll get you some almond leaves and a few rocks. You can use those to clean yourself."

I wait but Sister takes a long time to return. When she comes back, she says, "It's hard to see in the dark but I think these rocks don't have dog shit on them. Use these."

She opens the door and passes me the rocks and leaves. I wrap the leaves around a rock and wipe. I throw the rock and leaf down the hole. I wrap another leaf on a rock and do the same. When I finish, Sister and I return to the house. No one reminds me to wash my hands.

I go back to bed but soon wake up to another tummy ache. My youngest sister, Stacey wakes up with a loud cry, too. I think she has a tummy ache like me.

Stacey cries, "I want Mia."

Mother tells her, "Go sleep in the bed with Mia and Nika."

Stacey comes in and climbs in the bed. She says, "Nika, where's Mia? I want Mia."

This is when I realize Sister is not in bed. I yell, "Mother, Sister is not in bed and I don't know where she is."

Mother gets up and searches the house. Sister is not inside the house. Mother lights a candle and searches the yard. Sister is not in the yard. Mother wakes six of my seven brothers and tells them to go search for Sister. Matt wakes up, but Mother tells him he is too little to go searching.

Everyone in the house wakes up because of the commotion. But Father does not go out to search. I hear him and Mother talk in the bedroom.

"Did they find her?" Father asks.

"Not yet. Why don't you go out and help them look for her?" Mother says.

Father says, "You know I have pain in my legs. I can't go."

After using the outhouse, I search for Sister in the neighbor's yard. Mother tells us, girls, to stay home and my brothers are sent to search as far and wide as their feet take them. We stay up all night. Sister does not come home. The morning breaks and Mother is distraught. My brothers come back, and they are tired. We all worry.

Mother questions me because she knows I'm close with Sister, "Did Mia say anything to you, Nika? Did she mention she was going somewhere?"

I say, "She said she was going for a jog. She jogs almost every evening up and down the alley, but she never goes further than that."

Mother sits with a hand on her forehead.

She asks me, "What was she wearing when she went for the jog?"

"She was wearing a full-body slip. It was beige."

I shrug my shoulders then say, "Mother, I don't know."

Stacey continues to cry, "I want Mia." We don't understand what unfolds.

The pot cake dogs bark at two people who enter our back yard. One of them is the woman who lives in the alley just behind us. Her run-down, dilapidated, clapboard, one-room house is surrounded by bushes. This woman is so black and so fat. She wears a head-cloth over her afro. The curvy, full-body woman brings with her my missing sister who is covered in dirt. Sister is in shock.

The woman says, "I found her in a hole in my front yard. The hole is two-feet deep. She was asleep when I found her. I asked how she got in the hole. She said she doesn't remember."

Mother asks Sister, "What happened?"

Sister says, "I don't know. I only remember jogging up and down the alley. I saw a woman's head floating six feet off the ground. The woman had two really long plaits hanging down. Her head told me to follow. I don't remember anything after that."

Mother says, "Oh, no. You saw my mother. She came to give me a death warning. My mother was six-feet tall, and in her coffin, she wore two long braids that sat on her breasts."

The heavy-set woman who brings Sister says, "I don't know how your daughter survived the night without harm. Something protected your child. There are so many drug people who pass through my yard every night. My house sits in the bushes. People get raped, robbed, and even murdered in those bushes. Your daughter is so lucky no one discovered her in the hole."

Mother thanks the round, asthmatic woman. She waddles back to her home in the bushes.

Sister sits and stares off into space. I don't ask her anything. Mother tries to get her to say more but she only repeats the same words. "I don't know. I only remember jogging up and down the alley. I saw a woman's head floating six feet off the ground. The woman had two really long plaits hanging down. Her head told me to follow. I don't remember anything after that."

All of us sit together in the small living room and we ponder the things that make Sister this way.

Mother tells Sister, "Go change those dirty clothes and go to bed."

Sister obeys and then sleeps until late afternoon. The house is really quiet. We all talk in secret behind Sister's back. We don't understand how it's possible for her to see the head of a dead woman.

Later that evening, Mother calls her four sisters together and tells them what Sister sees. They all believe it's a sign. They worry death comes soon. Mother thinks she is the one who dies. She makes plans for her funeral and plans for us. Days pass and Mother worries more.

Sister is fine and is herself again, but Mother worries hard. Weeks pass and Mother's worry does not waiver. Months pass and Mother's worry deepens.

Strange things happen in the ghetto. Things words fail to explain do occur. We don't question how they happen. Mother believes what Sister describes. We all believe it. Mother says, "If you don't believe, you'll soon see. What she speaks is real. Spirits roam the earth."

I'm happy I never encounter a spirit. Sister must be so afraid of the dark because she encounters one. She is so brave. If I see a dead woman's head, I go the other way. I wonder if the spirit put a spell on Sister and this causes her to obey. But the spirit protects Sister as she sleeps in the bushes. No harm comes to Sister even in the most dangerous location – a dark, ghetto bush.

Horrific things happen in these bushes every day. No one is immune to the violent ghetto bushes.

These bushes lead to a densely wooded area. The trees are so big and so close together. Rainwater does not get through. Homeless people sleep in this wooded area and drug users go there to get high. One day, Amy takes me through the bushes to see this place. There are cardboard houses in there, and they are set up by adults, not children. We run out when we hear footsteps. Amy screams and we run home. Mother warns us never to play in the bushes. We listen because we are afraid of the evil that lives within them. There is much evil in ghetto bushes but there is much good, too. The woman who finds Sister helps her and brings her home safely. People want to do good deeds in the ghetto. They don't want to hurt. People look out for each other. Even Father wants to help keep us safe. He tears down the outhouse because he does not want to risk another incident like the night Sister disappears.

Chapter Twenty

This morning in February, I get up and participate in the morning routine. I wait in line for the bathroom and use the toilet while Edith showers. I like the smell of the soap Edith uses because it masks the stink I make inside the toilet.

"Nika, are you done? I'm ready to get out."

"Just a minute, Edith. I just have to flush."

"Hurry up, Nika."

I flush the toilet and Edith pulls the shower curtain open. She grabs a towel and wraps herself.

"You stink, Nika."

"Not for long," is my reply. I step inside the tub and pull the curtain. My eyes catch a glimpse of the green snot Edith leaves for me to discover.

"Hope you like the snot, Nika. I left it especially for you."

Edith knows I hate looking at other people's bodily waste. "I'll get you for this, Edith. You pig."

After my shower, I wrap myself in a towel and head to the ironing board that is set up in a corner in the living room. I press the wrinkles out of my school uniform before I put it on. Mother makes grits and tuna and we eat our small serving then we head out the door. Some of us walk across the street to the big yellow school. Some walk thirteen blocks to public high schools. The bright scholars take a bus to the private school in the South. My older brothers go to work at the construction site.

Sometimes, Mother makes a sandwich for our lunch, "slam-bam and bread." Bologna is cheap so Mother buys it every week. Other times, she gives us fifteen cents each to buy a "cup" and a piece of macaroni from the lady who sells lunch in the schoolyard. If we complain, Mother reminds us we can take the free lunch the government provides. I hate taking free lunch. The sandwiches are so soggy, and the kids laugh at me when I go up to get it. I prefer to go hungry to avoid mockery. My pride is a thousand times bigger than my need to eat.

Mother never packs us plastic juice cartons because she says, "The water fountain at school gives good water." Besides, she can't afford to buy juice or cartons of milk. Of course, lunchtime is not the best time of school for ghetto children who do not need a reminder that our bodies require food and water to live.

Recess is fun, though. I love to play outside with my friends. I love to run around. Sweat wets my uniform and I don't mind because a game of tag is a thrill and I'm always "it." When the bell rings for us to come in, we line up perfectly and orderly with our classmates and are quieter than a nosey watcher who wears bedroom slippers because we know teachers are permitted to discipline with the rod. I'm so quiet, I hear my lungs grow and shrink. Fear of the teacher's rod never leaves me after I receive six licks from the bamboo cane when I do homework at school one morning. Teacher says, "Homework is to be done at home."

We sing our multiplication tables in the line-ups outside our classroom door. Teacher patrols the lines and listens closely for silence. A quiet student who does not sing gets a crack with the yardstick, so we all sing out loudly. Woe to the one who can't recite the tables correctly. We all know them by heart or we face the punishment of a ghetto fool: embarrassment before our classmates – friends, enemies, and bullies.

School is fun but not as much fun as it used to be because I miss Makalo so much. I ask Mother if I could go see him. She tells me I can, but Edith must go, too. Mother doesn't like it when we walk the ghetto streets alone.

Edith and I walk to Makalo's house but he is not at home. His sister Trish tells us he goes to play with Tito and Jeremy. Edith and I walk home and, on our way, a pot cake dog comes at us. He growls and barks then I see his big, long teeth penetrate Edith's flesh as he bites into her thin thigh. I kick the dog. It runs away. Edith and I run home. Red liquid races down Edith's leg, she bleeds so much and cries. I feel sorry for Edith for the first time. Mother takes her to see a doctor while I remain home in shock. Even though Edith and I fight a lot, I don't think she deserves what the pot cake dog does. A vicious animal leaves its teeth marks in the flesh of a ghetto girl who does not deserve to feel its wrath. Even dogs of the ghetto have ghetto ways that make them harm innocent children who pass too close or trespass.

Grouchy neighbors leave their pot cake dogs loose to guard what is theirs. We ghetto children know better than to enter a yard when a pot cake barks. We play in neighbors' yards if there are no pot cake dogs, or we play in the vacant lots. But Mother tells us not to play in vacant lots that have tall bushes. The vacant lots with over-grown bushes give wicked watchers places to hide and provide the perfect crime scene that is hidden and private. There's a rumor that they find a newborn inside a glass jar in the bushes and another rumor that a teenager kills a Haitian in the bushes on a dare.

I fear bushes, pot cake dogs, wicked watchers, and Mother's switches. There is so much to fret and so little to comfort. Yet, there is some comfort when I think my future is bright. I go to school with the best intentions – to learn as much as I can. Teachers have a great deal of interest and help me develop my mind and one, in particular, is a saint. Her name is Miss Major. She picks me up every Saturday. Takes me to her quiet apartment in her car. Ensures I do homework and study for exams. What an amazing woman and how I appreciate her, but I don't fully understand. Miss Major tutors me on weekends at no charge and wants nothing in return. I think this is a part of her job, something all teachers do. But I believe she sees the real me who cowers inside the body of a ghetto child, the person who deserves an opportunity to blossom and become all that I can.

I hit the books hard. My grades are excellent, but I still love to play. Bat-and-ball, marbles, hide-and-seek, and rope skipping are so much fun. "Kick the can" is another game Makalo, Amy and I play. The best time to play is at night. Amy and I hide and the seeker (Makalo) puts down an empty soda can and then seeks us out. While Makalo searches, Amy and I run. The first one to kick the empty soda can wins the game.

It's a fantastic idea but the game can be dangerous. If someone steps on a rusty nail that sits with its pointy side up, the howl is intense, and the game has to end. One night, Amy steps on a rusty nail. Makalo and I hear her wretched screams.

"My foot, ouch! My foot!" Amy's screams are miserable.

Makalo and I run to her.

"Amy, what happened?" I ask.

"I stepped on a nail." Makalo and I look down. We can't see anything because of the darkness.

"How do you know it was a nail?" Makalo is so naive.

"Because I felt it go through my foot. How do you think I know?" Amy is justifiably impatient.

"Makalo, let's help her. Put your arm around me, Amy. Put the other arm around Makalo. We'll help you get home."

Fun and games in the ghetto are tied to stories of pain and the only park we know of is twenty blocks away. Sometimes, Amy and I walk to the park to play on the swings but after playtime is over the long walk back home in the heat is such a pain. We don't mind walking to the beach, though. I remember the day we practice for the Independence Day celebrations, Amy invites me to the beach house where her mother works as a housekeeper. She tells me the walk is fifteen minutes. It takes us over an hour to get to the beach house. We are happy the rich white people have lots of orange soda in their fridge.

Ghetto children love orange soda, especially an ice-cold bottle. Amy and I drink quickly and then we burp. Orange soda refreshes and quenches our thirst. Lemonade is our second favorite and the sweeter the better. We love sweets and ice-cream. The sound of the ice-cream truck makes our mouths water. Amy and I chase the musical truck with our pennies in hand and hope the ice-cream seller takes pity on us and gives us a scoop even if we don't have enough money.

"Mr. Ice-Cream Man, can I get a chocolate ice-cream please?" I'm nervous because I know I might not have enough money.

"Fifty cents," he replies.

"I only have forty cents and my friend has forty-two cents. Can we still get a cone each? Please, Sir." My tone is very polite.

"That's all right. Give me what you have." The ice-cream man takes our pennies, doesn't count them, and scoops our ice-cream.

"Thanks, Sir," I say.

"Thanks, Sir," Amy echoes.

Amy and I walk to my house and we sit under the tamarind tree.

"This ice-cream sure is good, Nika."

"I know."

"I'm glad you're my friend, Nika."

"Me too, Amy."

"I mean it, Nika. You're like my best friend."

"You're my best friend, too. Well, except for Makalo."

"Makalo's your cousin, not your friend."

"Oh yeah, right. You're my best friend and Makalo is my best cousin," I chuckle.

"Mmm, mmm, mmm. This ice-cream is so good. If it wasn't for you, I wouldn't have this ice-cream. Nika, you can convince anyone to give you stuff.

If I was by myself, I bet the ice-cream man wouldn't give me ice-cream if I didn't have fifty cents." Amy sings my praises as usual. After we finish our ice-cream, Amy and I play a game of hide-and-seek. Then I smell something so stinky under my bare feet – dog poop. There's no surprise I get worms that come out when I poop. The day my worms decide to come out is the day the water is shut off in my school in the South. I can't flush the worms. They wiggle inside the toilet bowl. The wiggly creatures are of a cream color and they are four to six inches long.

I feel my pride rise. It consumes me and so I cannot resist but to come up with a scheme. I tell the teacher I find worms in the toilet when I come in only to pee. She looks at me and I look at her. My eyes cannot lie, and I know she knows the truth. She says, "Nika, go wash your hands," and I remind her there's no water in the pipes.

Chapter Twenty-One

I tell my older sister, Chrissy about the worms that come out in my poop. We sit in the back yard just us two. She comforts me and says, "Nika, don't worry. I don't think you have any more worms in your tummy."

Chrissy playfully splashes me with rainwater from the barrel. She says, "Hey, I have an idea. Let's have a bath out here."

We use buckets to collect rainwater from the barrels and play a game of water toss in our swimsuits. Chrissy and I drench ourselves and splash each other. We forget water is not for childish games. Sister says water is the liquid of life. When the government water pump is shut off, survival demands us to find an alternative source. We rely on rainwater that collects in the barrels outside. We use the rainwater to wash dishes, clothes, the floor, and even our skins. But rainwater in the barrels is fun to play in, too.

"Get the soap and clean your armpits," Chrissy says.

We scrub our bodies until they are squeaky clean.

I throw a hand full of rainwater at Chrissy and then I giggle. She laughs the loudest when she splashes me with a bucket full. We dance around and sing Whitney Houston songs. Chrissy and I play in the rainwater that is supposed to last us a month. Father hears us and comes to see what gives us so much pleasure.

He yells, "What are you two doing? Are you crazy? Get inside and leave the rainwater alone."

His displeasure is obvious. We are wasteful ghetto children. We are impractical and stupid because we waste good, clean water. Father is right because water and power get shut off so often in the ghetto and they give us no warning. So, ghetto folk burn candles at night or kerosene lamps when the power remains out 'til nightfall. Wicked watchers love dark nights and they seek out their prey, so ghetto children huddle together around a candle in their rotting, clapboard houses in the dark. A ghetto is scary even when the lights are on. When the lights go out, Mother is angry if any of us is still in the streets. My evil brother Marcus disappears in the darkness these nights. He returns with a strong smell of "spliff" that ghetto children recognize right away.

After Chrissy and I dry off, Mother calls me to her. She sits on the couch and I sit on the floor between her legs. She parts my hair into ten sections and plaits each section, so I have ten plaits. My plaits are not long like Edith's or Chrissy's. They barely touch my shoulders. Mother complains that my hair is so difficult, and she says I need a hot, straightening comb to clear the knots completely. Mother goes to the woman down the road to get her hair straightened with a hot comb. The straightening lasts her a week or two. She curls her hair at night with sponge rollers and she manages to sleep comfortably with them. In the morning, she takes out the rollers and has a head full of eight-inch curls that frame her round face. The shape of Mother's face is one trait she passes to us. Regina, Chrissy, Edith, Belinda, and I have round faces, too. We look so much alike we often compare ourselves to one another. This creates a bit of friendly, sibling competition.

We compare to decide who has the longest nose, biggest breasts, and lightest skin. Regina and Sister have the biggest breasts. Chrissy has the lightest skin. They all say I have the longest nose and my nose looks like it detaches because glue holds it in a place like Ernie and Bert from Sesame Street. I don't mind it when they say this. I laugh and tell them at least my nose isn't long like the elephant Mr. Snuffleupagus from Sesame Street.

******

Three days after Chrissy and I get caught wasting good rainwater, we come up with another idea.

"Hey, Chrissy, you know what I think! I think we should cover the TV with colored paper, so we have a colour-TV."

"That's a good idea, Nika. I never thought of that." Chrissy gives me a "thumbs up."

"You think that'll work?" Edith jumps in.

"Yeah, Dummy," I reply.

I run to get some yellow cellophane paper from the kitchen table and then press it up against the TV.

"See." I point to the Sesame Street characters who are now all yellow.

"Nika, that's a good idea," Chrissy smiles.

"Well, I'll be damned. It does look like a colour-TV," Edith interjects.

"Edith, watch your mouth!" Mother yells.

We cover the TV screen with the yellow cellophane that Mother wraps the leftovers in from work. Mother does not complain. She thinks I'm very smart to come up with the plan in the first place.

Mother is very open to new ideas. She lets us explore and figure things out on our own. We learn that there is lead buried under the tamarind tree down the street in the empty lot. Edith, Chrissy, and I collect the pieces of lead and put them in an empty soup can. We make a small fire outside with brown paper bags, empty cereal boxes, and sticks. No one warns us of any danger. We watch the lead pieces cook over the fire until they turn silver. We also burn golf balls Mother brings home from work. The sight of the burning golf balls ignites an argument.

"Look at the wires inside the ball," Edith points as she speaks.

"Edith, don't be stupid. Those aren't wires, I quickly shut her down."

"They are wires, Idiot," Edith does not hesitate to strike back.

"You two knock it off. You're always fightin' bout somethin'," Chrissy breaks her silence.

"It's Nika. She started it." Edith gives me her mean glare.

"All right, Edith. That's enough. Anyway, those are elastic bands, not wires," Chrissy changes the focus of the conversation.

"See. I told you, Edith." I'm glad Chrissy agrees with me.

It surprises me that Edith doesn't say anything back. Then I realize it's because she is distracted by a boy who uses his arms to swing from the electrical wire up the alley. The electrical wires in the ghetto hang very low. Boys in the neighborhood sometimes climb up the wooden electrical posts and swing from the wires. One time the weight of someone's body causes the wire to break. Another long, dark night without power is the result.

Chapter Twenty-Two

The worst time for a blackout is during a hurricane. A strong hurricane comes this September. Mother sends Sister to buy candles, batteries, and matches. My first brother Vincent helps Father board-up the windows because Mother says there's no time for Father to do it alone. We stay inside the house for a week while the rains and winds put on a grand performance. Some people go to the big yellow school because their houses cannot withstand the strength of the wind. Mother tells us it's safer to stay home. When the news reports on the radio tell us the hurricane is over, we go outside to see the confetti mother-nature leaves after the hurricane's encore. Floodwater reaches the waistline, hog plum and coconut trees lie on their sides and reveal their roots, and electrical wires and poles lie on the ground. The story about the freak accident spreads quickly. A teenager pulls open the refrigerator door the exact moment lightning strikes him, and the power comes on. He dies from the electrical shock.

Freak accidents are a rare occurrence but when they do happen ghetto folks get all concerned about the end of the world. The next day, heavy, dense fog covers the ghetto, people say it's a sign of the end. "Clouds came down from the sky," they say. "The world will soon end." Ghetto people are the most superstitious. They are especially superstitious about dreams.

Mother is the most superstitious in our house and she is great at interpreting dreams. She says, "A dream about a wedding means death. A dream about front teeth falling out means death. A dream about weeping at a funeral means a wedding is coming."

I don't mind my dreams, except the dreams where it feels like evil spirits are trying to pull me into the other side frighten me. I have these kinds of dreams when I sleep in the position of a corpse at a funeral – on my back with hands that rest on my stomach. Luckily, I wake before they can pull me over. Mother says if I dream about a family member who is in the other world, I should not accept any invitation they offer in the dream. She says if I accept, it means I accept death and I die.

I love life and I don't want to die. I choose love, not death. I choose to live my miserable ghetto life and I live with hope that it will not always be miserable. Mother says hope is an amazing thing and when we lose it the path of our lives change. A hopeless life is wretched, and no one survives it. The ghetto is full of people who have hope and who refuse to become devoid of it. Hope helps to sustain the ghetto. But the reality is many turn to alcohol when hope begins to wane.

It's no surprise when Matt and I discover a bottle of gin in the fridge. He dares me to chug a glass full. I do it and it burns my mouth. It tastes awful. After a little while, I feel really weird and need to go have a sleep. A ten-year-old, ghetto girl should know better than to fulfill the dare of her curious eight-year-old brother.

My fourth brother, Joe who is very familiar with chugging liquor tells me, "You're drunk."

He asks, "Did you pour some liquor outside on the dirt and tell the spirits you offer them a drink?"

I say, "No."

Joe says, "The spirits will haunt you tonight."

I go to bed and believe his lie. I vow never to drink alcohol ever again. The fear of the spirits hypnotizes me and, in my mind, a drunk is a haunted soul.

There are many ghetto stories about spirits that haunt. A taxi driver says he picks up a woman from downtown and she directs him to her residence – the ghetto graveyard. He turns around to collect payment and the woman disappears right before his eyes. He speeds off in fear. Perhaps this woman dies because he refuses to drive her to her home on a dead-end street and she returns to remind him.

The next morning, I awake with a sickness in my stomach and my head throbs. I do not know how my drunken brothers (Vincent and Joe) are able to take this sick morning feeling each and every week. I slowly sit up on the bed and see Sister asleep. Then I hear Mother yell her reminders before she heads out the door for work. "Don't forget to wash the dishes, scrub the floor, hang the wet clothes, and get water from the government pump." Mother concludes with her final reminder, "Don't forget to go to church."

If we forget we hear Mother's long speeches when she returns from work. I prefer switches over Mother's speeches. They go on for hours and make you feel a murderer's guilt. Sister, Regina, Chrissy, Edith, Matt, Belinda, Stacey, and I walk to church together.

Church services are two and a half hours long. The women wear big, broad rim hats like the Queen and beautiful dresses made of satin. Men wear suits or dress pants with shirts and ties. Children wear beautiful dresses with lots of frills. On this ninth day of November, I wear my navy blue, A-line skirt and white blouse with a folding collar because I'm an usher. I stand at the door and pass out hymnals and bulletins. I get a glass of water for the visiting preacher who gives the sermon.

A woman in our church who has the gift of prophesy stands up and shouts, "Hallelujah, glory, and praise."

She comes to me, speaks out loud but directly to me, "God has a great plan for your life. Wait on Him and be of good courage."

I stand in my shiny, second hand, church shoes and my ten-year-old eyes refuse to blink. My lungs tighten until time forces them to relax. I'm embarrassed, confused, and afraid all at the same time. I do not know what to make of this woman and I do not know why she comes to me. Regina is far more religious. She is the one who should receive God's message. Why does this woman speak these words to me? There are one hundred and fifty others seated in the brown wooden pews. Yet God sends a message for the sinner who chugs her older brother's gin.

I do not question for more than a minute because I'm a ghetto child. I'm happy because this woman affirms me and reminds me there is a yellow brick road that leads me out of the ghetto. I must be patient and then I must be courageous when it shows itself to me.

Chapter Twenty-Three

I overhear Chrissy and Trish (Makalo's sister). They have a brown paper bag and some matches, and plan to make paper cigarettes. I ask if I could join them.

Chrissy says, "Come, but don't tell anyone."

The three of us walk to the open lot up the alley and hide inside my uncle's old, rusty, abandoned car. We roll the paper into cigarettes.

Chrissy and Trish are older, so they finish theirs before I do. They light up their paper cigarettes and smoke them. I finish mine and ask for a light. Chrissy lights my paper cigarette with a match and I take my first puff. I choke. Drop my paper cigarette on the front seat of the passenger's side. We are all in the back seat.

The front seat catches fire quickly because the seat fabric is torn, and threads hang. The fire spreads in a matter of seconds. We try to get out of the car using the door on the driver's side, but the door does not open. We cannot use the only other door because red, hot flames block it.

Chrissy, Trish, and I bang on the back-glass window of the two-door sedan. People gather because they see flames and smoke inside the car. Men, women, and children all gather. They try to open the car doors to let us out. The doors are stuck and do not open. We scream, cry, and bang on the back-glass window even more. Thick, dirty smoke fills the car. We choke. The smoke comes to us and fills our lungs. We cough and try to catch our breaths.

We are so hot. Sweat pours from our faces. I look out through the back-glass window and see the faces of people who fear the angel of death comes for us, three ghetto girls. Fifteen more people gather, and they surround the car but stay back from the front end because hot flames engulf it. They devise a plan to get us out.

A man returns to the scene with a crowbar and machete. He pries the trunk of the car open and cuts through the back seat. I lose consciousness. He pulls us out safely and carries me home to Mother.

******

I wake up on Mother's double bed and I hear familiar voices talk about the fire. My sisters come together in Mother's room to discuss the events. I hear Chrissy say, "She dropped the paper cigarette but I'm sure she didn't mean to."

I hear sirens. I jump up off the bed and crawl under it. I lie on my belly and cover my ears. I do not want to know what happens. I cry and try to understand the events that unfold because I'm naughty. I rub my hands together and I ask myself important questions. "What will Mother do to me? Will the police come to take me to jail? Will I go to hell?" I cry until I have no more tears and I remain under the bed.

My sisters poke their heads under and Edith says, "Don't worry. Mother won't beat you for this. She knows you're scared. It's okay." Edith is surprisingly sincere.

I refuse to come out. I look around at the dust balls under the bed and pull on the hanging threads from the old, rotting box spring. I gather dust balls in my hands and then flick them with my fingers. There is hardly any room to move around under the bed, but I manage to cross my bare feet one on top of the other. Then I change them around when the one on the bottom goes numb.

To pass time, I pull on my plaits and twist them around my fingers. Every breath I take I notice because my body presses against the hard-wooden floor. I roll over onto my back, but this is even more uncomfortable, so I quickly return to my original position. The spring coils creak in the bed as my sisters move around on it. I wonder if the bed might crash down and squish me. I don't care if it does. I prefer to have a bed squish me than to come out and face everyone.

My pride swells as time passes. I run my fingers along the rusty bed frame. It's cold to the touch. My eyelids are heavy. I yawn and turn my head to the left side and place my right cheek on the floor. My lids refuse to open. I fall asleep under the bed.

A few hours pass, and I wake to Mother's hard, strong voice, "Now she knows better than to smoke brown paper." She talks to my sisters who all pile on the bed.

Chrissy says, "But she's so scared. See if she's still asleep."

I quickly close my eyes and pretend to be asleep. Edith and Belinda poke their heads under the bed to check.

Mother says, "She's lucky to be alive. Thanks be to God she didn't die. Some children have to learn the hard way."

I hear Sister say, "She has such bad luck – the poor thing."

I twiddle my fingers on the floor quietly then fold my arms together on the floor and rest my head on them. I fall asleep again.

Sleep is a wonderful comfort when reality overwhelms. Ghetto children would never be awake if they fall asleep every time life presents a difficult situation. The two-year-old girl they find in the garbage pile inside a rusty old refrigerator falls asleep. They find her dead inside the old kitchen appliance two days later. She is unlucky because she closes the door and cannot get it open.

I'm lucky to escape death and survive for an unknown purpose. Although, I do believe ghetto children have a purpose to live. The old deacon Brother Leo teaches us our purpose is to know, to love, and to serve God. I think there must be another purpose that he forgets to tell us – to endure a treacherous life. I wonder what the purpose is for the wealthy. Do they have the same purpose as ghetto children or do they not need a god? I remember a preacher says it's hard for a camel to pass through the eye of a needle and this is how hard it is for a rich man to enter heaven.

******

My sleep under Mother's bed ends. I awake to a strong, familiar voice. My Auntie Zelda comes to see how I am. She pokes her head under the bed. When I see her face, I smile.

"Do you want to come home with me, Nika?"

I say, "Yes."

I crawl out from under the bed and grab onto my aunt's skirt. I do not look around and try not to make eye contact with anyone. I do not speak.

Auntie Zelda says, "I'm taking her home with me for the night."

"Go ahead, take her," is Mother's reply.

I cling to Auntie Zelda's skirt and follow her steps closely. We walk to her house six blocks away.

When we arrive at Auntie Zelda's small, clapboard, bright blue house, I say, "Will the police take me to jail?"

She laughs, "No, Child. What you did was an accident. Don't fret over it."

Auntie Zelda offers me some food – white rice and tuna fish. I eat it and then I ask, "Are you sure the police will not take me to jail?"

She smiles and says, "Come here."

I go to her. She takes me by the hand.

"Nika, I would never let them take you."

Auntie Zelda is such a wonderful comfort and I believe every word she tells me. I know she means what she says. She is such a big, tall woman. I'm sure the police are afraid of her. Everyone knows she is a strong woman.

Rumor goes around that she beats her common-law husband when he steps out of line.

Auntie Zelda has eight children of her own but today she gives me special attention. She lets me sit close to her until nightfall. I feel secure, relieve, and solace. These strange feelings a ghetto child does not understand but deeply appreciate.

******

A few months later, the news hits me like a ton of bricks. Auntie Zelda is in hospital. She has high blood pressure and they have her on a breathing machine in the ICU. She goes into a coma. Mother says I cannot visit. Children cannot enter the ICU. But I create my own images in my mind when Mother says, "She is in a bad way. Her head is swollen, and the machine pumps her chest."

Two weeks later, the real news comes. Auntie Zelda dies. She goes to meet my grandparents in the other world. Her unborn son is taken from her dead body. The news of her death is a dagger that enters my heart and then the stabber uses all his might to twist it a full 360 degrees.

Mother takes the death of my Auntie Zelda so hard because she does not suspect it's her who dies. Mother is the oldest, so she thinks her death comes first. But Mother is wrong.

My aunt who carries her unborn child is the death that comes first. The woman who tells me she would never let the police take me is the one who goes away forever.

I cry when I hear the news. Mother cries, too. Auntie Zelda has so many ghetto stories. Her stories die with her. No one ever knows about her suffering. She lives a life of poverty and only has forty-two years to find her yellow brick road. Too bad this road leads her to heaven and away from her children she loves deeply.

Auntie Zelda's story about when she falls asleep with her twin baby boys to wake up to one who breathes and the other who foams at the mouth, is dead and it's gone, too. Mother says she thinks Auntie Zelda sleeps and rolls over onto the infant. No one knows the pain my aunt suffers when she sees them lower her baby into the earth. No one hears of her life. But she must mean something to the grander story. What part does she play in it? Why does she have to die before she sees her youngest son take his first breath, make his first step, and say his first words? She does not deserve death – she lives and never really has a life. She dies before she lives. The woman who sleeps on her infant and watches them lower his body in the ground is the one who walks the yellow brick road to heaven.

******

The day of the funeral comes. I cannot control my tears. My cousins cry louder and much more because their mother lies in a casket at the front of the altar in the small, white church. Auntie Zelda sleeps with her hands on her stomach and she does not smile. She looks frozen.

Her skin looks green in some spots and her lips look like they crumble to the touch. The smell of stink death-fluid comes off her. They embalm her so much she looks like a gigantic, black figurine. The woman in the coffin is not my Auntie Zelda. She is some stranger. I don't know. Auntie Zelda never wears her short, nappy hair in curls like Mother and she never wears red lipstick. I don't understand why they try to make her look like someone she is not. Her hair is always in two braids and it's always messy with pieces that stick out in different spots. Why do they try to make her look perfect?

We all wear funeral colors. The women wear black dresses and the little girls wear white dresses. The boys and men wear black, grey, or navy-blue pants, white shirts, dark neckties, and some wear suit jackets. We all meet at Makalo's house.

I sit with Makalo outside on the weed-filled, overgrown grass in his front yard. Tears roll down my face. I wipe them away. Makalo doesn't cry or speak. He reaches over, takes my hand, squeezes it, and then puts it back on my lap. We sit in silence for about five minutes and then Makalo says, "I can't believe Auntie Zelda is dead." His face wears its usual big smile.

"Makalo, how come you smilin'? This ain't the time for smilin'." I'm a bit annoyed.

"I really don't mean to smile. My face just does it. Sorry, Nika," Makalo replies. He lowers his head.

"Don't feel bad, Makalo. I know you didn't mean to smile." I put my arm around his shoulder.

"Look, Nika." Makalo points at the two shiny, black limousines that pull up in front of his house. My first brother, Vincent yells, "The limousines are here to pick us up." How ghetto families pay for limousines at funerals is a mystery.

We arrive at the church and begin to process in. The procession is like paint as it dries on a wall. The weeping and wailing grow louder the closer we get to the casket. I begin to wail and cannot control the level of noise that comes

105

from underneath my stomach. I cannot look at the corpse very long, yet I cannot forget what it looks like.

After the funeral, we go to the graveyard and they lower Auntie Zelda into the earth. Graveyards are spooky and ghetto folks are theatrical at the sight of an open grave. People wail at the top of their lungs. The family enters the graveyard – a parade of weepers and screamers who take their time to walk in. The site is jam-packed with people because ghetto funerals draw enormous crowds. A community comes together to mourn the loss of a ghetto soul – a reminder that we are mere mortals.

There is a yellow brick road to heaven that's open all day and all night. The ghetto dead hope to walk that road and some do, I'm sure. God is gracious. He accepts ghetto people as they come, and he welcomes us all with open arms.

******

Six weeks after my aunt's funeral, I feel like I'm in heaven when I pull open my godmother's refrigerator door. She has so much food. Her fridge looks nothing like ours. When you pull our refrigerator open, you see lots of empty spaces, jugs of water, onions, and the brown sauce Mother use to make peas and rice.

My godmother's refrigerator looks like a supermarket. The front shelves have bowls and plates full of leftovers: peas and rice, macaroni, potato salad, coleslaw, fried chicken, steaks, and pork chops. She has the yummiest desserts – coconut tarts and guava duff.

The shelves in the door of the fridge have cartons of milk, orange juice, apple juice, fruit punch, and chocolate milk. There are orange cheese slices, ham, turkey, and bologna in the little drawer where she keeps sandwich meats. Three dozen egg cartons are stacked on the very top shelf and next to them are containers of butter, jelly, and peanut butter. A bowl of apples, oranges, and grapefruit catch my eyes. They look so delicious.

Mother lets me spend the weekend with my godmother this one time. Mother would let me go more often but godmother does not invite me to come back. She says I eat a lot for someone of my age and stature. She is busy and does not have time to spend with a ghetto child like me who enjoys food more than conversation.

Godmother hates my hair, too. She tries to comb through my knots and gets so upset, she pulls out a cooking Sterno and heats up the iron comb. Godmother parts my hair into twenty small sections, covers each section with hair grease, and runs the hot comb through each section. Dead hairs catch in the hot comb and I smell them as they burn.

I see and smell the heat and smoke come off the iron comb as she pulls it through my dry, thick hair. She tells me to hold my ears down, so she doesn't burn them. She burns my hand instead. I hear the sizzle and feel the intense pain but pretend to be fine. I'm tough so I never cry or complain. I twitch when I sense the hot iron is close to my scalp. My pain threshold grows, and I only flinch when hot grease falls on my neck after the hot comb goes through a section of hair at the back of my small, round head. Despite the moments of pain, I'm happy godmother uses the hot comb because it makes my hair soft, straight, and thin. I look pretty like Chrissy when my hair is done.

Hair is such a fussy thing for black children, but adults find so many interesting ways to style their hair. Auntie Zelda's oldest daughter Flora fixes hair well and she has customers who come for braids, extensions, weaves, and relaxers. One day, I ask Flora to put extensions in my hair. She does it and I look like a rasta when she is done.

I go home to show Mother. Mother is angry when she sees me. "Who told you to put that stuff in your hair? You did not get permission. You look like a crazy person."

I lower my head.

Mother says, "You better take out those extensions before I give you something to cry about."

I stay out of Mother's sight for weeks until I convince Flora to remove the extensions.

Mother is happy when she sees me without the hair extensions. She tells me, "Now you look like my child. You don't need hair extensions. You're beautiful just the way God made you."

Chapter Twenty-Four

A cry-baby in the ghetto is a bully's target. We never let people see us cry unless we are at a funeral. Even in the worst moments of pain, I fight back my tears. Amy and I play a game of Red Rover with eight other girls. There are ten of us – all nine and ten-year-old, ghetto girls.

We divide ourselves into two groups, five in each.

"Make two lines that face each other and hold hands with your group members," I speak like someone tells me I'm in charge.

"Listen to Miss Bossy," Amy is sarcastic.

We move apart so the two lines have about fifty meters in between. All the girls know how to play because we play this game two or three times a week, in the field at the big yellow school, after school hours.

All of us wear play clothes. Amy and I wear shorts and t-shirts, some girls wear skirts and blouses, and others, cotton dresses – clothes that have stains, holes, and patches. I call across to the other group, "Red Rover, Red Rover, let Amy come over."

Amy runs toward me and tries to break through the human chain we make with our hands held together. She does not break through, so she has to stay with our group and become a part of our chain.

We play for fifteen minutes and it's so much fun. The other group calls me to come over. I have great determination and plan to break through the chain. I run as fast and hard as I can. When I get to the chain, I hit the arm of one girl whose determination is greater than mine. She does not let go. I hit her arm with such a powerful force that gives me flight, in a backward motion, six inches off the ground. The back of my head hits the ground first and it sounds louder than when Chrissy's friend smashes her head with a rock.

I lie on the ground and do not move. The pain is like a million needles enter the back of my head at one time while a fork enters my back. I cannot move but I want to cry. I fight back the tears. I suck them in and use courage I do not know I have. This kind of pain does not warrant tears. Ghetto children play rough games. Only weak people cry.

All the girls race over and form a circle around me.

"Are you okay?" Amy's voice is shaky.

I don't respond. I lie on my back and stare up at the clear, blue sky. My face is devoid of expression.

"I think she's really hurt." Amy's shaky voice is quiet.

They try to lift me up off the ground.

I say, "No, let me be."

They put me back down and I lie there until the pain eases.

All the girls stay. They never leave my side. When Amy sees I look better, she points at me and smiles, "She's okay." Her voice is steady.

The girls laugh and Amy's confident voice returns, "You're so funny, Nika."

She begins to tease and mock my words, but all in good fun, "No, let me be."

I sit up and smile. "Why is that so funny?" I look up at Amy who chuckles.

Amy speaks with the Queen's accent, "No, let me be."

I stand up. "Didn't you know I'm the Queen of England?" My words, too, take on the British accent.

We all laugh. Amy hugs me and we walk home.

I have a lot of friends in the ghetto. But Amy is really close to me. She has so much talent and enjoys the arts, just like I do. We sing songs together and make up our own dance choreography that we perform for other friends. Amy has really dark skin but it's smooth like butter. Her hair is really short, and it only grows out three inches. Her mother parts it into five sections and makes five afro cotton-tails. Her teeth are so white and when the moonlight glows, they are very noticeable. At night, her face disappears in the darkness, but when she smiles, she becomes visible again.

I like Amy and she likes me. But there is another friend (Tabatha) who is jealous of our friendship. Tabatha wants to be my best friend and gets mad when she sees me spend time with Amy.

One day, we are at the government summer-day-camp at the big yellow school. I sit with Amy in the story-circle. The teacher gets up to get another book. Tabatha gets up and slaps Amy in the face. The surprise attack is effective. Amy does not know what hit her.

Tabatha and Amy fistfight, scratch each other, and pull on each other's clothes. The teacher separates them and tells them to go home. I worry because I don't understand what causes the fight. I wonder if Amy is okay. She has to walk home with Tabatha. What if Tabatha hits Amy with rocks, or stabs her with a broken, beer bottle? I worry Tabatha might plan to attack me, too. I'm afraid but I pretend to be fine. A surprise attack is an everlasting threat in the ghetto.

I think Tabatha is one of the heartless, so I worry. I must become heartless, too, if she attacks. I realize I might have to kill, and I accept this. I'm afraid because I know I accept it. If a heartless comes to take my life, I have to fight back to save myself. Fights between ghetto children turn bloody and often entice older siblings to join in. I don't want to kill but I will if I must.

I walk home from the big yellow school and I carefully watch everything around me. I do not see Tabatha, but I see some other girls on the way home and they say, "Amy is at home. She's fine. She made up with Tabatha. She admits she is weaker and can't beat Tabatha."

I cannot believe my ears – Amy cowers and does not become heartless. My pride denies me the option to cower. But I'm happy for Amy. She is wise and fortunate to be without pride. There are many proud people in the ghetto. Many of them are the corpses that lie in the caskets at funerals. Pride is so important to me I would prefer to be a corpse than to give it up. I would never surrender. If the attack is made on me, I fight back. Verbal attacks, physical attacks, emotional attacks, and psychological attacks, I engage in any battle.

******

A nine-year-old boy (Ryan) is the dirty-mouth bully and everyone knows him. He comes to interrupt our game of basketball. Amy and I play at the ghetto court my first brother Vincent makes (he cuts out the bottom of a plastic milk crate and nails it to the lamppost so we have a rim). Basketball without a net is very common in the ghetto.

Amy and I play with a basketball she "borrows" from the big yellow school. But Ryan takes the ball when it hits the ground after I shoot.

"This is my fucking ball now." Ryan hugs the ball.

"Give us back our ball. Amy and I are playing." My words are quick-tempered.

"Fuck, no."

"Please, Ryan, give us back our ball." I'm polite but stern.

"No. Are you fucking deaf, Nika?"

"Give us back our mother fucking ball before I kick your ass, Ryan." My words are impolite and humorless.

I put my hands on the ball and put my face to his. I flare my nostrils and widen my eyes. I stand with my feet apart and prepare for a physical battle. He knows I'm ready to fight for the ball. Ryan looks into my eyes and sees something that causes him to release the ball.

The next day, he tells Miss Major the words I use to get the basketball when she comes to pick me up for tutoring. Miss Major says, "Nika, did you say those nasty words?"

I cannot look her in the eyes. I cannot lie to her. I respect her so much. I feel shameful. I do not want her to know I speak the ghetto language because she encourages me to speak the Queen's language.

I look away and she knows the truth. I'm a ghetto child and the ghetto rages inside me. I'm prideful and pretend to be tough so I can survive in a neighborhood full of people who constantly test me.

She says, "Nika, your words surprise me. I don't want to hear you use them again. I cannot help a child who has no manners. You disappoint me very much."

Her words slice my soul. I disappoint the woman who believes in me. I'm so ungrateful.

"I'm sorry." My glassy eyes reveal my shame. The first teardrop falls, and I pretend to look at my feet. I cannot let her see me cry, but I want her to know I'm sorry to disappoint her.

"Promise me you will not use those words, Nika."

I don't promise because I know a promise is a lie.

"Okay."

I don't like when I'm wrong. I'm wrong because I use nasty words and because I refuse to be a bully's target. I wonder what Miss Major would do if she wakes up in my body tomorrow and experiences the same moment where Ryan takes the basketball. I wonder what she might say to him. Does she let him take the ball and cower to his nasty words? Does she fight back like I do? I know she fights back because she is strong like me. She tells me I disappoint her only to teach me a lesson but deep down inside she knows I have no choice but to fight back. If I do not fight back, what becomes of me? Do I die at the hands of a bully? I will never back down. I refuse to go quietly into the dark night.

Ghetto children must find a balance, stand up to bullies but don't become one of them. I become a bully when I threaten to kick Ryan's ass. I do not need to make threats. I only need to show bullies that I refuse to let them walk on me. A ghetto life is hard enough. I don't need bullies to make it even more difficult.

Chapter Twenty-Five

Matt and I climb the almond tree in our side yard. The tree is about fifteen feet off the ground. Its wide, green leaves make our side yard colorful and serene. The tamarind tree is right next to the almond tree but it's much taller and its green leaves are short and narrow. The two trees are so close together, we jump from one tree to the next. I think the trees talk to each other at night. The almond tree tells the tamarind tree that Mother uses its branches to beat us. The tamarind tree says, "That's a lie."

This third day of August, Matt and I pick almonds, eat off the yellow flesh, and throw the enormous seeds away. Edith comes to the almond tree and says, "What are you doing?"

Matt says, "We're picking almonds. There are lots of ripe ones up here."

Edith comes up to join us. The three of us stand on a branch. We pick, eat, and chit-chat. Then Edith starts an argument.

"Remember when you stole that money and Mother beat you?" Edith begins the conversation.

"I didn't steal it. I found it," I reply.

"Yeah. Whatever, Nika. That's what you say," Edith continues.

"It's true!" I yell.

"Edith, why you always pickin' on Nika?" Matt interjects.

"Because she's a liar, that's why." Edith flashes a mean look at me.

"You're a liar and a fool, Edith. You were the one who said it was five dollars. So dumb. Didn't even know it was twenty dollars," I jump in.

"Who you callin' dumb?" Edith responds.

"You. I am callin' you dumb."

"Come on, Nika. Don't let Edith get to you. Hey, catch." Matt throws an almond to me and I catch it.

Without warning, the branch that holds the three of us breaks off and we crash down in a matter of seconds. The fall amazes all of us. Fortunately, none of us is hurt.

"Holy cow, that was awesome," says Matt.

"I can't believe that just happened," I say.

Edith gets up quickly and runs toward the house. We hear her say, "Monkey uncle. I pee my pants."

Matt and I chuckle.

Chrissy, Regina, and Belinda come out of the house. "What was that noise?" they ask.

We tell them about the branch that gives us a magical ride.

Simon who watches us from the wall comes out because he sees the branch fall as he watches from his bedroom window. "I saw the branch come down," Simon says.

"I can't believe no one is hurt. I thought for sure someone would be really hurt," he says with a smile.

He asks, "How did it feel?"

Matt re-enacts the moment of flight and tells Simon it feels awesome. Matt, Chrissy, Belinda, and I pick almonds from the fallen branch and talk some more. Simon watches from the wall and joins in with our conversation. Matt and I use the fallen branch as a toy horse. We canter and gallop on it. Simon makes horse sounds. It's so much fun.

Father lets us keep the fallen branch in the side yard for months. When all the leaves change color and dry up, he drags it to the far side of the yard and burns it. Matt and I are sad our horse is gone. Father says it takes up too much space in the side yard. The almond tree branch goes away but Matt and I remember the glorious fun it gives.

******

The fallen branch gives much glorious fun, but the day of Matilda's wedding is the most glorious. The sun shines so bright and the sky is a lovely shade of blue. There are no clouds at all. Mother is happy there are no rain clouds because she believes it's bad luck for a bride to get wet from rain showers on her wedding day.

Matilda (my first sister) looks beautiful. She wears a long, white wedding dress and the train is four feet long. You cannot tell she is a mother of two and she carries her third son under her white dress. I think she is a black princess when she pulls the veil over her face.

Matilda has a huge wedding party. Six bridesmaids wear long, satin, mint-green gowns made by a local seamstress. Sister and Chrissy are bridesmaids. I wish I could be a flower girl but Belinda (my sixth sister) gets to do it. She drops white, carnation petals on the floor as she walks up the aisle in the small, white church. Matilda's biological father walks her up the aisle and Father stays home.

I'm happy today because Mother straightens my hair with a hot comb and then makes little ringlet curls all over my head. I look pretty. I wear a church dress that passes down from Regina, to Chrissy, to Edith and then to me. It will go to Belinda and then Stacey in a few years. The dress has lots of frills on the bottom, so I know Stacey will like it. She loves anything girlie.

After the wedding, we go to a beautiful garden to take pictures. Makalo is there, too.

"Nika, you look so pretty," Makalo says with his infectious smile.

"Thanks, Makalo. You look good, too," I reply.

"Tag, you're it," Makalo says and he taps me on the shoulder.

I chase after him and Mother sees me.

"Nika, stop that running. You might mess up your dress and hair," She yells.

"Yes, Ma'am," I yell back then signal to Makalo that I can't play. I move my lips and form the words (but do not speak them) while pointing at Mother, "I can't play now."

"Time for the family picture," says the photographer.

When we do the family portrait, there are more than forty faces that look out at the camera. Mother looks happy in the pictures. She is happy Matilda marries Donald – a hardworking, ghetto man who treats her daughter well. Matilda and Donald have two children together and a third on the way. Mother is happy Donald claims responsibility for his children. He does not involve himself in the drug trade but works as a chef at a fancy hotel. Donald is honest and will provide for Matilda and their children. Mother knows he enjoys beer – a habit that turns into an addiction. Matilda does not know she marries a drunk.

Drunks are common in the ghetto. This addiction is not as serious as addictions to crack or cocaine. Ghetto people believe drunks can quit at any time, but crack and cocaine addicts need rehabilitation. There are three different types of drunks in the ghetto: emotional drunks, crazy drunks, and invincible drunks.

Emotional drunks provide much to poke fun at. These kinds of drunks are not harmful to anyone but themselves. They love everyone and everything when they are drunk. My first brother, Vincent is an emotional drunk. He comes home, and the stink of liquor enters the house two minutes before he arrives. Vincent gives big hugs and kisses us on the cheeks.

"I love you all," he says. He slurs his words but continues to speak, "I love my sisters and my brothers. But the one I love most is Mother. She is my mother and the best woman in the world. I love her."

Mother gives Vincent a plate of white rice and he picks over it. He is already full. Liquor leaves no room for food. Vincent lights a cigarette, takes three puffs, and puts it out. He lies on the sofa and falls asleep. His nicotine urge wakes him at midnight, so he lights up a cigarette and tries to put it out on the arm of the sofa. Vincent is so drunk he falls asleep and leaves the lit cigarette on the sofa. The cigarette burns into the upholstery of the sofa, right next to his head. A fire starts.

Mother, who never really sleeps, smells smoke. She gets up from her bed and when she opens her bedroom door, smoke greets her with a curtsy. She sees Vincent asleep on the couch and sees the fire next to his head. Orange flames blaze while the blackface snores. Vincent sleeps on his back with his face to the ceiling. Mother runs to the fridge and grabs a water jug. She pours the water over the fire and tries to wake Vincent. He sleeps and does not wake even to screams and shouts from Mother. A drunk sleeps through everything.

Vincent is an emotional drunk, so intoxication makes him comical and hazardous. But crazy drunks are the ones we fear, especially crazy drunks who have cars. The man who lives across from us is a crazy drunk. He gets in his car and drives like a mad man. He speeds down the alley and skids his tires that leave long, black skid marks on the road of tar. Sometimes he drives off the road. Mother warns us to stay home when she hears his car make loud, screeching noises. It amazes that he does not kill anyone or kill himself. Crazy drunks in cars provide another form of surprise attacks. Innocent, ghetto children walk home from school and encounter these surprise attacks at least three times a week.

Invincible drunks are dangerous in the ghetto. They are the drunks who think they can conquer every obstacle. They believe their strength surpasses the strength of Goliath. My fourth brother, Joe is an invincible drunk. He sits on the wall at the street corner and challenges anyone to a fight.

Joe says, "You want to fight?" He stands up and stumbles as he tries to get himself ready for a physical battle. He cannot walk a straight line if his life depends on it. The one who he challenges punches him in the mouth.

Joe comes home with a bloody mouth and looks for a weapon. He takes a kitchen knife and tries to run back out. Vincent holds him down and takes the knife away.

Joe says, "Leave me the fuck alone. I'm going to kill that fucker."

Vincent continues to hold him down.

Joe continues, "If you don't let me go, I will kill you."

Vincent holds him down with more force.

"Don't fuck with me, Vincent. I'm going to kill that fucker."

Vincent says, "No, he is going to kill you."

"Kill who? Not me. He can't kill me. I'm a dangerous mother fucker." Joe slurs his words this time.

Vincent holds him down until he falls asleep. The next morning, Joe wakes up and forgets everything.

Each day, the ghetto awakens to the crows of the rooster. Morning refreshes ghetto folks. We feel like normal people in the morning. The sound of the rooster brings with it a fresh start. A new day gives us hope. Ghetto mornings are so quiet and calm. They are quiet because the partiers turn off their loud, reggae music and the gossipers use whispers. They are calm because people reflect on what they must do to survive. In the morning, we put the past behind us and begin anew. Invincible drunks forget the names of enemies. Emotional drunks apologize for burning sofas. Crazy drunks drive to work slowly. Ghetto children get ready for school and look forward to playing. Ghetto mothers go to work and toil with a smile. Rasta men sell newspapers and peanuts as they pace along the roadside. Women set up fruit markets with plantains, mangoes, pineapples, genip, and bananas. The sun brings with it a vibrant morning, a fresh start, and a new beginning. Ghetto folks are really hardworking, and they look forward to their toils. It's the one thing they can be proud of – one thing that keeps their joy alive. They never speak of retirement for death is the natural path that follows a life of labor. Boss-men and boss-women receive the most respectful manners from ghetto folks who must hold on to a job that pays less than a dollar an hour. "Time is money" is a phrase ghetto people use often. Yet time really is of no significance in the ghetto. The elders teach us that the difference between one hour and two hours is minuscule. It's better to arrive late so everyone sees when you enter. We like it when we are the center of attention except when the attention fuels gossip about our "niggerly" ways. Gossip spreads about the disfigured man like wildfire. "Did you hear his wife threw acid in his face for cheating on her with her sister?"

Beware the gossip of the ghetto. It is true forever and ever! The ghetto rumor labels Mother the stupid woman who can't close her legs. What is true equates what is rumor so be careful what they say. Words hurt and scar people forever in the ghetto because everything verbal is real. The Boggy Man, the Obeah Man, and spirits walk the earth. The people live in fear of them and even the wisest dare not deny. They'll say, "The Obeah Man put a spell on him and now he's lost his mind."

A mind is a terrible thing to lose in the ghetto. People poke fun at you for days and months and years. "You done lost your mind," is something no one in the ghetto wants to hear. People prefer to lose an eye, an arm, or even a leg.

As long as their mind is still in-tact, they accept their loss with only a flicker of the lashes.

Mother says the unlucky elders who "doubt" before they die are unfortunate, poor souls. No one comprehends their sickness, and no one understands how incredibly difficult it must be to wake up every morning a stranger. A grandmother strips naked and runs crazily through the streets. "Don't mind her," they say, "She's just a wacko, so let her go."

Mother is so glad she is of sound mind and I pray she takes it to the grave. She suffers enough in the intense heat and her blood pressure commits to high numbers. Each day, the unknowns give her something to ponder. A ghetto woman's mind is full of "what if" and "why me." She never really sleeps but rests at night. She dreams of *"in the sweet, by and by,"* and hopes for happier times.

Chapter Twenty-Six

Mother is not prideful like me. She tries to keep the peace and apologizes to the mean neighbor because her children eat his hog plums that fall off his tree onto the ground in her yard. If I'm Mother, I do not apologize. I tell Mr. Roker he is an asshole.

Only an asshole expects hungry ghetto children to watch good hog plums rot on the ground in their own yard. Only an asshole expects hungry ghetto children to pick up the hog plums and throw them over the fence back into his yard. Only an asshole expects hungry ghetto children to ignore the hog plum branches that hang across the fence in their own yard.

After Mother apologizes and tells us not to eat the hog plums, Mr. Roker becomes meaner. He takes a saw and cuts the branches that hang in our yard. He comes into our yard and retrieves the branches he cuts off. Mr. Roker picks up every plum that falls from the branches and takes them to his kitchen. He says, "Keep those snotty-nosed children away from my fence."

He sits on his porch and smokes his cigar as he guards his property.

Mother says, "Don't worry, Mr. Roker, I will keep them off your fence."

She does not know Edith and I plan to jump his fence when we know he is at work.

Mr. Roker leaves then Edith and I scale the fence to complete a mission – to take as many hog plums from the trees as we can. We climb one of the three hog plum trees and fill the plastic bags we bring. We quickly cross over into our yard when we hear Mr. Roker's pot cake dogs approach.

Hog plums are sweet. The sweetest are the ones we take from Mr. Roker's tree. Edith and I sit in our back yard and eat them. We laugh when Mr. Roker comes home from work. He suspects nothing. He does not know how many hog plums are on his trees. The ones we take, he does not miss.

We hear Mr. Roker grumble from his yard. "These are my trees. These are my hog plums."

"But these are my hog plums," Edith whispers to me and we snigger.

"And these are my hog plums," I gurgle.

Edith and I only get along when we are allies in an evil scheme.

"Nika, tomorrow we go again. Are you in?" Edith asks.

"I'm in. But just make sure Belinda doesn't see because she'll tell Mother."

"I know, Belinda is a talker and I'm a taker," Edith chortles.

"These are my hog plums," Mr. Roker yells as if he could hear Edith.

Edith and I laugh.

Mr. Roker isn't the only mean neighbor. Maxine is mean, too. She always wears a head-cloth and a cotton dress and cusses us out with the nastiest words if she catches us near her guava tree. The tree grows half in her yard and half in ours and a rusty, chain-linked fence separates the two halves. Maxine says it's her tree. She plants it, not Mother.

"Get your dirty, fucking asses out of my tree," Maxine yells.

Edith and I run away because we are afraid of her. She thinks she keeps this tree forever.

In spite of these mean neighbors, Mother reminds us this world is just a temporary place. She teaches us to be kind to others. We learn that we leave this world as we enter – naked and without possessions. Mother teaches wise lessons. We are fortunate she knows so much.

Mr. Roker and Maxine need to learn lessons of kindness. Perhaps they would be happier if they share their hog plums and guavas. For now, though, we have to put up with their unhappiness. I'm glad summer ends soon because the season for hog plums and guavas ends soon, too. Mr. Roker and Maxine are quieter when they know we are in school.

******

The first day of school comes and Mother gives me bus fare to ride to the private school in the South. Matt and I ride a bus to school every day. Today, the bus driver is an old man. He does not speed, and he plays soft, gospel music for his passengers. Matt and I get off at my school and we pay the driver. At lunchtime, I'm so hungry. I use the return bus fare to buy fried chicken, macaroni, and orange soda. I plan to walk home after school instead of taking a bus. This walk is more than ten miles.

After the dismissal bell rings, I see Matt get on a bus. The bus drives off and I begin my trek home. I walk down the nice, smooth, tar road of the South. I pass big, stone houses. I wonder what it feels like to live in one of them. I pass green lawns that are short and neat. There are only a few people out in the streets. There are no crowds like the ones that gather in the ghetto. I hear birds chirp because it's so quiet. The sidewalks are clean and don't have rusty, old appliances. I like the peace of this neighborhood. I think I stumble upon a Wonderland and wonder if a white rabbit will soon speak to me.

The hot sun beats down on the back of my neck. I feel so hot. Beads of sweat gather on my face. I see a woman in a sedan and she stops and waits at a corner. I arrive at the corner and she says, "Do you want a ride? I don't pick up strangers, but I can tell you're hot and tired. You're such a pretty, little girl and I wouldn't want some criminal to pick you up."

The woman looks like she works in a bank, and she wears a name tag, heavy make-up, and nice business clothes. I tell her, "My mother says never to ride with strangers."

She says, "Good. Make sure you walk straight home. Be careful."

I continue to walk, and she drives away.

I walk for an hour. I'm tired and hot but I do not stop. Fortunately, I do not encounter any criminals on the walk and no one else stops. My trek takes me over the highway and cars speed by. I like the cool breeze I feel when a car goes super-fast. It gives me a brief moment of relief from the heat.

People look out from their cars. I can tell by their faces, they think I'm crazy to walk along a highway. They know from my school uniform that I come from the school in the South. I continue my walk and the scenery changes the closer I get to home. The houses are smaller, the yards are messier, and the sidewalks have garbage. Two hours later, I arrive at my ghetto. I'm happy to be here. It means my walk soon ends.

I wave to people on the ghetto street as I walk.

"Why are you coming from this way?" says the nosey, old woman. "I thought the bus takes you to the other side."

I say, "I didn't take a bus today."

She says, "What? Child, don't tell me you walked home from the South."

"Yes, Ma'am."

"Your mother didn't give you bus fare?"

"Yes, but I lost it," I lie to conceal the truth. My belly is more important than the comfort of a bus ride.

I continue my walk and the scenery is very familiar. My ghetto, my home looks like heaven today. I see Makalo shooting marbles with Tito and Jeremy and I wave to him, "Hello, Makalo."

He waves back and says, "Hi, Nika."

I walk down the alley and I'm happy I only have forty more steps to get to our clapboard house. I take the fortieth step that takes me to the front door. I open the door and run to the fridge to get water. I drink from the jug and Mother says, "Why are you late?"

I tell her, "I lost my bus fare and so I had to walk home."

She says, "What! Are you serious? You walked home from the South?"

"Yes, Ma'am."

"My Lord. My child walked home from the South." Mother shakes her head in disbelief.

"Mother, I'm fine."

"Nika, next time if you lose your bus fare, go to the teacher and ask if she can loan you the money. I will pay her back."

"Okay, Mother."

I tell a white lie because Mother gets mad if she knows I spend the bus fare on lunch.

I change my school uniform, put on my play clothes, and I make a really important decision. I never dare spend my bus fare on lunch again. The walk home is too hard, and I can never do it again. I devise a new plan.

I wake up early the next morning, walk to the bus stop, and wait for the old man's bus. Schoolmates tell me he never remembers if passengers pay on the way in. If passengers get off, he asks, "Did you pay?"

They say, "Yes, I paid on the way in."

He says, "Okay."

The customers cheat him. They do not pay on the way in or out.

The bus driver who speeds and plays loud, reggae music comes to my stop first. He pulls over to the stop and says, "You need a bus?"

I say, "I'll get the next one. I'm waiting for a friend." I tell another white lie.

He speeds off. The bus I await arrives and I get on.

"Good morning," I say to the bus driver.

There are ten other passengers on the bus. I take my seat at the back because I want to be behind everyone when it's my time to get off. This way I can sneak off and the bus driver does not see.

The bus ride takes me downtown and I see women set up their displays at the straw market. They get ready to sell their straw baskets, straw hats, and other knick-knacks they weave with dried, palm tree leaves. White tourists visit the straw market in great numbers. The female vendors prepare for their busy workday while men ride their horses and carriages to the area where they line up. They wait for the white tourists to come as a policeman directs traffic. I watch the policeman because I think his red, black and white uniform looks so perfect.

The buses line up at a bus loop and many passengers come. Many are transferring from other buses, but some are getting off work from downtown hotels. I sit on the bus and I can see the big, cruise ships that dock in the downtown harbor. The robotic policeman gives a signal to the bus driver. It's safe to go.

The bus leaves and goes uphill then downhill towards the south. We pass a ghetto on the way. It looks just like my ghetto. Bright-colored, clapboard houses, graffiti-covered walls, and rusty appliances on sidewalks make up the decor. We pass high schools, churches, restaurants, gas stations, and bars. We pass really big, stone houses and I know we arrive shortly at my school. By now, the bus is full of other students who wear the grey and white school uniform.

One of the students at the front says, "Bus stop."

People in the front and middle seats stand up. They form a line down the center aisle and pay the bus driver as they leave. Some say, "I paid on the way in."

I walk behind the line. When the bus driver looks down to count change for a passenger who pays with a ten-dollar bill, I sneak off the bus. I walk behind the bus, so the driver does not see me when he drives away.

I feel guilty but by lunchtime, the needs of my belly become more important. I spend the bus fare on food. I cheat the bus driver again on my way home from school. For two months, I continue to cheat the driver. But one day, I'm ready to sneak off, and the driver sees me in his rear-view mirror. He says, "Hey, you little girl. You need to pay."

I say, "Yes, Sir."

I pay him and get off the bus. I'm lucky he catches me in the morning when I still have the money. If he catches me on the way home from school, I have no money and so I tell him, "I paid on the way in."

I feel guilty. I'm caught. The driver knows I'm a cheat. My pride swells. I can never take that bus again because the driver suspects I'm dishonest. I'm shameful. I cannot tell anyone what I do, and I bury the shame of the two months I cheat him in the graveyard in my mind.

I live with the shame and guilt. I'm a thief. A bright scholar does wrong. If Mother finds out she beats me harder than the last time. I'm a ghetto child and I'm no good. I cheat a bus driver and take the money to buy food. My belly causes me to do evil. I need to satisfy my belly with the small slice of macaroni I can afford to buy. I cannot afford to buy fried chicken and orange soda, too. I must learn to live within my means.

After school, I take the bus that plays loud, reggae music. I hate this bus. I don't feel safe in it. The driver passes cars when another car comes in the other direction. He is a reckless driver and I don't understand how he makes his license. He dates the young, high school girls and one of them bears him a child. These young girls come on the bus and they have arguments about who he is "with" now.

"Why are you sitting upfront on this bus next to my man," says one girl.

The other replies, "He was your man last month, but he is my man now."

They swear at each other and make threats. He laughs and says, "Bitches, calm down."

I'm happy to reach my bus stop. I get off the bus and wish I didn't have to take it again. I want to take the old man's bus. I feel safer on it. My pride denies me a safe ride to and from school. I cannot face the old man. He knows who I am. I'm a ghetto child who steals from a hardworking man. I don't deserve a safe bus ride. I deserve to ride with the crazy driver and if we crash, I deserve whatever befalls me. I carry the guilt and know I'm wrong. But pride gets in my way. I cannot apologize to the driver. I cannot be humble like Mother and admit I'm wrong.

The heart of a ghetto child is full of secrets. Secret sins we commit, we can never tell. We are not trustworthy, and we know it. This is why we go to the altar on Sunday and ask for forgiveness. I go to church and I pray about my sin. I ask God to forgive me for my ways. I cry because I want to be good. I do not want to lie or cheat.

The preacher says, "Come to the altar if you want to give your life and heart to Jesus."

I go up and join the fifteen other sinners who come to repent.

The preacher says, "It's good children want to come but they are too young to understand what this means."

I think to myself, "I understand. Please don't send me away."

The preacher does not send me away but separates the adults from children. The adults pray a grown-up prayer and the children pray a childish prayer. I do not want to pray the childish prayer. I want to repent. I'm a sinner. I say the grown-up prayer in my mind and I mean every word. I leave church that day and I feel better.

A few months later, I ride the old man's bus and I pay when I enter. I say, "Good morning," and take my seat. I never cheat him or any other driver again. I'm whole again. I rid myself of the evil that makes me forget the values Mother teaches. Honesty is important for good health and sound mind. I want to be good and do what is right. I'm happy I change my behavior before it leads to something terrible. Mother says a liar is a thief and a thief is a murderer. I do not choose this for my life. I choose to search for the yellow brick road that leads me to success. Poinciana trees grow along the sides of the yellow brick road and I'm eager to smell the sweetness of their flowers.

Chapter Twenty-Seven

Flowers are beautiful, especially in the ghetto. Hibiscus flowers grow wild and provide a colorful landscape. Amy and I pick them and pull off the green stem that conceals their sweetness. We suck on them and enjoy the sweet pleasure they give. Makalo, Amy, and I pick mangoes from the trees in the yard of the two-story apartment building. The people who live in the apartments are kind and say, "You can pick mangoes here anytime."

Matt, Edith, Makalo, Amy, and I pick avocadoes from the empty lot and we bring them home. Mother serves them with grits or we put slices of them between bread and eat avocado sandwiches. We are fortunate fruit grows well in the Caribbean. Ghetto children would never get all their nourishment if fruit trees go away. Pineapple, mango, guava, tamarind, hog plum, banana, sea grape, watermelon, genip, dilly, and soursop provide us with all the necessary nutrients rich children get from seedless grapes, strawberries, apples, oranges, kiwi, and cantaloupe.

Makalo and I live for fruit seasons. Makalo says, "Nika, I know fruit seasons better than I know how to shoot marbles. When hog plum season ends, mango season begins. What's your favorite season, Nika?"

"Mango season," I reply, licking my lips with my hungry tongue.

"Oh, yeah. Mango. Mmm. Mmm. I love me some mango," Makalo says, rubbing his tummy, licking his lips, and patting his head.

All ghetto children love mango season. It's the absolute favorite. We also know the difference between mango and "mangola." Mangoes are smaller and hairy on the inside. "Mangolas" are larger and smooth on the inside. "Mangola" trees are rare and people who have them guard them more carefully than Mr. Roker guards his hog plum trees. "Mangolas" are sweet and juicy. So Makalo and I don't chew them. We suck on them until they dissolve inside the mouth.

I remember one-time Mother's aunt brings her some "mangolas" and Mother hides them in the kitchen cupboard. She wraps them in brown paper, so they ripen quickly. She pulls one out and offers it to me.

"I can have a whole one?" I ask.

Mother says, "Yes, but don't tell the others I give it to you."

I hide behind the house and eat the "mangola" and I'm so happy to have it all for myself. Mother is kind and sometimes she does extremely nice things out of the blue. I do not question why Mother gives me a "mangola" just for me. But I enjoy that "mangola" so much, when I finish, the remnants consist of only a bare seed. Not one speck of flesh remains.

It's no surprise to Mother when I eat the "mangola" down to its bare seed. She knows I have a healthy appetite because I need constant reminders not to take second helpings. But the only day of the week Mother allows me to have a second serving of rice is Sunday.

"Mother, can I have some more rice, please?" I ask.

"Yes, Nika," The tone of her reply tells me she expects the next question.

"Could I also have another piece of chicken?"

"No, Nika. I told you there is only enough for everyone to have one piece."

"Here, Nika. You can have my piece of chicken." Sister passes her chicken to me.

"Thanks, Sister."

"You're generous to that girl. I don't know why. But you sure are generous," Mother says.

"Nika wanted the chicken more than I did. So, I gave it to her." Sister is frank.

"Watch it, Missy. Watch the way you speak to me." Mother gives her look that reveals she is in the mood for discipline.

"Sister, shhh...," I say because I don't want her to get in trouble with Mother.

"As long as you live under my roof, I'm the woman. You still a child, Mia. I know today is Sunday, but I will whip you if I must. Don't you backtalk," Mother's voice is firm.

Sister does not respond but continues to eat the rice on her plate.

I try to change the subject, "Look at all the colors on my plate."

Sunday dinner is a colorful food display. The dark brown peas complement the light brown rice. Bright orange macaroni and cheese provide a rich hue of spring, while the yellow potato salad glows like the sun. The dark red beets sit beside the multi-colored coleslaw and the fried, yellow plantain separates the meat from the salads. Brown fried chicken blends in with the brown rice and dinner is not complete without it.

Just like Sunday dinner, the colorful, underwater coral reefs are a beautiful sight, too. Our neighbor, George takes Edith, Chrissy, Belinda and me on his glass-bottom boat to see fish in their natural habitat. The beauty I see under the sea is glorious. Bright colors of every shade sit below the aquamarine waters.

The ocean floor is so clean. Fish swim in their schools – yellow, red, blue, orange, gold, silver, and rainbow color fish swim along, and they all look so content. There is no violence at the coral reef. The coral reef must be where the wealthy fish live. I wonder what the ghetto of the sea looks like. I wonder if the ghetto fish live the same ghetto life as me?

George drives us home after taking us out for the day on his boat. He is kind, but he has a crazy side, too. He lives with his wife and six-year-old son in one of the newer houses in the ghetto. His house is made of stone, not clapboard. I think George lives in the ghetto only until his house is complete in the rich neighborhood in the East.

A week later, my family gathers in the living room to watch a game of basketball. The Lakers beat the Celtics this game and Magic Johnson is the MVP. George places his bet on the Celtics. When the game ends, he unplugs his TV, opens his front door, and throws his colour-TV outside. We hear it crash down and we run outside.

George's voice is loud, "The Celtics are worthless fuckers."

Mother calls us to come back inside because she knows George is drunk. He is an invincible drunk. She knows he has a long shotgun because she sees him take it in his house the day they move in.

Mother says, "Don't go out there. Let George raise hell with himself."

We sit inside and listen to him cuss the wind, the air, and the trees. Edith and I cannot believe he throws out a colour-TV when we would gladly receive it from him if he offers it to us. His wife is wise. She takes their son and drives to her mother's house. The invincible drunk can only challenge himself to a duel. He goes back inside his house after sixty minutes of cussing. Fifteen minutes pass and we think George must be asleep because everything goes quiet.

The next day, George goes out on his glass-bottom boat and takes white visitors with him to see the beautiful, colorful reefs. We ghetto children go to school and some of us gather for spelling bees and speech contests.

Chapter Twenty-Eight

School competitions are colorful scenes just like the tranquil coral reefs. Students gather from schools across the nation and they wear their school uniforms. Some wear grey, navy blue, light blue, dark green, lime green, plaid, red, and patterns. All the different uniforms give us our identities. Everyone knows the green plaid is the uniform of the rich school and the blue plaid is the uniform of a ghetto school. My school in the South is a private school but it's the cheapest private school and the fees are low. Mother says it's the private school for the poor.

There is a war between the rich and poor schools. But the rich schools do not fight physical wars because the students are not from the ghetto. Instead, they fight verbal wars and use the Queen's English to attack. I expect there will be some rivalry today because students gather for the National Sports Day, so athletes can prove their school is number one. The rich, private school in the East always wins because they have the facilities to train their athletes. My school in the South doesn't have fields that span over a hundred acres that are always green and receive water from sprinklers. Our fields dry out from the sun and when rain is scarce, they dry out even more. High schools in the ghetto are even worse. They do not have real hurdles to jump or a rubber track that has the lines and markings of a real race track. Ghetto high schools have asphalt tracks or dirt tracks. Yet, ghetto children do well as athletes despite the lack of equipment.

My P.E. teacher asks if I could run the eight-hundred meter because no one else wants to do it. I say, "Sure. I'll try it."

Matt hears our conversation and approaches me.

"Nika, the eight hundred? Are you for real?" Matt is surprised. "You do know that means four laps around the track, right?"

"Yep," My reply is quite casual.

"Nika, are you sure you want to do this? I heard the eight hundred is a killer."

"What are you saying, Matt? You think I can't do it?"

"No. I know you can't, Sucker." Matt laughs.

I laugh, too.

"I'll cheer for you anyway. See you later, Nika."

The officials call us to line up before I have a chance to change my mind.

The first lap around the track, I'm really strong. I'm in third place. My leg muscles feel good. I sweat but just a little bit. The sun feels hot, but I can bear it.

The second lap around the track, I feel tired. I'm in sixth place. My leg muscles tremble. I sweat so much – my shorts and t-shirt are wet. The sun is hot, but I can manage.

The third lap around the track, I'm weak. I'm in eighth place. My leg muscles tighten and tremble. The sun is hot, and I burn inside.

The fourth lap around the track, my legs feel heavy. The crowd cheers for the runners who leave me far behind. Some runners finish and I fight with myself to continue. I want to quit but I'm no quitter. I suck-in air and blow. My heart pounds faster than the wings of a hummingbird. My leg muscles burn, and it hurts to move. I do not give up.

Another girl is in tenth place and I'm in ninth. She suffers like me, but she is stronger. She manages to utter a few words to me as she runs by, "Someone has to finish last and it is not going to be me." She runs to the finish line.

The crowd cheers for me. I'm in the last place but I continue. I have to finish this race. My pride swells. I refuse to go down in history as the ghetto girl who collapses before she reaches the finish line. My leg muscles feel numb. My whole-body aches and my throat burns. I breathe like an asthma patient.

I can no longer sweat. My body is dry, yet my clothes are wet. My eyes squint to avoid the bright sun rays. I can see the finish line and continue to move one foot in front of the other. I hear my feet hit the ground and see people along the side of the track with plastic cups of water and orange slices. This gives me the strength to go on. I run to the finish line and stop just in front of it. A woman shouts, "You have to cross over it." I use my ghetto strength and drag my feet across. Then I collapse.

People run to me with water and orange slices. They call my name. I say nothing. My eyes are shut. I just want to rest. My muscles are so weak they cannot form words. I only moan. Someone lifts my head a bit and pours water over my lips. The moisture seeps into my mouth. My tongue comes outside in search of more water. I receive more. My eyes still do not open. Someone puts an orange slice in my mouth. I open my eyes and see blurry images. I cannot make out the faces of the people who help me. These people are so kind. They pay me attention and care for me. They help me up and they carry me with my arms over their shoulders. They say, "Take your time. Catch your breath."

Someone else offers me more water. Another offers me another orange slice. I feel better.

I say, "Thank you. I think I'm okay now."

Finally, the images become clear and I see it's Amy, Matt, and Makalo who help me.

Long-distance is not something I'm good at. Ballet, jazz, and netball are my talents. I know my limits now and vow never to run a long-distance race again. I learn a very important lesson from my experience. A long-distance run is like a life in the ghetto. You start the race and you feel strong. As time passes you become tired and weak. You fight to survive and do not give up. But the difference is you choose to enter the long-distance race, you do not choose a life in the ghetto. Ghetto life is a gift, birth gives. We, newborns, receive it gladly. We cry when the doctor slaps our behind and this breath of life is our admission that we accept the gift.

Only one week after my long-distance race, Chrissy comes home with her baby boy. I ask to hold him. His yellow skin looks so soft and it's blemish free. He smells better than fried chicken. I want to kiss his soft, pink lips but Mother says it's bad for the baby. His body cannot fight colds yet. Mother takes him from me. Chrissy sits on the bed and she shakes his bottle of milk. Mother gives the baby to her and she feeds him. He sucks on the rubber nipple and I see his cheek muscles work so hard to pull milk from the bottle.

I ask Chrissy if I can burp the baby.

She says, "Yes, you can. Just be careful and hold him carefully."

She gives me a cloth to put over my shoulder and then she gives me the baby. I hold him over my shoulder and tap him on the back. After a minute, or so, he burps and then vomits. The white, stinky vomit soaks through the cloth and wets my school uniform. I give the baby back to Chrissy and say, "Ewe. Now I have to go change."

I go to change, and I hear the baby cry. I say to myself, "Babies are cute, but they are loud."

My cousin, Flora comes to visit and to see the baby. Flora sees me in the living room and says, "So, do you have a boyfriend or are you a sly fox? See what happens to your sister. She has a baby now. You look like a sly fox. I bet you have a boyfriend."

She makes me uncomfortable. I say, "No. I don't have a boyfriend."

Flora says, "I can tell you lie."

"No. I do not lie."

"Why do you get so defensive, Nika? Only people who lie get defensive."

I don't like the way she talks to me. I have no interest in boys. I'm too young for boys. I'm a kid. Why does she ask grown-up questions to me? I don't even have breasts or get my period yet. I still shoot marbles in the dirt. Boys are only friends and playmates to me.

Flora nags at me, "So, what's your boyfriend's name?"

"Flora, I told you I don't have one."

"Tell me and I promise not to tell anyone else."

"Please, Flora. Just leave me alone."

"I knew it. You do have one. What's his name? Did you kiss him yet?"

I roll my eyes at her. Flare my nostrils. Get up from the living room sofa and walk outside to the back yard.

I hear Flora grumble, "I bet Nika will have a baby before she's fifteen."

My pride enlarges, and I make a decision when I hear her words. I must prove Flora wrong.

The next day, Amy comes to see me, and we sit under the tamarind tree and talk. I tell about my conversation with Flora.

"Yesterday, Flora came over to see Chrissy's baby and guess what she said to me?" I speak without hesitation because I know Amy understands me.

"What?" Amy gives me her full attention.

"She asked if I was a sly fox."

"What? What does that mean?"

"She means I sneak around with boys," I lower my voice.

"What boys?"

"I don't know. I have no idea what she was talking about."

"Why would she say that, Nika?"

"I don't know. She said, Chrissy has a baby now, so I must have a boyfriend, too."

"What? Where would she get that from?"

"I have no idea, Amy. She made me so uncomfortable."

"Older women are so judgy."

"Yeah. And I can't stand that. Especially when I know what they sayin' isn't true."

"Flora sounds just like my cousin Mercy. She's always accusing me of doin' 'fresh' things with boys."

"I don't even understand why they would accuse us because all we do is play all the time."

"I know, Nika. But that's just how older women are. They're so suspicious."

Chapter Twenty-Nine

On a Saturday morning, Makalo's sister Trish comes to visit us at home. Mother and my older siblings are at work. I'm at home with Regina, Chrissy, Edith, Matt, Belinda, and Stacey. Trish asks if we want to walk with her to visit some friends.

I ask, "How far do we have to walk?"

"About an hour," Trish speaks like it's no big deal.

"Where's Makalo today?" I know the answer to my question but ask it anyway.

"Shooting marbles with Tito and Jeremy," Trish answers.

I agree to go with Trish, but my other siblings decide to stay home. We go for a long walk and I don't mind. I like Trish. She buys me orange soda when she has money.

Trish looks like the typical, black female with dark skin, thick lips, short, nappy hair, wide nose, and white teeth. She has a slender frame and walks upright like she balances something on her head. I'm eleven and she is sixteen.

We walk to another ghetto. I play with some of the ghetto children while Trish talks to a young man. I think this man is her boyfriend. Trish tells me to play Hopscotch. She and her boyfriend go behind a small, clapboard house to kiss and touch each other.

I throw my rock in the Hopscotch after I draw it on the tar with white rocks that mark like chalk. I hop on one leg and then come back to pick up my rock when I hear a little girl scream. I run with the other little girls who play with me to the place where we hear the scream.

A little girl points at a man who lies on the ground in the back yard of a small, one-room house. The back yard has no lawn, only black dirt. The man looks old. He has a long, slender body and wears a red, plaid shirt with buttons down the front and dark blue, long, polyester pants. His skin is charcoal, and his hair has grey patches. I'm afraid of his eyes because they are open, but he sees nothing. His body is still and looks stiff. The air around him is calm and it whispers words from the other world in his ears.

I say, "Is he dead?"

Trish and her boyfriend arrive at the scene and they pause to take in the sight. We stand like tree roots. Our eyes entranced by this man who lies on the ground. We wait to see if he moves.

Trish says, "Mister, Mister. Are you okay?"

The man does not reply.

Flies swarm and gather around his mouth.

Trish says, "You children get. Get back out front. You don't need to see this man."

I run back with the five other little girls and we are not in the mood for play.

"Do you think he is dead?" I ask the others.

They nod their heads and one girl says, "He has to be dead. Only dead people keep their eyes open and do not blink."

We walk to a wall that is only three-feet high and sit on it as we discuss what our eyes see.

"What makes him die?" I ask.

A little girl who seems to know a lot about death says, "I bet he is a drunk and dies from a stroke or heart attack. My drunken uncle looks just like this man when we found him dead."

I say, "I'm scared. I want to go home."

People come out of their homes and before long a crowd of onlookers watch this man as he lies on his back in the dirt. I hear a woman yell, "Did someone call the ambulance?"

Someone replies, "I called thirty minutes ago. It takes them so long to arrive at the scene. The ambulance drivers don't care if poor people drop dead."

It feels like a long time before I hear the sirens. They load the man in the ambulance and carry him away. Trish comes to get me from the wall.

She says, "Let's go."

We walk back to our ghetto but mostly in silence. I cannot get the images of the man out of my mind. I see him everywhere.

I say, "Was he dead?"

Trish says, "Yes. He was dead."

I say, "I know I will have trouble sleeping tonight."

I fret, worry, and feel afraid. I arrive home and tell my siblings about the vision I see. The dead man who lies in the dirt. I worry even more.

The night comes too quickly today. I do not want to sleep. I know the dead man awaits me in my dreams. He will invite me to come with him. What if I accept? I fight sleep, but this is a battle a child cannot win. My lids force themselves shut and I dream horrible dreams. I see the dead man. His frigid face haunts me.

I wake up in a pool of sweat and I move closer to Sister who sleeps next to me. I put my leg and arm around her. She pushes me away and says, "It's hot. Get off me, Nika."

I hesitate and then move over. I don't want to disturb Sister's sleep. I keep my eyes open and pull the covers over my head. I pray sleep does not come again. I doze off but this time I'm so tired I see nothing and have no dreams. I wake the next morning and I'm happy to see the light of day.

But I spend all day thinking about the dead man in the dirt. I think he looks even "more dead" than Auntie Zelda. Thoughts about the dead man and Auntie Zelda devour my childish thoughts. And I remember when they lower my Auntie Zelda's coffin into the ground. My cousins scream and threaten to jump in the hole. They cry, "No, don't put my mother in that hole. Mommy, Mommy. Oh, Lord, Mommy gone leave me."

The tears roll down my cheeks and my heart breaks. I want to fix my cousins.

Death brings a sadness that lingers for weeks. But the ghetto mourns really well, and people heal fast. Families move on and life continues. Yet, death does not bring inheritance like it does for the wealthy. People inherit more responsibility. Flora inherits the role of mother when Auntie Zelda dies. She raises her younger siblings just like Mother does when her parents die.

Because death is frequent in the ghetto, life insurance is a must and families struggle to pay it every week. Mother says, "Nika, I can't buy you a new pair of school shoes because I have to pay for the insurance. I cannot let it lapse."

Burial is an expensive event and ghetto people want to bury their families in the most expensive plots. They think it's better to rot in a cemetery where the grass is green, there is a shiny, chain-linked fence, and tall iron gates open to let the hearse in.

Thoughts about death linger a long time in my mind because Mr. Roker dies from cancer two weeks after I see the dead man in the dirt. Mother takes all of us to his funeral. Makalo comes, too. Mother says, "We have to show our respect for the dead. Even though Mr. Roker was grouchy, he was a human being."

After the ghetto funeral service for Mr. Roker ends, Edith, Makalo, Matt and I walk from the church to the graveyard with a marching band that plays loud, gospel music. I like to walk with the band. The music makes me want to dance. The hearse follows the mourners who walk. Some people dance as they walk. Some hold flowers and keep their heads low. Others continue to weep for Mr. Roker. Makalo and I dance but Edith and Matt walk with their heads down.

People talk badly about Mr. Roker's family when they realize we march to a ghetto graveyard instead of the one with tall iron gates. Some say, "They can't afford to pay for a better plot?"

Makalo whispers to me, "Don't these people know Mr. Roker can't afford to be buried in the rich graveyard?"

"Yeah. They should know Mr. Roker was broke," I whisper back.

I don't understand why it's so important to bury ghetto people in graveyards of the wealthy. A corpse cannot appreciate the green lawn. But it's the desire of many to have a plot outside the ghetto. Even Mother says she wants this, too. A woman who says she does not want wealth here on earth wants to have a decent burial and a quiet, clean graveyard to take her eternal rest.

I must admit it's lovely to walk in the beautiful, "rich" cemetery. It's so quiet and peaceful. The beautiful flowers and green lawn give it a park-like panorama. We forget there are souls who sleep beneath our feet. I hope Auntie Zelda is happy because she gets to rest in a beautiful graveyard. Poor Mr. Roker, he has to sleep in the ghetto forever.

Womanhood Begins

Chapter Thirty

Thirteen is not the typical age for a ghetto girl to move from childhood to womanhood. But there is very little about my life that is usual. A couple of weeks before mother-nature blesses me with blood that flows every month, I see a slimy, white discharge in my panties. I'm afraid because I don't know what causes it. I call Mother into the bedroom and show her. She says, "That's normal. It means you'll soon get it."

Two weeks pass, the blood flows very slowly when it first begins, and I only notice it when I wipe after I pee. I go tell Mother. She cuts up an old, white bedsheet and says, "Use these pieces as rags to catch it." She shows me how to fold the rags and put them in my panties. The rags look familiar. For years, I watch Sister wash her bloody rags and hang them out to dry. Mother cannot afford to buy us maxi pads.

A long shower soothes me because I feel dirty. I dry off then roll up a rag and put it in my underwear. I wear a cotton, knee-length dress because I don't want people to notice the bulge in my panties. Shorts are my usual first choice for attire, but the dress hides the new demand I must tolerate each month without privacy. I now share a bedroom with Regina, Edith, Belinda, and Stacey. We have two sets of bunk beds. I'm lucky I get a bed for myself. Belinda and Stacey have to share. I sleep in the top bunk above Edith. Gone are the days when I only have one roommate. I miss Sister's room. Mother says, "Things change, and we have to change, too." Sister marries and moves out and Chrissy takes our room with her cute baby boy.

The next day, Sister comes to see me, and we sit outside under the tamarind tree together.

"Mother says you got your period." Sister's voice is nurturing.

"Yes." I'm very solemn. I say nothing else.

I don't want to be a woman. Mother-nature gives unwanted gifts.

"You know what this means?" Sister takes my hand.

"Yes, Sister."

"It means you're a woman now, Nika."

"I know."

I don't desire to be a woman. I want to keep my childhood because it has fewer struggles. We all know a ghetto woman suffers more than a ghetto child. I don't want to suffer more. I yearn to keep the miserable life I have. I do not welcome the gloom a ghetto woman suffers.

A week later, Sister buys me my first set of books. The books are for teenage girls and they teach about menstruation, pregnancy, dating, and birth control. I read these six books every day and re-read them when I'm done. I want to learn everything about womanhood. Since I cannot return the bloody gift, I must learn how to live with it. Sister understands what I need. She always looks out for me. She can't believe it when I tell her, "My period lasted three weeks."

The first few months I get my monthly, I experience very little pain. However, every month it comes, the pain gets more intense. One night I'm unable to sleep. I toss and turn and rub my abdomen. I moan and cry because the pain is sharp and unbearable. I wake Mother, lie on the floor, and curl into a fetal position. Mother wakes Sister who spends the night away from her drug-addicted husband.

"Take her to the hospital," Mother says.

The pain is intense. I sweat. Moan. Groan. Cry. Sister goes with me in a taxi cab to the emergency. The long line at the government's hospital welcomes us. We wait for three long, endless hours before a doctor sees me.

He tells Sister, "There is nothing I can do for her."

He gives me a needle in my behind and says, "This will make her sleep. Hopefully, the pain passes when she wakes."

The next month I get my monthly. The pain is fierce. My head aches, and my stomach is queasy. I vomit on the bedroom floor. Edith and Belinda feel sorry for me. Sister takes me to her gynecologist's office. She pays my bill because she does not want me to have to wait for hours in pain. We only wait twenty minutes and the doctor calls us in. He says, "What is wrong?"

I tell him about my pain. He examines my abdomen with Sister in the room. He sticks a needle in my arm and holds it there. He asks, "Which pain do you feel – the needle or your stomach?"

I say, "Both."

He tells Sister, "There is nothing I can do for her."

He gives me a needle in my behind and says, "This will make her sleep."

Every month, I suffer the intense pain. Sister feels sorry for me. She gives me two little, blue pills and tells me to take them. The next morning, there is no blood in the rags. I ask Sister, "What are the pills you give me?"

She says, "They are birth control pills."

"Sister, I don't want to take them because they mess up my cycle." I fear I might have two periods this month.

The change from childhood to womanhood is unpleasant. My body changes before my eyes. I become a woman – a stranger. Breasts grow outward and now I require an additional undergarment. I don't feel comfortable in my new body. When I run, jump, and twirl, my breasts move. I must learn how to exist in this new body.

Other girls at school get their monthly, too. We all think this blood loss thing is no fun. An unlucky girl gets her period while she sits in class. Her grey skirt is bloody, and everyone sees when she gets up to go to the bathroom. A rumor goes around that another girl plays volleyball when her bloody pad falls out onto the court. Fifty or more spectators see it. She picks it up and runs to the bathroom. I'm lucky my monthly comes when I'm at home. I don't think my pride would allow me to return to school if blood stains soil my skirt.

******

I'm a neat-freak and I always keep my school uniform clean . People remark about how clean my white blouse is at the end of the school day. I don't play childish games anymore. I'm a young woman who attends to personal hygiene and ensures her appearance is of reputable standards. This is only after an unfamiliar man says to me one day, "You stink."

I make sure to change my blood-rags before they smell, so when I get my monthly, I have less time for friends. When I do have time with friends it's no longer for games but long talks. Amy and I share our stories about our monthly and we talk about boys.

"Nika, did you get your period yet this month?" Amy asks. The two of us sit under the tamarind tree in the side yard.

"Yes. Did you get yours yet?"

"No. Mine is supposed to come next week."

"Do you get cramps, Amy?"

"Not really. Not like yours."

"Amy, you're so lucky. My cramps are so bad."

"I wonder why yours are so bad. Maybe it's because your insides are too small."

"What do you mean, too small? You're skinnier than me, Amy."

"Nika, I know. But sometimes people look skinny on the outside, but they are wide on the inside."

"What! Amy, you can talk some fool."

"No. Seriously."

"So, you're wide on the inside, Amy?"

"I could be."

"Holy cow. I can't believe you think I get cramps because I'm too small on the inside."

"That might be a good thing, Nika."

"What? How is that a good thing?"

"I don't know. Maybe boys like it." Amy smiles.

"Well, if you put it that way." I laugh out loud.

Nowadays, I notice boys in a different way. I think I like them. I feel attraction toward one particular boy at school. He is one of the smartest boys in school. He grooms himself well. I never talk to him because I know I'm not good enough for him. I'm a ghetto girl, and he comes from a decent, middle-class family. I admire him and keep my feelings secret. A ghetto girl knows she can never win the heart of a decent man. I don't like rejection, so I never even dare show my feelings. I have my first secret crush.

Chapter Thirty-One

I secretly watch the boy from my chair and then my homeroom teacher calls my name as she reads from a list. She tells all the students who hear their names to take their school bags and report to the office. I walk to the office and I see Matt as he carries his school bag. He waves at me and I wait for him. He tells me, "My teacher told me to go to the office. I don't know why."

I say, "My teacher told me the same thing."

We arrive at the office and our principal speaks to the group of ten that come with their school bags. He says, "You, children need to go home. You have unpaid fees."

Matt and I take the bus home. Mother is at work. We stay home all day long and wait for her to arrive. The minute she steps foot in the doorway I say, "Matt and I got sent home today."

She asks, "Why? What happened?"

Matt says, "Because we have unpaid fees."

Mother gets angry. She says, "What! After all the fees I have already paid, they send you home because I'm late on this one." She shakes her head and turns up her nose.

The next day, Mother comes to school with us. She asks to speak with the principal. Matt and I sit out in the reception area, but we still hear Mother's words.

"Sir, I have fifteen children and I work hard to send the smart ones to private school, so they can have a good education. I plan to pay. Check the account and you will see I never have a balance at the end of June. I plan to pay. Please don't keep my children out of classes. Their marks will fall behind."

We cannot make out the principal's reply, but it must be positive. Mother comes out and tells me and Matt to go to class. They never call us out for late fees again even though Mother makes late payments. The principal knows Mother pays when she can, and he takes pity on her. Mother says she doesn't want pity. Her God makes a way for her regardless of the circumstances.

******

Two months later, I worry because Mother comes to see my teacher. My grades fall behind because I spend too much social time during class. The popular girl (Candy) is so pretty. Her long, soft hair, perfect teeth, and pretty face make me want to be friends with her. I try so hard to get Candy to like me. I carry her books and run her errands while I neglect my studies. I just want her to like me. If she likes me it means something. It means I fit in. She treats me like a caddy, but I don't care. As long as Candy lets me sit with her at lunch and during class, I really don't care about anything else.

Mother sits with my teacher and I stand next to the chair Mother occupies. The teacher says, "I don't know what is going on, but her grades have dropped very low. She spends a lot of time with friends and does not focus on studies."

Mother looks at me and says, "Really."

The teacher says, "We need to come up with a plan to get her grades up, where they should be."

Mother looks at the teacher and says, "Don't worry. I have a plan for her. Her grades will improve. You can count on that. She will not waste my money. I send her to you to learn and that is what she must do."

I'm quiet. I know Mother is mad. I disappoint her.

Mother leaves and I go back to class. I move my desk from the back of the class to the front.

Candy says, "Why are you moving away from my desk?"

I say, "I need to focus on school work."

When I arrive home, I run to Mother and tell her I move to the front of the class. I say, "I will study hard and will do better."

Mother says, "If I ever get another bad report from your teacher, you're going to feel pain. I will whip you. Do you understand, Nika?"

"Yes, Ma'am."

Womanhood does not spare me from Mother's rod.

The next day, I arrive at school and I see Candy. She talks with a group of girls. They look, laugh, and point.

Candy says, "Her mom beats her, and they live in a clapboard house."

This is the start of the torture I endure for six months. Luckily, summer break comes, and I get to spend it with Amy.

Chapter Thirty-Two

I put my lips to his and close my eyes. His lips are soft and moist. They feel like the flesh of a ripe dilly and taste like peppermint. I put my tongue in his mouth and he sucks it. I melt and feel giddy. I hear the soft wind play musical notes of lovers. Even with my eyes shut, I see a beautiful rainbow of colors. I did not know my first kiss would bring me such pleasure. This boyfriend (Theo) of six months has been such a gentleman. Theo is not a ghetto boy, but he is a bad boy. He quits school at age fourteen and moves in with another family because he does not want to obey the rules his parents demand. Chrissy's boyfriend introduces us. Theo and I are both fourteen, but he has more experience with girls than I do with boys. We normally meet under the dilly tree in the empty lot down the road but today we kiss in the side yard of Amy's house.

After a year of dating this bad boy, I know I'm in love – my first "puppy" love. This boy is so handsome. He is not the average black boy. Theo's milk chocolate skin and pointy nose complement his stunning smile. His voice is a couple tones lower than mine. He talks about sex but does not force the conversation on me. I tell him I plan to wait until I graduate high school. He is patient and gentle. We only kiss and that's all. I like it when we kiss but I love when our hands touch and when he hugs me, even more.

One day I go to a party at the house Theo stays at. When I arrive, I ask for him. I hear him call for me from the bathroom. He says, "Nika, come here."

I go in and the shower curtain hides his naked body. I say, "Theo, I'll wait for you outside."

He says, "Stay for a while."

I put the lid down on the toilet and sit. We chit chat and then he says, "I'm done." He pulls the curtain open and reveals himself to me.

I get up and say, "I'll wait for you outside, Theo."

As I leave, I hear him say, "Sorry. I didn't mean to frighten you, Nika."

The next week, I meet Theo under the dilly tree. He rides his loud motorcycle to my ghetto to visit me. We sit under the dilly tree and talk. He says, "I have something important to tell you."

I say, "What is it?"

"I have another girlfriend and she has sex with me."

Theo's words are hard to hear.

I say, "What?"

I cry.

"Why would you do this to me, Theo?" I take off the Gucci watch he gives me as a gift. I give him the watch.

"I'm sorry but I couldn't keep this from you. You're such a nice girl, Nika."

"Great. Being a nice girl causes you to cheat. You will soon tire of that girl. You're both too young for sex. What happens when you get tired of her, Theo?"

"Nika, a man never tires of sex."

I go home and cry myself to sleep but I hide my sadness from everyone, especially Mother. Mother does not know I go to the dilly tree to meet a boy. Chrissy, Edith, and Matt know but they keep my secret and share it with no one. I'm hurt. But I don't understand the pain I feel. It's a new kind of pain. Period cramps, headaches, and stomachaches are not like the pain I experience. Medicine heals these kinds of pain, but nothing eases the pain of heartbreak.

Time passes, and I meet another boy. I date him for only three months. He demands I return his gold chain when I tell him I would never have sex with him. I give it back without hesitation. I don't love him. I still think about my first kiss and my first love. I want to be with Theo.

I worry because I hear nasty rumors. I hear Theo turns to evil ways. Rumor goes around that he kills a man and buries his body. I don't know why he becomes evil, but his evil ways lead to his death. They find his dead body as it floats in the sea.

Chapter Thirty-Three

We go to a beach picnic, my schoolmates and I, to celebrate the end of another school year. It's a glorious day for the beach. Thirty of us sit under a coconut tree and talk about the events of the school year. Only a few of us swim. A boy, named Tate talks to me. He likes me. I can tell. I only think of him as a friend. Some years ago, I notice Tate and his big, wide smile but this is before I'm a young woman. He never considers me for a girlfriend because he sees me as a child. He is three years my senior. But now Tate looks at me differently. Unfortunately, I'm not ready for love. I still nurse the wounds of my first love.

"Nika, you sure are pretty. Do you know how pretty you are?" Tate smiles at me.

I blush and smile back. "Thanks, Tate. But you don't have to lie to me."

"Lie to you? It's the truth. Don't tell me no one has ever told you?" Tate's smile grows, and his eyes speak to me.

"Told me what?"

"Your skin is the color of a brown paper bag and your rounded button nose stands out amidst your thin upper lip. Dark brown hair reaches the nape of your neck and is short by North American standards. But to the people you know as your own, you have 'good-length' hair with natural copper highlights. You wear a chemically straightened style with loose curls – products of the hot-curling rod. You, Nika, are gorgeous."

"My goodness, Tate. That was the cheesiest pick-up line I've ever heard." I walk away.

"Hey, Nika. It wasn't a pick-up line. It was the truth." Tate smiles and winks.

Tate continues to woo me, but I think it's a friendship. We spend a lot of time together and we talk about everything: food, family, friends, the future, and dreams. We jog together around a park on a school field trip.

When we return, the gym teacher says to me, "So, did you sleep with him yet?"

I don't reply. I'm really angry.

The gym teacher is a wicked watcher. He likes young girls and says inappropriate things to us. Tate sees me and knows something is wrong. He comes to me and says, "What happened? What did he say to you, Nika?"

I tell him the gym teacher's words and he becomes even angrier than me.

The next day at school, I come out of my classroom to go to the lunch line. Some of Tate's friends come to me. They say, "There's trouble. Come quick."

I follow them. As I get closer to the front of the school, I see Tate. He throws big, heavy rocks at the gym teacher. I turn around and run back to my classroom. I'm afraid. Everyone runs to the front of the school to watch the rock-fight. I'm alone in the classroom. I wait until students return. They come back, and they talk about what unfolds. Tate throws rocks at the gym teacher and some hit him. There is bloodshed. The principal intervenes, and he asks, "What is this matter about?"

The gym teacher speaks with a bloody mouth and says, "It's about a girl."

Tate says, "No, Sir. This is between me and the gym teacher. The girl has nothing to do with this."

Tate protects me and refuses to let the gym teacher drag me into trouble.

Tate's parents come to see the principal. They are wealthy people and know how to handle these kinds of things. I'm happy when Tate comes back to school after a week of suspension.

The principal now knows there is something not right about the gym teacher, but he gives him the benefit of the doubt. The gym teacher remains on staff but in a matter of months, his nasty ways show themselves again. He calls Candy into his office and talks to her about her gym marks. She thinks this is the reason for the meeting. He then asks her, "Are you a virgin? Would you like to know what it's like to be with a man?"

Candy leaves his office and is upset. She goes to the school reception area and calls her mother. We don't know what happens but in a week's time, we see a picture of the gym teacher in the newspaper. He announces his resignation.

The news does not surprise us. We know the gym teacher is a "fresh" man. He fondles the girls' breasts when he teaches how to do crunches. He looks under our shorts while we do crunches. This nasty teacher tells us if we don't do the crunches, he gives us an "F."

I see the gym teacher touch Candy's thighs when he explains about leg muscles. He touches another girl's ass when he teaches how to bump a volleyball. His bad breath does not discourage him, and he comes close when he talks to his female students.

The gym teacher never touches me. I'm not sure why. Perhaps he knows my ghetto ways are more dangerous than his wicked touches. He knows I speak my mind and I have no trouble with words. I'm glad Candy tells her mother. She saves so many others from the hands of a snake who slithers on his belly in search of prey.

Chapter Thirty-Four

I hear the crow of the rooster and feel the warmth of the sunray that touches my arm as I roll over in my top bunk bed. Soft, gospel music plays on the radio that Chrissy turns on to bring in a typical Sunday morning. Mother is at work because she takes an early morning shift from 5 am to 3 pm. I get up and walk down the narrow hallway to the tiny bathroom. There is no line-up because my siblings all sleep-in on Sunday morning. Most are tired after late-night partying on Saturday or some are tired from late-night shifts at work.

Father leaves to visit his brother just up the street. After I use the bathroom, wash my face, and brush my teeth, I go to the kitchen to make a bowl of corn cereal. We eat corn cereal on Sunday morning because it's cheap and it's the only cereal Mother buys. Also, Sunday is not a day for a big breakfast because we save our bellies for Sunday dinner.

I sit at the kitchen table and eat while siblings get up and do the same Sunday morning routine – head to the bathroom and pour a bowl of corn cereal. After thirty minutes or so, there are nine of us awake. We sit around the house – some at the kitchen table, some in the living room, and some on their bunk beds.

Matt, who is now a teenager, has a friend (Leroy) over and they sit in the living room to chit chat about their night at a party. Leroy spends the night at our house almost every weekend because he and Matt are very close.

I join in with their conversation in the living room. Matt, Leroy, and I sit and talk about nothing important, but the conversation is happy. We laugh quietly so we do not wake any siblings who continue to sleep. Marcus comes into the living room and yells at Leroy, "What are you doing here?"

Leroy says nothing. Matt and I look at each other and wonder why he asks such a stupid question. He knows Leroy visits frequently. Marcus walks out of the living room and then returns immediately. He pushes Leroy so forcefully that his head goes through the drywall.

Leroy chases Marcus outside and they begin a bare-backed fistfight.

I yell, "Stop it!"

The fight escalates because Matt joins in to help Leroy. By now the entire household is awake. Vincent (my first brother) joins in to try to separate the fighters. Now the fight is in the front yard on the hard-concrete walkway and then it moves to the sandy driveway. Edith runs to get Father. He arrives and helps to subdue Marcus who continues to give hard punches to any who tries to restrain him.

"I'm calling the fucking police. I'm tired of this shit." I don't care if Father hears me curse.

I call the police and they arrive but after the blood spills. Matt bleeds from his mouth and his eye is swollen and bruised. Leroy bleeds from his mouth and has bloody scratches along his back. Marcus bleeds from his mouth and spits red saliva as he curses, "Leave me the fuck alone. I'm going to kill all you fuckers."

The police arrive in their car with lights that flash but no siren. They know my evil brother by name. My father and Vincent let go of Marcus who they pin on his belly in the dirt in our front yard. The two young police officers pull Marcus up off the ground. They pull his hands behind him. He fights back. They handcuff him and say, "Listen, we don't want trouble. We just want you to calm down."

Marcus yells, "I'm not going back to jail."

The police tell him, "If you don't calm down, we'll have to take you in."

Marcus says, "I didn't do anything."

The police talk to him and I go inside the house to get ready for church.

By now the nosey old woman and a crowd of neighbors gather to see what happens. They only know that a fight broke out and it involves males from our household. They do not know what really happens. I do not know either. Why Marcus attacks Leroy is a mystery. It seems like Marcus is jealous of the friendship Leroy has with Matt. But this makes no sense because heartless people do not experience emotion. Perhaps Marcus isn't heartless but pretends to be.

The police leave after they calm Marcus. He stands outside the front yard of the house and is quiet. Nosey neighbors return home. I walk past Marcus and head off to the small, white church. I tell him, "You need Jesus."

I see Leroy in the neighbor's yard and he yells at Marcus, "This isn't over."

These words frighten me. I do not want Leroy to involve himself in fights with Marcus. I know a heartless ghetto soul lives within this brother and to fight him is a dangerous thing. Leroy is wholesome like Matt. He does not want trouble but wants to be a boy and that's all. I hope he gets a good night's sleep and forgets about this Sunday morning.

I walk to church and I feel angry. This walk brings me wicked thoughts. I want to kill Marcus. These thoughts follow me to church but by the end of the service, they leave me. I'm thankful that evil thoughts don't stay. They come and then they go. Yet, the image of black men fighting in the dirt is one that never leaves me. I can still see these images when I have flashbacks that take me to these violent moments. I believe I choose to keep these violent recollections because they strengthen my desire for success.

Violent memories remind me of the wretched childhood mother-ghetto provides her children. Mother-ghetto is like mother-nature when she unleashes a tornado that kills thousands of women and children. But mother-ghetto is more powerful because the souls of the children she kills do not pass peacefully to the other side. Our souls must live even though we die.

Chapter Thirty-Five

Tonight, I have such a wonderful dream. In my dream, I see Makalo's face up against the window screen and I wake in Sister's room. Makalo says, "Nika, I come to shoot marbles with you."

"I'm comin', Makalo." I jump off the bed and run to meet him in the side yard.

"Nika, how come you so excited this mornin'? Most mornings you don't get so excited. Sometimes I have to shake the sleep off you."

I hug Makalo and squeeze him real hard, "I'm excited because you come to play."

Makalo puts his arms around me but does not squeeze.

"Squeeze me, Makalo. How come you never squeeze me when we hug?"

"I don't know. Because…"

"Because why, Makalo?" I let go of him.

"Because Tito and Jeremy say boys and girls shouldn't hug so close if they're family. We're cousins, Nika."

"I know. Whatever, Makalo. It doesn't matter because Tito and Jeremy are so stupid."

"Why you say that, Nika?"

"Because they always tellin' you stuff and they don't know nothin'."

"But they're my friends, Nika."

"And I'm your cousin."

"I know, Nika. You want to shoot some marbles? I'll give you a rollie pollie because I have two now. Yesterday, I win one from Jeremy."

"Yeah. Let's shoot some marbles."

Makalo and I play marbles in the dirt under the tamarind tree for about ten minutes and Amy arrives.

"Hey, Nika. Hey, Makalo."

"Hi, Amy," I say.

"Hi, Amy," Makalo says and his gigantic smile follows.

"Can I play, too?" Amy asks.

"Yeah. You have any marbles?" Makalo asks.

"No."

"Here, Amy. Take these." I pass Amy five small marbles.

The three of us play and Makalo wins. His right pocket bulges with his winnings.

"Hey, let's play hide-and-seek," I say. "Amy and I will hide and Makalo you count."

"But I don't want to count."

"Why, Makalo," Amy asks.

"No reason." I can tell Makalo is embarrassed because he doesn't want Amy to know that he can't count past eleven.

"I'll count, Makalo. You and Amy go hide."

I jump in quickly to save Makalo from the embarrassment, "One, two three, four, five, six, seven, eight, nine, ten, eleven, twelve, thirteen, fourteen, fifteen, sixteen, seventeen, eighteen, nineteen, twenty. Ready or not here I come."

I find Makalo hiding behind the tamarind tree and then the two of us search for Amy. Before we find her, I wake to the smell of home-made bread as it bakes. It's a Saturday morning. We are fortunate the woman who lives to the right of us bakes bread and sells it to customers. The wonderful homey aroma makes us happy. One loaf is three dollars. But this morning the drooling smell of home-made bread does not make me happy. I'm sad because my dream of Makalo and Amy ends. I love it when I have these sweet dreams. Happiness comes when I remember that today Amy, Makalo, and I plan to spend the day together at the beach to celebrate Makalo's birthday. The smell of home-made bread becomes pungent. I take a deep, long breath to take it in.

I wish Mother would bake bread, but I know she is too busy over the hot, metal, gas stove at work. Mother wears a white apron and uses it to dry her hands after she cleans her work station. Sometimes she has to load the dishes on the automated dish tray, so the dishes are clean. They roll out of the machine scalding hot. Mother uses her hands to clean the giant, iron pots that have hard layers of pot cake stuck to the bottom. She is not only a cook but a dishwasher, too. She toils and saves her money for the trip to Miami. Mother goes on the trip to shop. She tells us it's so much cheaper to buy meat, toiletries, clothes, kitchen utensils, and bathroom items in the Flea Market in Florida. Mother returns from her trip and she brings home chicken, steak, and pork chops that fill the freezer.

Regina, Chrissy, Edith, Matt, Belinda, Stacey and I gather in the living room to watch TV and do not hear when the thief comes in. He takes all the meat Mother buys and leaves a trail of chicken legs that leads to a tall fence at the left side of our backyard.

We hear Mother scream, "Lord, they steal all my meat."

We go to see. Mother stares inside the empty freezer and holds both her arms up in the air. I run out the kitchen door to see if I can get a glimpse of the thief. The only thing I see is the trail of chicken legs the hungry, mingy, pot cake dogs now eat.

Mother says, "That's okay. The Lord knows all things. Let them take the meat. They must need it more than us."

Mother does not even call the police.

She says, "Call the police? What for? The police can't do a thing to help me now. The thief is gone."

Thieves are plentiful in the ghetto. We have our very own living under our roof. Our thief is called Marcus. A thief is like a thorn in a rose garden – something expected but forgotten. We suck on our fingers as they bleed after the thorn pierces through our skin. Mother forgets the thorn of the ghetto and she bleeds as a result – not real blood but figurative blood that causes ghetto women pain.

The countless hours of toil over a hot stove in weather that makes the skin sweat are for nothing now. The meat Mother buys will not nourish her belly or the bellies of her hungry children. A thief enjoys the meat and his belly does not complain that the food is that of others. The thief will chew. Regurgitate. Chew some more. Swallow the stolen meat just like we would because he is just like us – a hungry ghetto child. Then he will take a nap.

Mother thinks the thief is the teenage son of the poorest woman in our ghetto. She is so poor she has no furniture in her one-room house that leans to one side. Termites eat away the wood that is the siding of her house. They sleep on the floor and have no indoor plumbing. The woman and her five children have an outhouse that we see them enter and leave when nature calls for its fecal deposit.

Mother is happy the thief is not her own son. We know Marcus does not steal the meat because he sleeps on the living room floor with chains that bind him to the wheel barrel full of heavy rocks. Father chains him to keep him out of trouble. Marcus is a criminal who spends time in jail for stealing running shoes. Mother lets the police take him because she thinks jail time might cure his desire for evil. He steals everything from us. Gifts from boyfriends are his favorite target. He steals watches, gold chains, and gold rings.

The day arrives when I'm a victim of the evil ways of this brother. One minute I wash dishes and the next minute Marcus asks, "Have you seen my red shirt?"

I say, "No."

After I clean the last pot, I realize my watch is gone. I run to the street corner and ask everyone if Marcus passes by. They all say, "No."

I know I will never see my watch again.

Two days later, Marcus returns home and I ask about the watch. He says, "I don't know what you're talking about."

Perhaps he really doesn't know. The drugs mess up his brain cells. Perhaps he knows and smiles in secret because he takes another item and trades it for his white powdery pleasures.

Chapter Thirty-Six

Good smells of the ghetto bring many pleasures to all. The wonderful smell of fresh bread as it bakes gives my palette pleasure that moistens the inside of my mouth. The strong smell of marijuana gives the ghetto boys pleasures that make the whites of their eyes turn pink. They talk slowly as if they hear music in their heads. I hate the smell of ganja but love the smell of cocoa butter because it reminds me of Sister. She moves with her husband and father-in-law into an apartment in the South. I'm happy because she lives close to my school. She does not work, and she carries her first child.

I walk with two of my friends, Lily and Tina, to Sister's apartment. I wish Amy could come but she goes to a school in the ghetto. Lily and Tina go to my school in the South. Sister feeds us when we arrive – sweet bread and red Kool-Aid. Then we watch the video of the Pointer Sisters (a famous group of negro sisters who sing and make music videos in America). Lily, Tina, and I learn their song called *I'm so excited*. We go to Sister's apartment to practice. Sister agrees to help us prepare for a lip-synching contest. They tell us the winnings might be five hundred dollars, so we practice really hard. I take the role of the lead sister in the group and pretend to sing the words, "*I'm so excited.*"

Sister says, "Nika, make your mouth really wide when you form the words. It's better. People will not know that you lip-sync."

My reply points out the obvious, "But it's a lip-synching contest."

We all have a belly laugh. I laugh so hard tears form and roll down the side of my face.

Lily laughs so hard she collapses.

"Nika, your sister's a trip," Tina chuckles.

We practice for weeks and Sister loves when we come to see her. I think she is lonely. Sister is at home alone all day. She does not know what it's like to be alone. At our home in the ghetto, she never has a moment alone. I'm always at her side. But now she is lonely in this apartment she shares with her husband, father-in-law, and two brothers-in-law.

Sister has sweet bread and Kool-Aid ready for Lily, Tina, and me every time we come. I look forward to the sweet bread. Mother cannot afford to buy it. It tastes so good in my mouth. When I chew, the bread softens. I half swallow. Regurgitate. Take a sip of Kool-Aid and swallow again. Sister is such a wonderful woman. She welcomes me and my two friends and expects nothing in return.

Today, I go to Sister's apartment alone because both Lily and Tina are sick with the flu. Sister is happy to see me.

"Come in, Nika. Where are your friends today?"

"They're both sick with the flu."

"Well, lucky for you, you didn't catch the flu, too."

"I hope you don't catch their flu, Sister."

"No. I'm fine, Nika. Come in and have some sweet bread."

Sister closes and locks the heavy door behind me. I put my backpack on the couch and sit at the small kitchen table. Sister passes me a slice of bread and a glass of red Kool-Aid.

"So, how was school today, Nika?"

"Good." I can't say much because my mouth is full of bread.

"Nika, any exciting news to share?"

"Well, actually there is, Sister. I talked to Monique today. You remember Monique?"

"Yes, Nika. She is the girl whose uncle is organizing the contest, right?"

"Yeah, yeah. She said her uncle plans to raise the prize money to six hundred dollars."

"Nika, are you sure about this? I'm beginning to think this is a scam. Why is her uncle doing this?"

"No, Sister. It's no scam. Her uncle plans to make money from ticket sales."

"I see. I knew there was a catch. Anyway, it doesn't matter. You're doing this for fun, right, Nika?"

"Fun and the money, money, money." I smile really big. Sister chuckles.

"Don't forget you will have to share the money with Lily and Tina."

"Yeah. I know."

Two months pass quickly, and the day of the contest arrives. Lily, Tina, and I are nervous because there is a man who wears full make-up. He looks just like Boy George, except he's black. We think he must be a professional. We watch him perform and are so impressed. The man does not look like he lip-syncs. We are sure he really sings.

"Wow. He's really good." Tina pipes up.

"I know," is all I can say.

"Nika, do you think we still have a chance to win?" Lily is worried.

"Hell, yeah!" I look at Lily and smile.

The announcer calls us to come up on stage. I'm nervous but excited, too. I love the stage. It transforms me into someone else. I have no past when I step out on the stage. I feel like a new creature. The music starts, and we begin our performance. I'm out front. Lily and Tina are my backup singers. We spin around, and I kick up my feet. I wear Sister's turquoise shoes.

One of my three-inched, high-heeled shoes flies off into the crowd. The crowd cheers louder. They think it's a part of our act. Sister does not mind that I kick off her shoe. She smiles and cheers in the audience, too. I see her, and I know she counts on me to perform well. I kick off the other shoe and the crowd goes wild. We lip-sync every syllable and I dance like a superstar. We do a great job.

After the last performer finishes, the announcer takes the microphone. He calls the third-place winner, then the second-place winner. The man who dresses like Boy George is second.

"The winners are the three girls who lip-sync the song of the Pointer Sisters, *I'm so excited.*"

We all jump up and scream. The crowd of two hundred goes wild. Sister gives me a hug and I run up onstage with Lily and Tina.

"The winner receives fifty dollars." The announcer waves a small, white envelope in the air.

I look into the crowd and I see Sister's face. She lip-syncs, "Only fifty dollars."

I take the envelope with the cash and go to Sister and say, "You should have this."

She says, "No. We'll split it into four equal parts. Don't feel bad that it's only a fifty-dollar prize. You did great, Nika. I'm so proud of you."

Sister and I smile and dance to the music that plays while people leave the arena.

We win this night and it feels great. The money isn't much but it's a fun experience. Lily, Tina, and I always remember the days we walk to Sister's apartment. We have much to laugh and talk about. But now I miss the visits with Sister. I only see her when she comes to see us in the ghetto and this is only on weekends.

Now that I can't talk to Sister, I talk to Edith a lot more. We don't fight anymore. The last fight we have is when I wear her red blouse. She pushes me into the wall, but I push her right back. Edith and I are mature now and prefer to talk about boys.

"Nika, do you know Dion?" Edith begins the conversation.

"You mean Dion whose dad works at the corner store?"

"Yes."

"What about him?" I ask.

"Do you think he's good looking?"

"Not really."

"Well, I think he is."

"Edith, you know we don't have the same taste in boys. I like boys who are milk chocolate, not charcoal. Dion's a bit too dark for my taste. And his buck teeth don't help either."

"Skin color doesn't matter, Nika. You sound just like Pa."

"Edith, shush. Suppose he hears you."

"He won't hear me. But it's true. Pa is so hypocritical."

"What do you mean?"

"Look at how dark Mother is. For someone who always complainin' 'bout black, black people. He sure marry one."

"Edith, shush."

"Don't worry, Nika. He can't hear me."

"Edith, stop or you'll get in trouble."

"I ain't scared of trouble. You should know that by now."

"Well, I don't want to get in trouble, so shush."

"Fine, I'll shush. So, do you think Edward is good looking?"

"Edward? The guy who works on the glass bottom boat with crazy George?"

"Yeah."

"Now that one is fine! Do you know if he has a girlfriend?"

"Of course. He is very much taken."

"Too bad."

"Yeah, too bad."

"I don't understand why you asking about these guys. What about Dave? Aren't you two goin' out?"

"Yeah. We're together."

"Does Mother know yet?" Edith gives me the look that swears me to secrecy.

Eventually, Mother finds out about Dave because he invites Edith to his prom. Dave comes to ask Mother's permission. Mother lets Edith go because Dave is decent and comes from a wealthy family. I tell Edith she needs to thank me and my tonsils for our role in her destiny. The first time Edith meets Dave is at the hospital. Edith goes with me to the hospital for swollen tonsils and Dave is at the hospital for a bad flu.

Father does not want Edith to go to the prom with Dave, but Mother talks him down because she wears the pants in the family. Edith and I hear him grumble from his bedroom, "These girl children will only bring babies into this house if you let them go out with boys." Father doesn't talk much and when he speaks, he is only pessimistic. In my mind, he's incapable of affection. The solace of a father's embrace is a fairy tale to me. My sisters and I do not know the paradise of a protected girl child who sleeps like an angel as the love of her father surrounds her. The love of a father is a deep desire because family is everything. If a father fails to love his ghetto children, people don't see because ghetto children receive love from mothers, sisters, brothers, teachers, preachers, friends, and extended family. But Father does not inflict pain on us because of his actions – he hurts us with his lack of action.

Chapter Thirty-Seven

I have a bad flu and have to stay home from school. This bug is awful. It makes my muscles ache and I cannot keep anything down. Mother is good with bush medicines. She tells me which bush to drink when I have ailments. This time, Mother gives me a piece of aloe to fight this flu. The slimy, bitter piece of aloe tastes awful, but it brings me good health in a matter of days.

The next time the flu bug grabs hold of my bones, I ache everywhere. Mother brings me a plate of corned beef and white rice. I eat it, but it comes back up as soon as I finish. I never eat corned beef after this day. Every time Mother makes it, I say, "I can't eat that because it makes me feel sick." I eat white rice and butter instead.

When my body returns to full health, Mother tells me to make Sunday dinner because she has to work. She permits me to stay home from church, so I can cook. Regina, Edith, and Chrissy cook on Sundays, too. We take turns, but it seems like I'm the only one who does dishes. I can't stand a dirty kitchen, so I clean the dishes even though it's not my week. Chrissy and Edith pretend they don't notice they miss their turn to do dishes. I remind Edith and she says, "Why should I clean them? When I'm done you come behind me and clean them again."

I say, "It's because you don't clean them properly."

I'm a bit of a "clean freak" and Saturday is my personal chores-day. I wake up. Wash my face. Brush my teeth. Then I pick up the broom. I can't stand a filthy house. I clean for four hours. Mother comes home from work and she says, "Thank you, Lord, for a child who cleans."

Mother never worries about chores. She only has to cook specialty dishes for us. Regina, Chrissy, Edith, and I can make peas and rice but only Mother knows how to make the soups and stews we love.

I come home with the news and Mother is in the kitchen making chicken souse. "They plan a beauty pageant in the neighborhood," I speak like it's a royal announcement. "The politician wants to do something for his constituents, so he gives money to organize a beauty pageant."

Mother says, "Do you want to go in it?"

"Yes." I don't even hesitate.

"What if they cheat you a second time, Nika?"

"Mother, fame isn't important. I want to enter because I like being on stage. I don't care if they cheat. Besides, prizes are awarded to the winner and runners-up."

Every day after school, I go to the big yellow school to practice with the other contestants. We are all young, ghetto women between the ages of fourteen and eighteen. The beauty pageant gives us something to look forward to. I size up the competition and I feel pretty confident. The elegant woman who comes to teach us poise says I'm really good. She says I walk like a queen.

Mother pays a seamstress to make me an evening gown for the pageant. It's royal blue with streaks of silver and it fits me well. This time they do not cheat. I win the contest and they crown me queen of the ghetto.

As ghetto queen, I focus on community events. I organize talent shows and become active in the Young Progressive Group. They even pay me money to choreograph dances for community events.

I focus on my community work and I don't have time for boys. Besides, I don't like when ghetto boys look at me. Their eyes reveal they want to devour my flesh if only they have an opportunity. They do not keep their desires secret. I hear so many words that give me pause.

"Hey, I want to fuck you."

"Hey, you have such a nice ass."

"Hey, you look delicious."

"Hey, I wish you could sit on my dick."

"Hey, I want some of that."

"Hey, pretty girl. Come here let me show you what a real man feels like."

"Hey, my cock is so hard right now. You have no idea."

"Hey, I want to lick you all over. I'm a pussy-eater and I'm not ashamed to say."

"Hey, come here let me suck on those nice breasts you have."

I cannot escape the verbal torture and I'm careful never to walk the streets at night. But some ghetto men don't care if it's daylight. A car pulls up as I walk home, and a young man says, "You want a ride?" He is the passenger in the small four-door car. The driver has a wicked smile.

I say, "No," and begin to walk faster.

The passenger says to the driver, "That's the girl I told you about. That's her."

The driver says, "Sexy, come go for a ride with us."

I say, "No."

I walk even faster. He looks at me like I'm his next meal. He licks his lips and then smiles at me.

The guy in the passenger's seat says, "You can't escape me forever, Nika. One day, I'll get you. You better watch your back."

I know he means what he says. He is a stalker and a wicked watcher who has the potential to become heartless. I run home. I'm afraid but I don't cry. I have to be strong. A ghetto woman wears skin as thick as the shell of a tortoise. I cannot let him intimidate me. He speaks words of terror, but I refuse to be a victim. I do not think of him for more than one night. I'm fortunate I do not encounter him in a dark alley, but he leads the mob that attacks my new boyfriend.

Chapter Thirty-Eight

I stand at a bus stop and my boyfriend, Chris, sits as a passenger in his brother's car that drives past. He gets out and comes to talk to me. Chris is from another ghetto. The jealous stalker yells, "Let's get him. He's talking to Nika. She's the one I want. That fucker can't have her."

The jealous stalker and a mob of ghetto negroes chase Chris who manages to outrun them. Minutes later, Chris returns and fires his handgun at the jealous stalker. I remain out in the street and I tell Amy what happens.

"Amy, I cannot believe what just happened."

"What?"

"I was at the bus stop and I saw Chris. He was with his older brother. They were driving by. Of course, Chris saw me, and they pulled over. Chris came to talk to me and then I see this guy across the road. It's the guy I told you about who was in the car the other day who threatened me."

"What happened?" Amy's face reveals she knows my news is very big and very serious.

"The guy calls like six or seven of his friends over and I hear him say, 'Let's get him. He's talking to Nika. She's the one I want. That fucker can't have her.'" I continue, "The next thing I know there's like twenty guys chasing Chris. They must be a gang or somethin'."

"Are you serious, Nika?"

"Yes! They chased Chris all the way down the road and guess what? Chris comes back with a gun."

"A gun. What the hell, Nika."

"I know, right. Shit. I can't believe this. That's not even the worst part. Chris fires the gun at this guy – the guy from the car. I don't even know who this guy is. He's a frickin' stalker. I think he's been following me. Amy, I'm frickin' scared."

"Nika, girl you better go home."

"I'm going home. I can't believe this is happening."

"Shit. Nika, run!"

"Holy shit." I turn around and see the mob and the jealous stalker leads them. They chase after me. I run.

Innocence has no voice amongst a mob. A mob of young, uncultured, ghetto negroes is dangerous. Curse words combined with black angry faces unite in a mob for a wicked cause. Evil consumes heart, mind, soul, and body. The mob chases me with every intention to harm. The rage of the ghetto burns deeply within and sweat drips from their faces. The whites of their eyes fill up with red veins as they take heavy breaths. Both male and female make up this irate group in pursuit of revenge. They gnash their white teeth and chase after their prey. Like the antelope, my life depends only on the speed of my feet.

Ghetto girls understand how things happen in a flash. One minute, I'm at a bus stop in a casual conversation with my boyfriend and the next minute, my boyfriend runs for his life as a mob of gangsters attack him. A minute later, my boyfriend returns. Fires his gun and flees. Then the mob decides to reciprocate by attacking the innocent girlfriend. The fact that I'm a good student makes no difference. The fact that I'm innocent makes no difference. The fact that I'm one of them makes no difference. The mob is angry.

I run so fast I lose consciousness and adrenaline consumes me. My feet take me home and the mob waits in the alley. Father warns them and says, "Stay off my property." They dare not enter the yard of a true ghetto man. But they arm themselves with broken, beer bottles and rocks. They pace back and forth. They stake out my house for two sluggish hours until the ghetto rage calms. The feral negroes leave. I pack some clothes in a garbage bag. Matilda drives me to her house in another neighborhood. For seven weeks, I fear I might encounter the mob's rage. Finally, two months after escaping the mob, I have a good night sleep. But my good night sleep lasts only one night. I return home to my ghetto the next day and my sleep returns to its restless condition because the news of Amy's death brings me a tsunami of turmoil that compounds the wretchedness of my existence.

******

"Amy's dead," Mother's words sting.

"What!" I think she must be mistaken.

"Tabatha stabbed her over some boy just yesterday." Mother's words hurt more than her switches.

"What!" The only word that comes from my lips seeks a retraction.

"The funeral is next week," Mother delivers the final blow.

"What!" I'm numb inside and out.

The news of Amy's death makes me realize how savage a ghetto life really is. My feelings muddle together. I cannot distinguish fear from anger. Sadness from despair. How could Amy be gone? How is it that my best friend is dead at fifteen? Tell me how I'm supposed to understand that Amy is gone forever. Fuck you, Yellow Brick Road!

******

A ghetto story full of gloomy, miserable, heartbreaking scenes is all I offer because I'm broken in so many ways. Being whole is something I can never claim. There are so many pieces of me that are still missing. I search for the piece of me that believes in innate goodness. The part of me that welcomes pity or empathy is long lost, too. Like the average ghetto teen, I question my worth each moment I hear of someone's passing. Amazing graces keep me here yet another day.

Amy's gone but I see her everywhere. Leaning on the graffiti-covered walls. Standing in the garbage-filled front yards. Sitting on rusty appliances on sidewalks. Gazing at the rotting clapboard houses. And sitting in the abandoned cars in the bushes. Amy and I are daughters of the ghetto. But I'm the lucky one. I continue to withstand the torrents that lead to the ghetto rite of passage.

Today, I take the bus to my school in the South. I find a book on the bus. It is a diary. I say to the bus driver, "Someone left a book here."

The driver says, "Take it. That book was there for three weeks. It belongs to a white visitor. She is long gone back home to the States or Canada or some place. Take it. Read it. I can tell you like to read."

The driver is right. I like to read. I stare at the book. On the cover, it says, *Meredith's Diary*. I wonder who she is. I wonder if she is from the ghetto, too. What things does she endure in her life? I take the diary. Put it in my bag.

When I get home from school, I sit under the tamarind tree. I don't stop reading until I come to the end. Meredith's diary teaches me some new lessons.

Meredith's Diary

April 10th – My Awakening

What the heck is life about? It comes with so many contrasting experiences. Love, hate, happiness, sadness, pleasure, pain, lust, constraint, shame, pride, and even good fortune can be thrust at us in our waking moments. Why the hell does it have to be such a tug and pull journey? Do I sound angry? Shouldn't

I be angry? Why the hell aren't you angry? Is breath really a gift or is it a curse? Damned the breath that gives life to the pain of living! Why does life have to have such white and black moments? Why does joy and sadness have to exist in the same space and time?

How can you appreciate joy if you don't know sadness? You want to experience joy and never even be aware that sadness exists?

Why do you sound so philosophical? Stop trying to be a pseudo-scholar.

Really? You should stop using words that are hollow in their attempt to explain what you really want to say. Perfection is a lie. Just go ahead and frickin' say it. Stop trying to cover it up with this bullshit. Pseudo-scholar. Who the hell understands that shit, anyway?

I do. I understand the need to speak for the refined. The educated needs dialogue suitable for them. Dialogue, they can muse over.

You certainly seem impressed by your superior vocabulary.

Why are we talking about this? We were talking about life and how it is such a bowl of shit.

Shit can be good. It can be good if you haven't been able to do it for weeks. You see. It's all about context. It's all about the circumstances. For example, under what conditions have you been led to have such a terrible conversation with yourself? Do you not know that people would see this as an act of craziness? You could be locked away for having such a conversation.

Why are you answering back? Shush. You better not respond. Ponder on what it will mean and what significance? Are you losing your mind? Shush, I say. Don't answer this plight of self-damnation. I want to remain sane. Keep quiet!

If you want my silence, at what price will you bid?

Stop it! I cannot withhold judgment of my own thoughts. I must speak to them. I am not crazy because I can have a conversation with myself. Many famous and infamous have had moments as such. Let me be. Let me devour this moment of real reflection. I just came home from the movies and the movie struck a chord with me.

It matters to none, this chord of which you speak. Listen. You cannot negotiate with yourself. You are losing your grip if you think this is the kind of behavior that would be considered normal by others. Have you ever heard a person say, "I need a moment to talk to myself?" There is great shame in this. Stop. I want no part in this self-destruction.

Who the hell do you think you are? You can't claim me. You cannot predict my demise. You are but a faint voice that somehow manages to sustain. Why do I even bother? Why do I even give you the opportunity of attention? No more from you. I mean it.

Tell me about this movie you saw that struck the chord which led to this awakening.

It was a movie about how life passes us by without us knowing. A woman was dying. She had an affair. Her kids hated her. Her husband was always too busy, and the marriage was over. Yet, he loved her and spoke of how she was his pain and his joy. How frickin' unbelievable is that? How can pain be joy? Why can't joy be joy? Why can't pain be pain? Don't you dare speak! Don't say a word. I hate it when you try to analyze things.

If you hadn't seen that movie, would you feel this way?

Yes. I was feeling this way before the movie. It just gave me the words to speak my thoughts.

Your thoughts? What about my thoughts?

Shut up, I said. You are just a faint voice that is beginning to nag. We need to end this conversation now.

When I shut up, you will cease to be human. Your conscience makes you who you are. I am faint, but I am here. And thank heavens. Without me, you would be like the waves of a rolling sea crashing down trying to make a path in the sand but failing to see that you cannot clear a path because all things change. Nothing stays the same. You are changing, too. I am changing alongside you. I am becoming more self-aware.

Stop it. Just shut the hell up. You are becoming self-aware? You are no self. How the hell can you be self-aware when you are nothing?

I am you.

How dare you? You are just a distraction – a waning thread that will cease to connect anything. Soon, I will put you away for good. I will never utter another word nor answer to your irritating beckoning. Go away and never return. I don't want you. I don't need you. You are a nuisance and such an incorrigible son of a bitch.

But I am you.

You are not me! You are damned to the silence that is coming.

May 15th – My Struggle

Today, I spoke with my daughter and we had a fabulous time.

What did you speak of?

There you go again. Talking like some Shakespearean wanna-be. Why can't you just be normal? Why do you always have to turn these conversations into such complex discourse?

Complex discourse? What the hell? You're the one who is using words you don't understand. I would know. If I don't understand them, you don't understand them. Shakespearean wanna-be. Remember, I am you.

See what I mean? There you go again with the "I am you, bullshit." Please. Let's just stop talking.

So. What did you and your daughter talk about?

She is feeling a bit worried that the baby might come when Timothy is away. He has to go to Paris for some kind of training and he will be gone for three months. He might be in Paris when the baby comes. So. Of course. She is worried. I suppose it is a natural feeling. Being worried is a normal human reaction.

You are now an expert on what's normal?

What's that supposed to mean?

It means what you think it means. You aren't normal. Listen to yourself. Listen to me. Does this seem normal that you are talking to yourself?

It is normal to talk to yourself. It isn't normal to talk back. So. Shut the hell up, then!

Why did you have a fabulous time?

Who said anything about a fabulous time? You are such an idiot. Fool.

I'm no fool. You are such a short-tempered imbecile. Quit jumping on me for no reason.

My daughter and I went for a walk today. It was a glorious day. The sky was so blue, and the sun was shining down like it wanted to light up our day. It did, too. We laughed, walked, and talked together. It's so easy being with her. She is such a comfort to me. I am so proud of her. She is a loving wife and she will be a wonderful mother. She is such a blessing to us.

Which us?

Me and Noah. We are us. Did you think I meant you and me? You really must think I'm crazy. I would never refer to you as us. I bet you would like it if I did. Don't hold your breath waiting for that to happen. We will never be us.

But we are.

I am trying to keep calm, but you need to take that back.

Take what back?

Take back what you said.

What did I say?

You said we are.

We are what?

You said we are us! Take that shit back. I mean it. Take it back, or else.

Or else. Or else. What are you going to do?

Don't push me.

Push you? Why would I need to push you? You are too busy pushing yourself.

Damned you! Irritating. Nagging. Blood crawling. Son of a mother…

Go ahead. Say it. Say the word. Are you scared? I dare you. Say it. You want to.

Do you have nothing better to do with your time? Do you enjoy watching me become enraged?

Enraged? You are not enraged. If you were enraged, you would say the word. Why can't you say the word? I am patiently waiting for you to say it. Mother…

Just stop it. Please. You know I won't. You know I can't. It's a dirty word. I hate that word. That word will defile me. That word makes me sick to my stomach. That word is so nasty.

Sometimes you need to let yourself be nasty. Just say it.

Please stop!

Say it. You will feel liberated. Say it. You will feel good all over. Say it. You will truly be one with me.

May 22nd – My Acknowledgement

I'm sorry for being so mean to you the other day. You know how I get when I become frustrated. I sometimes say things I don't mean. Like yesterday, when I told Noah that I didn't care if we separated. Divorced. I really didn't mean it. I'm so glad he never believes a word I say. I would be devastated if I lost him. He is my best friend. I know he needs me, too. Are you listening? Are you there? Don't give me the silent treatment.

Silent treatment? Don't be so self-absorbed. I was having a nap. Resting my energy and preparing to make those big decisions we are facing.

What are you talking about? What big decisions?

Don't pretend you don't know. If I know, you know.

Know what? What do you know?

I know Noah hasn't been the kindest to you lately. He has been treating you badly. Not encouraging you to follow your dreams. We always wanted to take piano lessons. I know Noah thinks you are too old and it's a waste of time and money. Wait. I mean to say we are too old.

Too old? You have to be kidding me. Where did you get the idea, he thinks I'm too old?

I said we. We are too old.

Please. Don't start this again.

Start what again?

This you, me, us, we shit isn't going to work today.

It already has.

I knew it. Go ahead. Call me an ass.

You're an ass.

STOP!

You said I could call you an ass, so I did. I only did what you said.

I am not too old. I mean. I am not an ass. See. Now you have me all befuddled.

Shall I get the dictionary now? What did I tell you about using the language you don't really understand? Speak to yourself at your level.

Come on. Stop this now. I don't want to fight again.

Fight? It takes two to tango. Are you now admitting there are two of us?

No.

So. What exactly are you saying when you speak of fighting? I always thought a fight involved conflicting parties. Are we conflicting parties?

No.

So. What are we?

I don't know.

Yes. You know. You know exactly what we are. We are us. We two make us.

Please. Listen to me. I will never admit to this. So. Stop. If I admit to this, it means I am crazy.

By whose standards will you define yourself as crazy? Certainly not by mine. Certainly not by yours. So…

So… So, what?

By whose standards are you crazy if you admit that you have a spirit, a soul, a conscience?

Spirits don't talk back. Can we change the subject? Please. I want to talk about Noah.

If you insist. We can talk about the love-hate relationship that exists between the two of you. So. Do you love him today?

Quit that. Don't make fun of this.

I am merely speaking of what I have observed. By my ears and eyes, I have received this vital truth.

Would you stop it? You're no poet. Stop pretending to be something you are not.

At least I admit to the facts. I am no poet, but I love pretending. You are a great pretender yourself.

What do you mean?

Were those moans real last night? Was Noah leading the two of us to ecstasy?

I can't believe you are bringing this up. Were you there? Are you spying on us?

Which us? You and me? Or you and Noah?

Damned you! Evil piece of shit. You know I mean Noah and me. I have told you there is no us! Stop trying to persuade me to think differently. And, yes. Noah was leading me to ecstasy, since you must know. Didn't you feel it? Oh, yeah, right – you can't feel anything. You are a mere figment of my being, desperate for recognition. You played no part in my moans because my moans were physical, real. You are but a fleeting thought trying to anchor in reality.

Who is the poet now? You see. I am real because you are real. I am the part of you that makes you reflect. Judge. Care. Question. The part that is truly living. Don't underestimate my importance to your existence. To rid yourself of me is to rid yourself of heart. Do you choose the life of the heartless? It is because of me your answer will be "No."

June 6th – My Acceptance

I need to talk to you. I need to hear what you think. Can we talk about my day?

Of course! I am always here for you. You can count on me to listen. What's on your mind?

I had a good time today playing the piano. My instructor Mr. Elliot is a really nice man and such a great teacher. He is so encouraging. I wish Noah could be like that.

What do you mean? Like that?

I wish Noah was cheering me on. You know? I wish he understood my passion. We are so different.

Really? You think so?

Of course. We are.

Fine. I agree. No argument from me. How are you two different?

He likes to sleep in. I am up at 5:00 am every day. He raises his voice when he talks. I am subtler in the expression of my feelings.

Sorry. I have to interrupt. If you are going to talk to me, then, please. Talk to me. Don't sugar coat things by using those fancy words you learned in law school. Subtle in the expression of my feelings – what the hell does that mean?

It means I don't normally yell. I speak calmly. Like this.

Just because you don't physically yell, doesn't mean you don't yell. You yell at me all the time. Or should I say, you don't speak subtly in the expression of your feelings towards me?

I yell in my mind. I know. I feel safe with you, so I feel it is okay to yell. I don't feel safe with Noah.

Now, wait a minute. He might not be the best at supporting you, but he has never done anything like that! He sounds like a bear. Deep down inside, he is really a lamb. In fact, he should be afraid of you. You're the one who is ready to blow. It's because you don't allow yourself the freedom to express yourself fully.

What do you mean?

You never truly react. You calculate your reactions, your words, your thoughts. Well, at least you used to. Before I spoke up. I had enough of you suppressing me.

People who are civil act rationally. Screaming, swearing, words without thought, these are all irrational behaviors.

They are human behaviors.

I know but they are imperfections of humanity.

Really? Are you serious? Are you now admitting it? You're a perfectionist.

Stop it. We are supposed to be talking about Noah. Why do you always turn things around on me?

You know what they say? The truth hurts. We are talking about Noah but in order to fully understand him, you need to understand you.

I understand me.

You do. Yes. But you don't accept who you are. You are educated. A beautiful fifty-year-old with a successful law practice and you are a wonderful mother to Emily. You will be a wonderful grandmother to her baby. However, your relationship with Noah is weak. You don't really talk to him. You always prepare yourself for conversations with him. How can he really understand your passion for music if you never share it with him? Stop blaming him.

I never thought about it like that. I always thought he was jealous of me. How can a janitor feel comfortable in a marriage when his wife is a lawyer? I keep telling him to go back to school, but he keeps telling me he loves his work. How could you love cleaning up after people? That's a cop-out.

See. There you go again. You don't respect what he does. I always knew this, but I never understood why. He is happy. What's wrong with that? Tell me, are you happy in your work?

Well. Yes. Most times. Most days. Mostly. Of course. I am.

Really? If I had a brain half the size of your hesitation, I would say you love playing the piano more than practicing law.

I do love playing the piano but that isn't real work. Somebody had to teach Emily about real work. Noah isn't doing it. She needed a role model.

She needed a mother. I know how guilty you feel about the fact that you didn't have much time to spend with her while she was growing up. You were too busy building a practice. You were always jealous of her relationship with Noah. He raised her. Not you.

Stop that. Just stop that. Damned you to hell for saying that! I had to provide. I had to make sure we had the money to pay for this way of life. I wasn't going to let her go to an inner-city school. I made sure she had the best of everything.

Yes. She had the best of everything except you.

Enough. I have heard enough of your inaccurate logic. Your summation is inconsistent and irrelevant.

My summation. Oh, no. You mean our summation?

You bastard… You mean bastard!

June 17th – My Denial

I'm so happy today. The jurors came back with a verdict of not guilty. Mr. Robinson is a free man.

Why are you so happy? You know deep down inside you thought he was guilty. You are happy that justice was not served? I thought you were rational?

It's my job. I have a duty. I have a responsibility. I signed an oath.

Oath, my ass. Why don't you quit pretending?

Pretending?

Yes. Quit pretending you like what you do. Your instincts were nudging you all through the trial. You know Mr. Robinson killed his wife. Why did you speak on behalf of a vicious criminal?

It's my job. It's what I do. Innocent until proven…

Right. Proven guilty. That should be your new bumper sticker. In fact, you should put up a bumper sticker that says, "Hey, I'll make sure you get off. Commit the crime and do no time."

Please. Cut me some slack. The law is not based on intuition, instinct, feelings, and assumptions. It is based on facts.

Right. The fact is your gut was telling you he did it.

That doesn't matter. There was no real proof. No evidence.

You need evidence? What evidence do you have that I exist? Can you prove to anyone that a soul is real? Does this mean I don't exist? Does this mean you are crazy?

No. I am NOT crazy.

I know. You don't have to convince me of this. You are human, and you have instincts.

I am human, but I am also a responsible adult. I have a job to do. My client entrusted his life in my hands.

Your hands? I thought it was the hands of the law, justice. The marvelous legal system.

Fine. We don't have to agree on this.

Agree. We do agree. We agree that you protected a vicious criminal. I have not heard you speak in defense of this.

I shouldn't have to defend myself, especially to you. You faint, fading voice that utters meaningless lines that echo inside the abyss of nothingness.

That should have been my line. It sounds so melodic.

Stop it! You think this is a joke? This is no joke. This is my life. You are trying to ruin my life.

You mean our life. You are trying to ruin our life.

No. I refuse to let my conscience be my critic.

That's my duty, my responsibility, my oath.

Now you're mocking me.

No. Not mocking. Just reiterating words.

Those were my words.

They are mine, also.

No. They are not. My words are not your words.

Of course! They are. Remember, we are us.

Why do I do this to myself? Please, God. Help me to stop.

A prayer. Finally, I succeeded in guiding her to a prayer. Continue my child.

Silence this voice. Overcome this moment. Silence this voice. Overcome this moment. Silence this voice. Overcome this moment.

I told you. It's my duty. I cannot remain silent.

Silence this voice. Overcome this moment.

It's my responsibility.

Silence this voice. Overcome this moment.

Silent night. Holy night. All is calm. All is bright.

Please. It is my duty. I have no proof. If he is guilty, his conscience will not let him rest. I am innocent of his crime.

You're right. You did what you had to. Would you do it again? Would you protect a vicious criminal again, if I spoke up? What if Timothy killed Emily? Would you defend him?

Dear, God, please forgive me!

July 2nd – My Promise

I plan to pray for Mr. Robinson. Last night, I made the decision. He needs my prayers.

When will you pray for us?

I pray for me every day. You know that I do.

Really pray. Pray honestly – without hiding anything. For example, "Dear God, I know I haven't been attending church, but I realize I am a sinner. I haven't been there for my daughter, especially in the most important times of her life. Like, when she got her period. I was away attending a very important and prestigious conference that I couldn't get away from. You see. I was one of the keynote speakers. My poor husband Noah had to buy her maxi pads and teach her how to use them."

Why do you insist on torturing me? I don't deserve this. I told you, I had to work.

Of course. You did. So what else did you decide last night?

I decided that I want to be there when the baby comes. I want to be with Emily. I plan to ask her today if she would be okay with it.

I'm sure she will be fine with it. She loves you. You are her mother. She understands that you had to work. She doesn't hold anything against you. Thank goodness, Noah raised her.

What's that supposed to mean? Are you suggesting that I harbor grudges? Are you suggesting that if I spent more time with her, she would not have turned out the way she did? Are you suggesting that I played no part in forming her? Are you alluding to the notion that she was better off not having me around, anyway?

Hold your horses, Missy. I am not alluding to anything. At least, I don't think I am. Well, if alluding means the same as suggesting. What did I tell you about using these elephant words with such minuscule definition? Why not just say suggesting if that's what you want to say? Mumbo jumbo doesn't make things crystal clear. You should know this. I am but a simpleton who speaks the language of simpletons and understands the words of simpletons. The real Meredith would never use such fancy words and I know the real Meredith. I am the real Meredith.

Don't call my name. Don't claim my name. I am Meredith.

I am the real Meredith. I am the essence of Meredith.

I knew it. You want to be me. All this time you have been trying to convince me to say "us" just so you could be me. I should have known you were up to something. You will never be me. I am Meredith.

Fine. You can be Meredith while you speak. I will be Meredith when I speak.

No! There is no compromise. I am me. Not you.

Whatever you say, Meredith…

Stop this. This is ridiculous. Do you realize what you are doing? Stop being such a fool.

I'm not a fool.

I'm not talking to you!

Who are you talking to?

Me. I'm talking to me.

Wow. We can really complicate things.

Fine. If you want to pretend you're me, go ahead.

I love pretending but…

But what? Can't you keep the peace for a minute? I wanted to be there for Emily. I cried for weeks knowing that I wasn't there for her. I wanted to be there. You have no idea how hard it was for me to accept that Noah shared that experience with her. I don't want to miss anything else. I plan to be there when the baby comes.

Even if you have to work?

Yes. Even if I have to work. I will cancel the appointments. Move things around. I will be there for her, especially knowing that Timothy might be gone. She needs me to be there. I will not let her down this time.

Good. I will hold you to it. Remember, oath. My oath.

Right. Your oath. I don't really need you for this. I can do this on my own. I don't need you nagging me about it.

You don't need me. What a hoot. Ha, Ha, Ha, Ha, Ha.

I mean it. I don't need you for this. I have made a conscious decision to be there for Emily when the baby comes. I don't need my unconscious thoughts to remind me.

That's what you think of me? I am not just your unconscious thoughts. I am the vibrant part of your existence. When will you accept me for who I am? You need me. You need me desperately. You have no idea how much you need me. Without me, you could never make a conscious decision to do anything. I didn't want to say this, but I have to. Mr. Robinson is a free man because you didn't listen.

Listen? Listen? To whom? Listen to what?

You didn't listen to me. I told you. He did it. I wish you would have listened. You wouldn't have to carry this burden. You are already burden-ridden.

Burden? I am not carrying any burden.

July 18ᵗʰ – My Burden

I can't believe it. I just can't believe this is happening!

What? What's the urgency?

The urgency? You know, damned well, what the urgency is. I'm sure you are celebrating. You love being right, don't you?

Being right? What are you talking about?

For Christ's sake, please. Don't make me say it. You were right. Okay. Just don't make me say the words.

Say what?

Silence this voice. Overcome this moment.

Boy, oh boy. Here we go again. Meredith is going nuts!

Silence this voice. Overcome this moment.

Nuts. She really is nuts!

Fine. You want to hear it? You want my lips to form the words? You want my vocal cords to echo the lines? Fine. I'll say it. But I want you to hurt when you hear it. You will feel like you are being butchered by the rotating saws of the meat cutter when I say them. You will not receive them with ease.

Is that a threat? Are you threatening me? Be careful, Meredith. I am warning you. Don't make empty threats.

I can't do this. I can't say it. I can't repeat words that damn me to hell. Why didn't I listen?

Hush, Child. Hush. You are only human.

No. I refuse to accept that crap. I am supposed to know these things. I knew. I always knew. I could feel it… But I had a job to do.

Yes. You did your best.

My best? How can you defend me?

I understand you. I understand why you do what you do.

How could you understand this? Do you even know what I'm talking about? There is no understanding. Not this. No understanding this shit!

Calm down. Don't become irrational.

How can I stay calm? How can you be calm? You are such a sick, frickin' bastard.

Calling names won't make this better.

No. But it makes me feel better. Remember, you told me sometimes I need to be nasty.

Yes. But not to yourself. Not to me.

Why shouldn't I be nasty to you? You deserve it?

I deserve it? No. I think you meant to say, we deserve it.

Mr. Robinson came into my office and thanked me for getting him off. He asked me if I wanted a cut in the insurance claim. He said he never met a lawyer so convincing. He thanked me for persuading the jury in his favor. He winked at me. Do you hear me? He winked at ME!

You didn't have to say it. You really didn't. I was just teasing but I realize this is not a good time for such behavior. How do you feel now?

I feel awful. I feel dirty. I feel terrible. I feel like I, too, am guilty.

You shouldn't feel guilty. You took an oath. It was your duty.

My duty? It wasn't my duty to let a criminal, a murderer go free. He needs to pay for his crime. His wife needs justice.

She will have justice. Just leave this in the hands of powers greater than ours.

Where are these great hands? Why weren't these great hands in the courtroom? Why didn't these great hands direct the jury to find him guilty?

Perhaps the great hands were busy helping you win your case.

Please. Please. Please. Don't say that.

What do you want me to say?

I want you to say, "I told you so."

Why should I say that?

Say it, you lunatic. Say it. I know you want to.

Fine. I told you so. I told you to listen.

You're right. I need to listen. I wish that I listened. I now have another burden to carry. I can't do this alone. Will you help me?

I already have.

July 26th – My Offer

I had a really good evening with Noah, Emily, and Timothy. We went to a nice restaurant and had a lovely dinner. We said farewell to Timothy and wished him the best in Paris. The lucky guy. Who goes to Paris for work? Emily was glowing. She is such a beautiful expecting mother and she seems to be coping well with Timothy leaving and all. Three months is a long time for them to be apart. Noah and I have never been apart for more than four weeks. I really hope she takes us up on our offer.

Who?

Emily.

What offer?

Noah and I offered her the spare bedroom for the next three months. I would love it if she stayed with us. That way, I would get to see her every day.

That's a great idea. What did she say?

She said she wants some time to think about it.

Think about it?

You know how she is. She never wants to be a third wheel. She thinks Noah and I need time alone.

She's right.

What do you mean?

You need time to really work on your marriage. Having Emily there will only give you both a good reason to postpone the inevitable.

What is the inevitable?

The dialogue. The talk. The teary-eyed session you need in order to move on. You need to talk about why you have been avoiding him.

I haven't been avoiding him.

Not physically but mentally.

How can you say that? How do you even know? Wait. Don't say anything. It's because you are me, right?

No. Because we are us.

You are a stubborn son of a bitch, aren't you?

Isn't that a rhetorical question?

Who's using fancy words now? I was telling you about the wonderful dinner we had. How is it that we are talking about how I am avoiding Noah?

You mean us talking about Noah?

I'm not avoiding him. I just need time to deal with my burden.

You didn't tell him?

I will. I will tell him when I am ready.

Ready? You need to tell him. He needs to know what's bothering you.

I'm not ready to tell. He won't understand. He might not want to share this burden with me.

How do you know? You need to give him a choice. How can he choose to carry it with you if he doesn't know?

Perhaps he doesn't need to know.

He needs to know why you are avoiding him.

I can't take him yelling at me.

He won't yell at you. You didn't do anything wrong. He only yells when you do stupid things. This wasn't your fault. You had a responsibility. Mr. Robinson is the one who will pay. He used you.

I helped a criminal go free.

Not consciously. You didn't have the facts to prove your hunch.

That's no excuse. I can picture Noah yelling that at me.

Why picture it? Tell him.

He'll say things like: stupid lawyers, idiots, damned, twisted legal system. He'll ask me that question.

What question?

He'll ask. Why?

Why you do it? You do it for him. You do it for Emily. Don't you?

July 30th – My Shame

Emily called this morning. She decided it would be best if she didn't stay with us. She wants to spend time getting the nursery ready for the baby. She found out the sex. You know?

Oh. Do tell. Is it a girl or a boy?

It is a boy. Timothy is so excited. Noah jumped up and down. So happy! He will soon have a grandson. I was a bit disappointed. I wanted it to be a girl.

Why? So that you could try to re-live Emily's childhood through her? Believe me. The great hands at work know best.

You're right. I was hoping to do some things with her that I didn't get to do with Emily.

With her? There is no her. It's a boy!

Why do you have to be so curt? I know it's a boy. I was expressing my feelings but as usual, you have to step all over them. Dance recitals. Christmas pageants. Band concerts. Prom night. I missed so much.

Don't feel sorry for yourself. You made the decision to work, work, work. You are the sophisticated lawyer who had to prove so much.

See. There you go. Rubbing it in my face. Where were you while I was working? Why did you just get the courage to speak up now? Where was your courage back then when I needed it?

I told you. You are changing and I am, too. I wasn't confident back then. I was afraid of you.

Afraid of me? Why?

Because you were so successful. I thought you must have known better because everything you went after, you got. I felt useless.

Known better?

Yes. Better than me. You were so smart, and I was only a faint voice. You were so strong, and I was yet only a faint voice. I wasn't strong enough. You overpowered me.

What's changed?

You've changed. You've grown weary.

Weary?

Yes. Who could sustain a life focused on work, especially criminal law? I knew you would get tired.

I don't feel tired.

Not physically tired. Emotionally tired. Spiritually tired. Consciously tired.

Why am I so tired?

You are tired of making everything around you seem perfect. You finally can accept the flaws of your life.

What exactly are these flaws?

Let's see. Your need to control everything: the money, what Noah wears, how Emily sits at a table and choosing Timothy for her.

How dare you say that! I did no such thing.

Was it a coincidence that Emily happened to be invited to the party of the most sought-after, law school graduate? You had nothing to do with that?

I just want her to be happy. Timothy is so good for her. He is so good to her. She shouldn't have to go through what I went through with Noah. Always feeling guilty about my success.

Really? Is that ALL you went through? Please. Share your sad stories with those who care. You went through nothing with Noah. He went through hell with you. He was never good enough. Never knew the right words to use. He could never please you. Well. Yes. In that way he did. But in the most important way, he couldn't.

What the hell are you saying? Are you saying that I'm the one who has been at fault all these years?

Aren't you? Why don't you go, play a song on the piano? It will soothe you. You need something to calm you. I can feel you are getting really tense. I don't want you to be upset. I know how much you wanted Emily to come, stay with you.

I did. I really did. I mean. I really do. Perhaps I can still persuade her to change her mind.

Don't do it. Don't put yourself at risk like that. You know how much you hate rejection. Do you need me to remind you of that time?

Don't you dare speak of it! She was only five years old. She didn't know any better.

Of course. She did. She just wanted the parent who spent time with her to comfort her that night. Nightmares can be hard on little kids. You know that. I wasn't surprised when she asked for Noah to tuck her in that night. I wasn't surprised that she woke Noah up instead of you. I wasn't surprised she screamed "Daddy, Daddy" instead of calling for you. She knew Noah would be there for her. You would be amazed at what children know by the time they have spent five years on this earth. You were never around. I wasn't surprised at all, but the rejection made you squirm. How could Noah comfort her? Why didn't she want her mommy? Has she ever called you that, anyways, Meredith?

Stop. I don't want to hear you. Why do you have to dig so deep? You were silent all those years. It's your fault. It's because you were the coward. Everything that happened was ALL YOUR FAULT!

August 3rd – My Preparation

I did what you said.

What did you do?

I told Noah about Mr. Robinson.

Good. I'm glad. What did he say?

He didn't say much. He just gave me a hug and said it wasn't my fault. I was really surprised by his reaction. He said he knew something was bothering me. He thanked me for telling him.

See. What did I tell you? You need to give Noah a chance. He is really not that bad. He did a great job raising Emily.

You're right. I just psyched myself up and made him out to be this big, bad wolf character. I know he really isn't like that.

You would never have married him if he was a big, bad wolf.

I know. I can't believe we've been together for thirty-four years and married for twenty-eight. Do you think I would have married him if we weren't high school sweethearts?

Sure. You would have. You love Noah. Everyone loves Noah. He is such an easy-going person. And happy. No one is as happy as Noah. He loves his work and his family. He adores his Emily. You know what I think? I think Noah is the best thing that happened to the two of you.

What do you mean?

Noah is a blessing for you and for Emily.

I have something really big to share with you.

Really big? You have some news?

Not news but something I have been thinking about.

Go ahead. Spill it. Let me hear it. Don't keep me waiting.

Why do you have to do this? Do you have to make fun of everything I say?

Fun? No pun intended.

Why would you say that? Anyways. I am thinking of going to visit my dad.

What? Oh, no! You're not! You are not going to Shady Oaks. I can't take all those old folks. They make me feel stupid.

Why do they make you feel stupid?

Because they have been around a lot longer than me. That's why. When I look into their eyes, I can hear their souls poking fun at me. I'm glad you only go there once a year. You already did your time this year. Why would you want to go there a second time? Can't we wait until next year like we normally do?

See what I mean? Some days you can be so angelic and other days you are the devil's advocate. I thought you would like this idea.

Why would you think that?

Because it is a good thing to do. It is a righteous thing to do. Since Mom passed and Mark moved to Australia, he really only has me.

Mark? Who's that?

My brother. How could you forget Mark?

Oh, Mark. The brother you haven't spoken to since your mother passed away. How long has it been? Ten years?

I refuse to entertain any discussions that raise such hurtful experiences. Can we move on and talk about Dad? I think I should go visit him next week. Maybe even take Emily.

What for? He doesn't know who you are. Do you think he would have the slightest idea who Emily is? Face it, Meredith. He's already gone.

Why do you speak like that to me and about my father? He is NOT gone. I hate you. I hate how you are.

I'm sorry. Sometimes I can be too honest.

Honest? Is that what it is? How about just plain mean? Is that word plain and simple enough for you to understand? What about malicious? Despicable? Unpleasant? Callous? Cruel? Should I use those words as well?

You have every right to be angry. I have every right to be truthful.

Stop that. He is NOT gone.

Meredith, I'm trying to help you prepare. You need to prepare for this.

Prepare for what?

His death.

September 15th – My Agony

There is a message on the machine from Shady Oaks. They say it's urgent.

What are you waiting for? Call them back.

I don't want to. I mean. I can't.

Why not?

I don't want to hear.

You need to call.

I can't.

Meredith, I'm with you. You are not alone.

I feel alone.

Come on. Noah is there for you. Emily is there for you. Timothy is there for you.

I still feel so alone.

You are not alone. Make the call. Please.

Why don't YOU make the call?

I would if I had fingers. I am limited in my abilities. I only have the power of influence.

Well. You are doing a terrible job right now.

Fine. Don't call. You don't need to know that your father is DEAD.

SHUT UP!

Don't yell at me. Make the call. Then, I'll shut up. Deadman needs his daughter.

Please. Stop. Why do you have to do this?

It's for your own good.

Fine. I will make the call. Only if you promise you will never repeat those words again.

What words?

The words you just spoke.

It's for your own good?

NO!

Don't yell at me. What words?

You know I can't say them.

Why not?

I don't know.

A lawyer can't say, "Deadman needs his daughter?"

Please. Stop. He isn't dead.

How do you know? You haven't called.

I will. When I am ready.

You are ready. We've been preparing for this for a long time.

Stop it!

I told you.

Told me what?

You needed to prepare. Death was coming. He was dying.

No. I don't believe you.

Believe me? You don't have to believe me. Make the call.

I will tomorrow.

Are you serious?

Yes. Tomorrow. I will call.

Does Noah know?

Know what?

That your dad died.

My dad is not dead. Stop saying that.

I wish he wasn't. But he is. You need to make that phone call.

If I don't call, it's not real. I don't want it to be real.

It is real, Meredith. Please. Call to find out when it happened.

I don't want to know.

You already know. Stop this. You are acting like a fool.

I am a fool.

No. You are not a fool. You are a fifty-year-old woman who is mourning the loss of her father.

Silence this voice. Overcome this moment.

Not that shit again.

Silence this voice. Overcome this moment.

October 27th – My Miracle

Today was the best day of my life.

Why? What happened?

My miracle arrived today. Emily had her baby. She named him Peter.

How wonderful! Were you there?

What do you mean?

Oops. Meredith did it again.

I was there.

Really? You were there during the birth?

Well. Not exactly.

Not exactly? What does that mean? Go on. Explain yourself. Make your excuses.

I knew you would try to wreck this moment for me.

You said you didn't need me. I told you. You do.

I was in the middle of a trial. I couldn't just leave.

I thought you made a promise. You never keep promises.

I couldn't just leave. It was a hearing.

It doesn't matter. You never keep promises. I thought I was making progress.

I tried. I arrived at the hospital only fifteen minutes after the baby arrived. I was practically there.

Go ahead. Lie to yourself. Make it sound okay.

It is okay. I tried. I couldn't leave.

Yes. Like, you had to defend Mr. Robinson. A man who brutally murdered his pregnant wife?

Stop it. Please. I can't handle this today. Don't ruin this for me.

I'm only asking a question.

That's not a real question. Your intention was to make me feel guilty.

Do you?

Do I what?

Feel guilty?

I had to work. Why can't you accept that?

I can accept that as an excuse, not an explanation.

I am not making excuses.

You are.

Fine. It is a damned good excuse.

Certainly. You had to work.

Alright. I feel terrible that I missed it. I just don't know what to do with myself.

You need to start listening to me.

What's that supposed to mean?

You need to give up the work, Meredith. There isn't much time left for us.

What do you mean? Stop being so negative. Let me enjoy this day. My miracle arrived today.

You were supposed to witness the miracle, not hear about it, after the fact. You might never have the opportunity again.

Of course. I will have the opportunity to witness the other births.

What other births?

Emily's babies. I know she hopes to have more.

November 27th – My Declaration

It's been a month now since Peter's birth and he is growing up so fast. He smiles and coos when you rub his feet. He is a true Armstrong. Both Emily and Noah love having their feet massaged.

You finally use the last name you refuse to carry? Did Noah ever forgive you for that?

He has forgiven me. He understands that it was important to my father to keep my maiden name. Besides, Emily didn't mind being Smith-Armstrong.

Sure. That's why she was so eager to take Timothy's name. She couldn't wait to be Mrs. Jenkins. Now you and your long-lost brother Mark are the last to bear the Smith's name. What a shame.

What do you mean? Why is that a shame?

It's a shame Mark never had kids of his own. It's a shame your career was so important you never had time for more than one.

Okay. You need to shut up now.

Why? Did I step on a sensitive spot?

I mean it. Shut up.

Don't tell me to shut up. I have to remind you about the poor decisions you made for us.

There is no us.

I wanted more kids. Noah wanted more, too.

Silence this voice. Overcome this moment.

I refuse to be silent now. Why did you have to kill our baby?

How dare you?

How dare I? You were the one who went to that butcher and had him kill our baby. I will never let you forget that.

I had to. Please. Stop.

You didn't have to. Your career was so frickin' important that you had to kill him. Emily was already two years old. You would have managed fine. How could you keep this from Noah? You need to tell him the truth.

I can't. He'll hate me.

I don't hate you. I know what you did. I think you owe him the truth.

No! I can't.

If you don't tell him, I will.

What? What are you saying?

I will tell Noah you aborted his son after the first trimester.

You can't.

I will find a way. I will not let Noah die not knowing the truth. One day, I will tell him.

Please. I beg of you. This secret has to die with me. I mean. With "us."

You must really think I'm stupid. I know you said "us" because you want me to side with you. You are not truly admitting that we are "us." I'm no fool.

I know you're no fool. But, please. Don't push this issue. Noah can never know.

He must know.

Fine. Then, you better figure out a way to tell him because he'll never hear it from me.

I promise you. I will tell him. When I do, you will have to beg his forgiveness.

What do you know about forgiveness? Why can't you forgive me? I was so busy at work. I had just taken on four new cases. I couldn't do it all – work, raise Emily, and take care of a newborn.

Raise Emily. You didn't raise her.
Please. Stop.
I'll stop when you admit to your bad judgment.
You are right. I was wrong to hide the pregnancy from Noah.
And.
I was wrong for killing my baby.
And.
I was wrong for not telling Noah what I had done to his unborn son.

December 26th – My Deliverance

Yesterday was such a marvelous day. It was the best Christmas I ever had.
Yes. I agree it was a lovely time.
It was so nice to have everyone together – Timothy, Emily, Peter, Noah, and me.
What about me? I was there, too.
Fine. Whatever.
Emily looked so happy. She must be so relieved to have Timothy back home for good.
Yes. She is thrilled about it.
Little Peter is such a cute bundle of joy. He is looking more like Timothy nowadays. How adorable!
Yes. He is a beautiful boy.
Did you like the gift Noah gave you?
I love it.
Really? That surprises me.
Why does it surprise you?
I never pictured you as a quilter. I figured you wouldn't like a year's worth of quilting lessons.
Now that I'm a grandma, I plan to do some quilting. I already have my first project planned. I'll make Peter's first bed quilt.
Really? When will you find the time to make a quilt?
Once the practice sells. I'll have plenty of time.
Are you serious? You're going through with selling?
I have to. It's time to focus on family.
I have to admit, I am a bit reluctant to believe you will go through with it.
I'm ready. When I hold Peter in my arms, I feel it. I know it's time.
Good, Meredith.
Good. Is that all you have to say? No pokes or jabs?
No. I'm happy for you.

That's all. Nothing else?

No. That's all.

Alright. Let me just get to it, then. The decision has nothing to do with my diagnosis.

I know.

Just because I have breast cancer doesn't mean my career has to end.

I know.

Lots of women survive and return to work.

I know.

I just know it's time to focus on more important things now.

I know.

I want to spend time with Emily and Peter.

I know.

Why don't you say something?

I don't have anything to say.

I know it's burning your tongue. Say it.

Say what?

When are you going to tell them you're sick?

January 30th – My Liberation

I've made a decision to tell Noah about the baby.

And the cancer?

No. I need more time.

More time. Cancer means you have no time.

Don't say that.

It's the truth, Meredith. Why can't you face the truth?

Because it's hard. I don't have the energy.

I will help you. Don't worry.

Don't worry? How can you speak those words to me? How can you even form your lips to say those words? Oh, yes. You have no lips. You're not real. You're a figment of some pseudo-reality that I created to deal with my messed-up life.

Meredith, I am warning you. You better stop this train of thought.

Silence this voice. Overcome this moment.

I refuse to be silent now.

You must be silent. I will not let you overpower me.

I can, and I will.

Watch me. This wrinkled face, 130-pound, fifty-year-old will never let you win.

Okay. I give up. I realize I can never beat you.

What do you mean? You can't give up. I want a fight. I demand you fight back. You bitch!

Silence this voice. Overcome this moment.

What?

You win, Meredith.

Alright. I will tell Noah about the cancer. I will tell him everything.

You mean you'll tell him the truth about your feud with Mark. You'll tell him that you stopped talking to your brother because he blamed you for your mother's death.

What did you just say?

Well, Meredith, your mother only started to drink heavily after she found out about the abortion.

Stop.

She never would have died in the car crash if she wasn't drunk.

No.

Your mother told Mark the truth. You knew. Didn't you?

Please.

The car crash was all your fault.

Stop. You're a liar.

I am incapable of lying. You know that? Don't you?

Silence this voice. Overcome this moment.

No, Meredith. We need to face the truth.

Never.

We must. We are dying. This is the time to free ourselves of the pain.

Pain. You can't feel my pain.

I wish that were true.

Silence this voice. Overcome this moment.

February 14th – My Confession

I told Noah.

What did you tell Noah?

I told him about my cancer.

Meredith, I'm sorry.

Why are you sorry?

I'm sorry, you're sick.

Don't be sorry. These things happen.

I know. But it is going to be a difficult journey.

I'm ready. You know I'm a fighter.

Did you tell Noah about the abortion?

No.

Why?

Silence this voice. Overcome this moment.

Please don't try to avoid this. You have to face the truth at some point.

Don't you think I know that!

What are you so afraid of?

I'm not afraid.

Yes. You are.

Fine. I'm afraid.

Fear is a natural response. You need to embrace your fear and prepare yourself for whatever comes.

No! I can't.

If you don't tell him, I will.

There you go again making threats.

This is no threat. I mean it, Meredith.

Why can't you just let this rest?

Rest. I can't rest holding on to such a terrible secret. I am the one who carries all the pain of it.

What are you talking about? I am the one who bears the shame and guilt. A faint voice carries no pain. How dare you make a statement like that!

Now, Meredith. Let's not forget who I am. I am the part of you that feels.

Stop it.

No. I will not stop. You need to hear me. I am your conscience.

Silence this…

Silence. You be silent. You murderer!

Silence this voice.

Never. I will never be silent.

Please. Stop.

I am no use to you if I don't remind you of the malicious things you have done to yourself. You are a murderer. Tell Noah what you did!

Okay, you win. I'll tell him.

Good.

Now, please. Let me rest awhile.

Fine.

Thank you.

March 27th – My Ordeal

Noah and I are going on a boat cruise to the Caribbean next week. I need some sun before the surgery next month. I thought I would be more excited about the much needed vacation, but I'm really scared. I can't get the cancer off my mind.

I know. Things will go well. Don't worry. Let's stay positive.

Positive. Easy for you to say. You're not the one whose breast will be cut off. You won't feel anything.

I know. But I will be there with you.

I don't need you there.

I know you don't need me. I want to be there for you.

Why?

I want to help you get through this.

Why?

Meredith, I don't like your tone.

My tone? Am I scaring you? Maybe I don't want everything to go fine.

You don't? Emily does. Noah does. Timothy does. And...

And what! I deserve to die.

No one deserves to die.

Maybe I am just ready. I'm tired.

Tired. I'm the one who is tired. I'm tired of having to be the strong one. Lately, you have just given up. What kind of mother gives up when she knows her child needs her? Emily needs you. Peter needs his grandmother. This does not surprise me. You never come through for Emily.

Take that back. You fucking bitch!

Never.

Everything I do is for Emily. She means the world to me.

Do this for her. Fight for her.

I can't.

Really? Are you serious? You have never cowered to anything. Now suddenly you have become weak. I can't believe this. Fine. Let's die, then.

What?

I'm fine with dying. Let's do it.

How can you say that? How dare you!

Mmmm. Can't wait to keel over.

Stop it.

Heaven, here we come.

Stop.

I wonder what the spirit world will be like?

I'll fight.
What did you say?
I'll fight.
Sorry. I didn't hear that. Can you repeat it one more time? Please.
I'll fight. I don't want to die. Emily needs me.
I'm glad to hear you had a change of heart.
Promise me. You'll be there.
I promise.
I love you. I forgive you, Meredith.

Chapter Thirty-Nine

Meredith's diary teaches me that life comes with hard punches and ghettos look different for us all. Meredith's ghetto is not physical. Hers is psychological. Yet, we have the same choice. Choose to contend or choose happiness.

The constant torture of my ghetto life continues but there are moments I feel joyful. I'm thankful for Mother. She works hard and wants the best for me. Mother does not live her life for herself but for her children. She toils every day and is content because she knows I walk the yellow brick road.

There is a joy unspeakable that I carry. My woes do not define me. Ecstasy, bliss, pleasure, and delight rise with me every morning. Who am I? I'm a ghetto child. A ghetto daughter. A ghetto woman. I am survival. I am resilience. A plethora of happiness incinerates the evil encounters. Elation comes, and it satisfies me. I'm happy! – When I dance. Win a netball game. See the light of a new day. Listen to Mother's olden day stories. Spend time with Sister. Listen to a good joke. Eat Sunday dinner. Hear a good sermon at the small, white church. Perform on stage. Reminisce with Makalo. Share stories about Amy. Hang out with Matt. My life is what it is. I live like I know how to – on the edge of my seat. I look forward to when *my yellow brick road* reveals itself to me.